EPISODE EIGHT

MEGAN MARX

First published in Australia in 2019

ABN: 42 408 220 115

The right of Megan Marx to be identified as the author of this work has been asserted by her in accordance with the Copyright Amendment (Moral Rights) Act 2000.

ISBN: 978-0-646-99713-1 (paperback)

ISBN: 978-0-646-99741-4 (e-book)

Edited by: Beverly Hotchkiss

Cover Design by: White Deer

Cover Images: Eeemotja

Printed by: Longxiang Group Limited (China)

To Mum, Anna and Will.

Dad, there're some things you shouldn't know your daughter knows.
So maybe give this one a miss. I love you.

And probably you too Gran.

PART ONE

"The world is a vampire, sent to drain
    Secret destroyers, hold you up to the flames
    And what do I get for my pain?
    Betrayed desires, and a piece of the game"

- Smashing Pumpkins "The World is A Vampire"

CHAPTER ONE

(Henry)

Every morning when the day begins my alarm goes off. It's not a clock. It's not a badly tuned radio dial crooning out static and noise. It's not something I punch on a bedside table. It's not my iPhone set with a thousand reminders. It's a thin, electric sheet that vibrates beneath my flesh, humming like a drone. If I amp up the settings it's more like a convoy of tanks pummeling up the drive, pounding shocks through my thighs, my ass, and throbbing up my spine. A violent, vibrating reminder of my circumstances.

I spilt whisky on the off-lever on the side of the bed about two months ago, so now I'm forced to get up if I want it to stop. If I'm too drunk or hungover to feel it, my dog acts as a second alarm. He wakes up with a startled rise of jowls, lunging his tongue all over my bare chest and face. I let the vibrations throb a few more times before dragging myself up onto one elbow. I take Clyde's face between my hands and rub his ears. When Clyde jumps down and wanders into the living area I get up and sit on the side of the bed and turn the alarm off at the wall. I sit hunched and naked, I rest my arms on my thighs and exhale my nightmares.

Eventually, I stand-up and walk to the window. The panes are crusted with sand and salt. The windows are morning-foggy. I use the side of my arm to wipe away a patch of condensation. I can see Bondi Beach. Already there are surfers belly down paddling boards on the water and tourists with morning coffees and mothers with prams. The earnest and efficient getting sun and exercise before the day really starts. The ocean stretches out, yawning, slack with calm. Lazy. I'm envious of its uninterrupted state, its gentle lolling. Today's anniversary is already jamming my spine with shame.

It has been six months since I lost my hearing and I wonder if I'm starting to get that dull, slow, round and loose drawl that some deaf people claim. The kind everyone imitated when they were a kid, or if I'm lucky and my persistent practice, and my years of enunciation, have overshadowed the accident. I'm inherently aware that my voice was noticed. It was like a strong jawline. People would say that I had a handsome voice, a masculine voice, the voice of a man who is certain of his position in the world. Now for me, there's only a pulsating hum in place of that memory. The muted, dull sound of piss hitting the side of a toilet bowl.

Every morning I can't help but recall the last magazine article written about me before the accident. It's etched in, like teenage fingers sinking the words 'fuck you' into drying concrete. *Henry, a voice like a magnet, like sex, like Nick Cave reincarnate.* There are photos of me alongside a stream of black text. I am standing proud, noxious, swarming with self-love. The title and quotes are in bold red. The journalist mentions the voice I can't hear anymore with such unflinching and ardent flattery, that I'm able to momentarily transcend my self-loathing, and roost on the hope that my words still have some kind of magnetic ability to get what they want.

Once she had successfully flattered me, it was mainly an article to appease the female masses by degrading herself (I have no idea why women love this stuff). She talks about how she doesn't have the body shape to be on the show and says that her hands are too ugly to be given an engagement ring on TV. She adds that even so, she can't help but be moved by the cheesy love stories that develop and cry hysterically throughout the series with her other apparent 'romantically ill-fated friends'.

I walk away from the window. I've lived in this apartment for about three months. It's high on a hill overlooking the ocean. The apartment has old, white, stone walls, high wooden ceilings and resurfaced timber floors. I don't think the building was originally designed to be apartments, but investors managed to revamp it, skirting strict state heritage laws, and it now has four separate residences catering to smug-upper-middle-class lives and stories. I purchased the top floor unit, and it's furnished with brown and mustard leather couches, old collectors lamps, books and weird abstract paintings that match the decor perfectly. The rugs, the accent tables, the light features, well everything – everything was chosen by Jonas the art director from The Eligibles. After Jonas finished adjusting the final painting, he sat down, smiling, and slowly opened a case of cigars, eyes wide and proud. He said that it was the kind of home that should smell of expensive cigars. They were from Nicaragua, he kept telling me. Expensive. *Nicaragua.* Did I know he had been there before? Dated a Nicaraguan man. It was very dangerous. Saved the cigars for a special night. I politely smoked two of the suckers despite my abhorrence for tobacco, abhorrence for the whole lung-burning experience. I leant back and gave him the cocky wink and stance I knew he thought they should be smoked with. I poured him whiskey on the rocks and we drank and smoked and I stroked his ego with words I couldn't hear.

I should add that it was nice of Jonas to help me out with the redecoration, but let's not kid ourselves, it was also a strategic and somewhat tactless move of self-promotion on his part. News of his 'charity work' swarmed social media like berserk, rapacious locusts. Charity for the 'handsome handicap bachelor' the 'sensory disabled', headlines I was still getting used to. Now, I'm left with a home that makes me feel like an imposter, as if some pious, irritatingly sanctimonious writer or artist lives here, not the deaf ex-reality TV star that I am. I'm the man with the strong voice who made the majority of his money off other people's misfortune, and a little off my own set of misfortunes. An opportunist, but for what?

I wonder if pretentious is the kind of home Jonas thought I'd suit or if it's just that the apartment is so vacant of any permanent or consistent company that all the furniture feels a bit too self-important for me - the sad handicapped host who inhabits its walls.

Admittedly, I do have women back here occasionally, but I prefer them not to stay the night. You could say I now relish in a desensitized give and take, a sort of dull and repetitive in and out, the one-night-fuck, the badge of manly conquest and esteem. I don't like waking up with naked women in my bed anymore. They suck at the little energy I have for the day. They giggle nervously and try to have conversations, often forgetting that I am deaf. I'll turn around to see their lips moving and I'll have no idea how long it's been going on for. Or they'll come up behind me when I'm standing in the kitchen and wrap their arms around my waist. I almost punched one once when I was making her coffee. No matter how many times they sneak up with little cold hands from behind it still scares the shit out of me. 'I'm fucking deaf, you stupid bitch!' I've screamed on more than one occasion. They feel shocked and then sorry, and of course then I feel like a dick. Besides, the skin-to-skin contact feels prickly and too intimate and too odd on waking. The mornings still punch me with my new reality and sex makes no sense, there's no room for anything except for me to try to grasp how fucking quiet everything is.

Mostly I prefer to be alone. Peeling off my clothes at

night and throwing them on the floor when I'm alone is less painful than doing it with someone else. It is like deleting the world. I am like a snake shedding its skin. I am removing the mask. It is a ridding of the useless circus of my life. I am no longer a charlatan. There is no one to accuse me of being good, of being brave or of being better than I am. I am completely naked with myself - well myself, Clyde, and usually a few empty whiskey bottles.

As I stare at Bondi Beach, I think about the radio interview I have later today. I hope the hosts remember to face me when they're talking. Sometimes I swear the bastards purposely cover their mouths with the black foam of the microphone or turn away so that they can then ramble seemingly genuine apologies. Sometimes they mouth words so incredibly slow that there is not a chance in hell I could lip read. I'm not fucking retarded. Maybe it's for them to draw attention to my handicap, my weakness, so they can let the audience know, which then helps to boost their ratings: 'I'm so sorry, it's just your voice... sorry it's so easy to forget... he's *deaf*. Then they'll smile and wink at me like we're mates and as if I'm unaware of what's going on. I make a damn good story.

I remember the first radio show, about three months after the accident. The host or someone involved with the show, had the enterprising idea of bringing in a hand sign specialist, as if somehow suddenly being deaf brought with it an understanding of whatever the fuck bending fingers and flailing arms meant. Remembering still makes me cringe—the so obvious incapacity I'm still refusing to accept and get used to. When we finished our chat, the same host had asked me what my favourite song used to be. He sat there staring at me—I swear there was amusement in his eyes. It took all my strength not to punch him and even more not to cry. I ended up suggesting Sampha, *Close But Not Quite*. Probably a bit depressing for this particular show, but fuck them with their stupid questions. I wondered if Poppy was listening.

I throw some clothes on; shorts, sweats, t-shirt, grab my water bottle from the fridge and head to the beach for a quick run with Clyde and then it's off to the gym. Some routines don't change just because we do. There's maybe four other people lifting, one stares at me shamelessly as I walk in. I pretend not to notice. I head over to the bench press and start warming up. As I lift, I rehearse in my head everything I think I will say on the show later today. It's a habit. I always rehearse. I'm trying to make it sound less banal, less sad and pathetic, less how I feel. I put another 20kg plate on each end of the bar. I remind myself it's a job, that it's just work. It's what's expected. I tell myself that some members of the public want to wank off to my cliché rubbish about how traumatic and heartbreaking the accident was. I'm so tired of making the story sound fresh. It's the same script. I do a lead up to the show, to the day, to how we were filming and then to how it is possible for something so horrific to happen on a reality show. It's similar to my rehearsed, half-in-the-bag pick-up lines I use at the clubs.

Being on the radio requires that I'm on. That I act like the nationally described 'go-getter' that has triumphed over tragedy. That I act like the man I used to be. That I am someone who has made the most of their situation. I call bullshit. I violently miss the sounds of my life. The sound of the ice swirling and clinking in my glass as I pour in my favourite 21 year aged Glenfiddich whiskey, the sound of Dark Side of the Moon playing on my brown Micracord turntable, a gift from my Mother on my 21st birthday. I even miss the awful hum that sung along with the music after I fucked up the needle. I miss the sound a woman makes when I'm down between her legs. The guttural moans as her hips rise. I miss the sounds of the ocean, the spitting crackle and whoosh of the waves in and out. Rain, I miss fucking rain, hitting the tin roof at night with its dings and pings, like popcorn dancing on a stove top. I even miss the sounds we don't notice when we hear, like our feet on a wooden floor, the groans and sighs or whistles we randomly make throughout a day. The simple sound of our own breathing. It's so silent in here now. So eerily silent. It makes time slow, spacious and empty.

What is really bizarre is to be at a nightclub that is strewn with drunks and pulsating lights and thumping music, everyone's mouths open wide like an Edvard Munch as they scream over the noise to each other. And all I can do is feel the floor throbbing at my feet and into my chest, the red and white flashing lights burning my eyes through to the back of my head and down into my throat. I'm cast in a silent film where no sound enters and there is always a barrier between me and them. I find myself staring at people's ears. Their folded, puckered ovals of skin over cartilage, like thin towels thrown on the floor. Little abysmal black holes stuck in the middle, holes that link inside lives to outside lives. Except for mine. The small bones and flesh attached like buttons to the outside of my skull are just pretenders, actors, con artists.

I have nightmares of drunken strangers reaching their greedy little fingers and hands into my mouth, pulling at my tongue, their little balled up fists crammed down my throat. Then suddenly, I hear better than everyone. Teeth clashing against glass on the other side of the room as a young girl giggles and takes a sip of her cocktail. She's been accidentally bumped in the arm by a boy whose huffering too close, like a helicopter ready to land. I can hear the panting of a couple thrust up against the hallway wall as they dry hump oblivious to anyone squeezing pass on their way to the washrooms. I can hear the bartenders scraping bank cards across the bar and into the open plastic palms of the EFTPOS machine.

I wake up sweating. I know that I'm missing out on something extraordinary. It's not just a distraction that sound brings, it's a whole other dimension. Sound has light and shadows. It sort of travels around us. Moves like an ethereal waterfall up and down our bodies. Sinks and reverberates inside of us.

Yes, I know, I know. *I'm lucky. Other people have it much worse. Try not to think of being deaf as a disability but an opportunity.* Blah, blah, blah.

I am trying. I am. I am trying to fill the spaces where music and laughter and chatter and the general banal hum of sound used to crowd my life. Whisky, random women, silent porn and nightmares aren't working anymore. Yet, on the radio, on TV, while I'm on show, I paint a story of gratitude and redemption. Like any good storyteller it has its highs and lows and in the end the hero triumphs. He or she rises above the ashes and claims the glorious prize of … of what? If only life would actually wrap up like a story.

CHAPTER TWO

(Ten Months Ago)

I arrive at the Crowne Plaza in Adelaide, South Australia, where I am immediately led up to the highest floor and ushered into a large, mauve conference room with tall, gold engraved doors. My photo is taken by a shy assistant with a square face and square torso. What we would all call a boxy woman. With her teeth showing, she gives me a happy four-sided smile that seems to stretch the lower half of her face, and with her short, stubby fingers and a blush, she hands me a name tag and I am then ushered into a smaller room that is filled with about twenty or thirty other men. They are all between the ages of twenty-five and thirty-five. Just as advertised. There are also two women, whom I assume are the casting agents.

One woman is older than the other. I would guess she's in her mid-50s. She's all business with her short grey hair and black, wide-rimmed glasses. They are like a shield propped on her face. She looks like a school mum from Harry Potter. It's evident that she is in charge as she smiles at us. You can feel her scrutiny as she cinches her eyes. She doesn't hide judgements and assessments as she scans me up and down. She's already slicing and dicing. Her mind works fast. You can tell that she's exceptional at reading people and piecing together the potential of their interactions. It's her job. She clasps her hands in front of her long, pale pink linen dress, the only thing that softens her approach and moves her gaze around the room. The other woman is younger, brunette, kind-of pretty. She's seated at a computer close to the back of the room. She has her doll-like lips pursed, her cup-like cheekbones clenched into a tiny little grimace as she types. You can tell she's trying to look important, but she's too bangable to be taken that seriously. I'm the last one to arrive. Always like making an entrance. I smile. The commander-in-chief asks us to stand and to form a circle so we can begin.

"Welcome everyone." She keeps the same smile and pushes her glasses back with a long finger as she looks around at all of us. "How about we start by going around the room. Just say your name, age and occupation?" Everyone kind of shuffles and smiles at one another. We are not sure who should start. The woman frowns. "Okay, how about I start?" There's a slight sternness to her voice, hardly noticeable, kind of like a mother who is losing her patience. She looks around at us again and takes a breath. This time I think I detect a hiss. "Hi," lips smiling again,

"I'm Peta, I'm fifty-two years old and I work as a casting director!" The smile still holds as she motions to the man to her left. And we are off.

"Hi, I'm Ruben. I'm 31 years old and I'm a heavy machinery mechanic." We go around the circle. My turn is next. I haven't really listened as I've been rehearsing different answers in my head. *Hi, I'm Henry, 31-year-old sleazebag looking for some fast cash. Hi, I'm Henry the man of every woman's dreams. Hi, I'm Henry what the hell am I doing here?*

"Hi, I'm Henry, 31 years old and I work in finance." And before you know it it's off to the next guy.

After that we engage in what amounts to basically a bunch of social experiments. In one exercise we are placed in front of another applicant and asked to say something we like about them and something we don't like about them. I get the impression that Peta is hoping we don't just say something banal, such as 'I like his smile but I don't like his hair'. Her eyes have narrowed, and it has given me the impression she is looking for something controversial, something insightful or different. I'm paired up with Ruben. On first impression I'm not sure if I like him at all. Maybe I should just say that? He is tall and fit and has green almond-shaped eyes that remind me of ripened and halved avocados. Avatar eyes. Sitting above his eyes are dark straight eyebrows. There's a permanent half-smile pinned to his face like a cartoon caricature and to be honest, I wouldn't mind knocking it off his face. Cocky bastard. His hands are jammed into his pockets giving the impression that he is either really uncomfortable or just doesn't want to be here. When it's my turn, I say "I think 'Ruben-my-adversary' looks over-confident and we all know that means possibly–an egomaniac." His half-cocked smile twitches and a few people grunt and look at each other shocked. I grin, "Actually, this has made me both like him and not like him." Ruben and I stare at each other for a nano second. Everyone nods and smiles. Some let out little nervous laughs. Ruben relaxes and smiles too. "He's competition," I say and wink at Ruben.

When it's his turn, he tells me that my hair is wanky but that I seem pretty ballsy. People that say it like it is – he respects. I make a joke and tell the room that my Mum still cuts my hair so he'll have to take it up with her. Everyone laughs and Ruben relaxes even more. He removes his hands from his pant pockets. Some of the other guys fumble when it's their turn and some say 'pass' even though that was never given as an option. There's a skinny guy with glasses to our left, Thomas, who stutters, and Ruben looks at me and quietly mimics him with a dry, sarcastic tone, "Hiiii... I... I'mmm... Thoohh..." He's good at the imitation and I can't help but smile even though a part of me feels bad for the nerdy kid of the group. I am not unaware of the unkindness of our exchange, I guess I'm just not good at standing up to that shit.

Next on the audition roster is a 'discussion', which in reality TV terms means a heated exchange at least and a full-blown crusher at best. Peta draws our attention back to her and asks, "If you could spend ten minutes on the moon or have a one year all-expense paid trip to Europe which would you choose? Think about it. I'll give you thirty seconds to choose and then I want the moon people on my right and Europe people on my left." Easy enough question, surely it won't cause too much trouble.

I don't need thirty seconds, I immediately go to the moon side. Chatter has already started. Peta claps her hands, everyone goes silent. "Discuss!"

Surprisingly, the first guy to speak up is poor Thomas the stuttering engine and even before he speaks his face has turned a bright shade of red. "Well obviously Eu...eu...rope because wh...wh...wh....at's ten minutes compared to a ye...ye...year of something....of ...of... of... experiences," he says, "... like... awesome."

A guy called Benny, who is standing beside me speaks up. "Quality over quantity mate. Who would you rather fuck? A dozen starfish or a moaning porn star? Someone who just lies there or the one who likes to cum?" Everyone laughs. "It's gotta be the moon, mate. Not everyone gets to go there." Ruben's smiling and pipes up, "Hard to believe you could make a woman cum Benny in the two minutes you would last." Everyone laughs even harder. I look at Thomas. I give him a smile. When the laughter dies down, I pipe up. "Seriously though, think about it. You can go to Europe for a year anytime, on your own schedule, but you sure as hell can't tee up a trip to the moon on Skyscanner. Not unless you're friends with Wallace and Gromit." A few people laugh. I see the pretty brunette who is sat in the back look up, smile and then start tapping away. I'm thinking I passed. This is so strange. I can't believe how eager to please we all are.

The debate goes on for a while. Then there's a few more games. Peta explains the premise of the show because a few people pretend they've never watched it. They're here for an audition to be on the goddamn thing but are apparently too good and too smart to watch reality TV. She doesn't flinch or call bullshit even though most of us know they are wankers. She explains anyway.

"We've chosen a lady – of course a very beautiful, intelligent and down-to-earth girl – who would capture any man's attention, as The Eligible. I can assure you, she's nothing like me." It's the first kind-of joke she's told but no one laughs. Peta claps her hands together and ignores the lack of response to her one-liner. "On the first night all of you get to meet her, one by one. She'll be dressed like heaven, because she *is* heaven, and we'll try to spruce you up all James-Bond-like too. Every week, one of you or maybe two of you will get eliminated."

"And how does that happen?" Someone asks.

"Well, there will be times you can hang out in a group, and then she will also choose one of you a week to spend some alone time with her." A few guys elbow each other. Peta frowns, "I can assure you she's a lady, and it's not that kind of alone time, thank you." The guys who were grinning are now looking down at the carpet, hands clenched in front of them like naughty school boys. "At the end of the week there will be a cocktail party and the special lady will have a certain amount of coat pins. Throughout the course of her conversations and interactions that night, she'll slowly hand them out. The pin represents the fact that she would like to get to know you better. Towards the end of the night, there will be two unlucky gentlemen without pins, and only one pin left. The man without a pin will have to go home. It's up to you how you want to play it if you're in the bottom two. Comprehendé? Yes?"

Everyone nods.

Finally, Peta says, "Okay everyone, thanks for your participation. Dana and I," she motions to the girl at the back, "We are just going to leave for a few minutes to have a brief discussion to see who will go on to the next round of auditions." Peta and Dana are gone for what feels like less than three minutes. When they come back, they choose only four of us out of the men who are there. I can't believe it is so few. Though you could pick out a dozen pretty quick who you knew weren't going to make it. Too skinny, too short, too stuttery, too pale – it's a weird game. Crossing the finish line it was me, Ruben, a guy I knew they'd pick on account of his good looks, and surprisingly – Thomas. I guess stuttery doesn't matter or maybe it adds drama. I immediately think they want him on the show just to shame and ridicule him and to make the audience cringe. He is nice looking though so maybe it's more about that. Thomas has a large smile pinned to his face, like the twisted head of the donkey on the pin-the-tail-on-the-donkey game; some of the other guys slap him on the back.

The rejects are shepherded out of the room like cows in a stockyard. Peta hands out a few handshakes and some 'thank-you for coming ins'. Peta then tells the remaining four of us to stay put, to not leave the room, to not give out our details to each other, and to keep the talking to a minimum. Supposedly, they were interviewing another group who went in earlier. For a while we are reasonably well-behaved, but after about half an hour I think *fuck this*. I'm beginning to wonder if they are just doing some kind of experiment on us, like rats in a trifling crate and they just want to see how we'll behave. I end up asking the boys if they are up for something to drink other than the bottles of water set-up neatly around the room. I flash a good grin. They are all up for it. I stick my head out the door and stop a plump, middle-aged broadly smiling housekeeper. With some rolled up notes I ask, "Hey m'lady you mind bringing us a few beers?" I give her a big tip.

We're on our third round and getting pretty rowdy by the time Peta comes back – even Thomas has relaxed. He doesn't stutter as much when he's not nervous. She seems genuinely surprised when she sees the empty glasses. "How did you get these? There's security at the stairs and elevators making sure you guys don't leave." She's glaring but there's amusement in her eyes too. I give her a wink and a smile, "If there's a will there's a way." Everybody laughs. I can feel the charm of my voice and good looks working. She softens even more.

I'm asked to follow her and I'm taken to another room. More lab experiments. At the front is a long table with five people, two women and three men. They are sitting on swivel chairs that they are slowly undulating in, back and forth, like slow waves on the water. The room is barely lit. There are three cameras that look like some-thing from The Transformers. All of them pointing towards a single, lone, wooden chair – front-lit by lights and reflection panels. It feels like I'm under an investigation with the Australian Border Security or about to be questioned and tortured by some kind of street gang.

I walk in and shake everyone's hand and introduce myself. I make eye contact, smile and keep my back straight. The production crew seem pleasant enough. They look at me with half-smiles – or are they smirks? I fidget a little and clear my throat before taking a soldier's stance.

Peta breaks the tension. "It's the ringleader here." She gestures toward me, "Seems our boys got themselves a few rounds of beer." She's smiling. I immediately feel at ease. Everyone smiles. They seem impressed. I'm steered with a wave of the hand and offered the seat in the spotlight.

"How did you get beers?" The guy sitting at the far right of the table asks. He's leaning forward on his elbows and grinning.

"Flirted with the housekeeper," I grin. Everyone lets out a little laugh.

The team take their turns introducing themselves and explaining what they do. There are two casting agents, Peta and Dana, the Network Director, the Production Director – he's the one who asked about the beer – and a Producer. Peta takes the lead. "To start I just need you to say your full name, age, town of residence, and occupation. If you can, just stare directly into the camera, and then after that when we have a little discussion, you can look at us. Okay?" A man is suddenly in my face with a rectangular chalkboard. It is snapped and I'm motioned to go.

"Hi, I'm Henry Vedder. I'm thirty-one years old, hail from Adelaide, South Australia and I work in the very exciting business of stocks." I grin but no one laughs.

"Very good, that was great," says Peta. Sean, the Network Director leans over and whispers something in the Production Director's ear.

"Now we're just going to go around the panel and ask questions," continues Peta, "just be as honest as you can."

"Brilliant" I reply.

Sean starts. "If you could choose any female celebrity as your ideal woman, who would it be?"

I don't hesitate even though I've never been the kind guy to salivate over celebrities at all.

"Wonder Woman for sure." Sean tilts his head and gives me a curious look. No one says anything so I keep talking. "I know she's not a real celebrity or person for that matter but man she's a Goddess of Love, isn't she?" I feel myself start to blush a bit. "She's fearless and fights to the death but she's also calm and warm and smart. It's kinda what you want in a relationship." *Where the fuck is this shit coming from?* I think to myself. I've never thought about Wonder Woman before, well maybe as a boy with a comic book. Pretty sure she was the first 'woman' I ever wanked to at twelve years old. Torch jammed up under my left armpit, covered with batman sheets. The book in one hand and my cock in the other.

Sean smiles and leans back in his chair. His right arm is stretched out in front of him resting on the table and his pen taps away. "Any other reason you love Wonder Woman?"

I look directly at him and smile, "Well, she's got a pretty smoking, kinky hot outfit and a killer rack. What kind of man doesn't like that?"

Everyone laughs. Sean keeps his eyes on me, "I'm not sure we can arrange that." His eyes narrow. He reminds me of my place. He has the power. I fidget a little in my seat and lean back. As we continue to go through the questions, I think about Junip. Maybe it was the Wonder Woman comment and my cocky attitude. She would have hated what I'm doing – all the attention that's premised on appearance and some weird superficiality, the push of archaic gender roles. I push the thought from my mind and remind myself I need this. Fuck it.

There's a month between being told I'm on the show and flying to Sydney to undergo filming. In that time I have to undergo two psych assessments, a medical that includes six vials of blood and a urine test. Fucking lab rat. About ten pages of results come back. I guess it's nice to know I'm healthy. Not even an STI – surprising considering the general sexual rampage of Henry Vedder. I consult with a stylist, get photos taken in my 'favourite' outfits to send off, and fill out a bunch of publicity questionnaires. I watch a few seasons of the show to prepare myself for what's about to happen and I have sobering moments where I nearly pull the plug on the whole thing.

I can't remember being very curious about who I was going to meet. I am told that it's someone unknown who hasn't been on a season before, but of course that she is amazing and beautiful and funny, and all the things that men put in their dream-girl case.

The truth is my financial situation is pretty dire. That's kind of my focus. I haven't really worked for four years. I had made some money investing in stocks but I have recently lost most of what I had in a venture that went really fucking south. I was never very good at speculation – the research killed me. I had just enough cash to keep my rent and my whisky and what most women would call my 'man-slut' lifestyle up for tops three more months. And without a fallback trade or degree, I was anxious as fuck about what I was going to do. The last thing I wanted to do was go on the TV Show "The Eligibles" starring Henry Vedder as one of the twenty or so other desperates. It was some chick that I picked up that gave me the idea. "You look like one of those guys from 'The Eligibles'" she had swooned. And Bam... I saw it as an open door to easy money. That's banking that everything goes well and that I'm portrayed okay. Hell, it could be fun, an adventure of some kind. Who knows, maybe I'll start working in TV or radio. My mother always said I had a voice for radio. There sure as hell was no way I was going back to any kind of criminal behaviour. I got a flash of my life before trading stocks.

I'm not sure how I feel about all the risks I've taken to get here. There are things I've taken, things I've gained and things I've lost. What I do know is that I take risks, and that I've been lucky. Opportunities have knocked and I've grabbed at them with my two greedy hands like a reflex. I certainly didn't go on the show to meet a woman or to find someone I could love. As far as I knew, it wasn't possible to love like I had already. The love ship had sailed.

We're prepped for filming, mollycoddled, as my Gran used to say. Dana, the girl who typed away in the back of the casting room, meets me at the airport. She leads me to a bus with five other guys from my state, who I presume were on the same flight but I didn't notice them. Maybe I should've been looking out for the 'competition'. There's also a security guard. Fat and bald but friendly. I grab a seat. We start to introduce ourselves and shake hands but the security guard says, "Hey can I ask you to please not talk to one another." He smiles an apology. "I'll also need your phones, passports and wallets for safekeeping until you leave the show." He hands out plastic zip-up bags with our names scrawled in black letters across the front. I have a minor twitch – what have I signed up for? I place my things inside the bag.

The bus ride takes about an hour. We drive over the Sydney Harbour Bridge. I haven't been here since my Mum and Dad brought me for a holiday when I was about twelve. I remember them holding hands and Dad smashing ice-cream in Mum's face that day, and we laughed a lot. The only good memory really I have of my Dad.

We arrive at the hotel, drive around the back and enter through the employee entrance which is a large, steel garage full of boxes and moving equipment. Once inside they have 'minders' who take us separately to our hotel rooms. My minder is a young, quiet, skinny guy with flat, slightly greasy brown hair. The kind of guy you forget. He tells me that I will be sharing a room with a guy named Maverick. We are not given key cards because we are not allowed to leave our rooms for the three days we are there. After giving up my passport, phone and wallet I feel a bit like I'm going to prison. When I enter the room, Maverick, a tall, muscular and fit guy with a wide face, a wide smile, and some slight balding edging up the sides of his forehead, stands up and thrusts out his hand. He starts talking and for someone who looks rather brooding and intimidating he never stops. I hear all about his obsession with cars. He starts on about all the old cars he's rebuilt and sold – a Mustang '66 Coupe, a '65 Mustang Fastback, a '67 Shelby GT350, and a bunch of others – to rich old men and then he rattles on about the magazines his cars have been featured in. I've never given a shit about cars, but I feign interest. I'm so relieved I've brought my iPod with me – the only one we were allowed was one without Bluetooth or Wi-Fi and they're sure as hell hard to find. I eventually place the headphones over my ears. He keeps nattering. Fuck. I shove a book in my face. I'm reading this crazy crime novel I picked up at the airport before we took off. And still, he keeps talking. I'm getting sick of listening to him. Mav, shut the fuck up. It never ends. For three long fucking days it never fucking ends.

The days include preliminary filmed interviews, stylist consultations, meetings with various magazines and publicists, safety officers, lawyers and producers. It's a lot more work than I anticipated. Most of this is done solo, but occasionally, we are with some of the other guys. We never get a chance to talk really though. I always relish leaving the hotel room. The whole room fucking smells of Mav. I start to really miss the smell of a woman.

When the day comes for us to meet our lady, we are all bussed from the hotel to some generic, grey-bricked community center near the shows apparent mansion. I have makeup applied for the first time in my life, save the time I tried out my Mum's lipstick when I was six or seven. Smeared it all over my face. I have put on a custom-fitted slate grey suit that a stylist named Krista and I chose. A phone-sized electronic pack is placed on the back of my suit pants and the cable edged up through my front side and a small microphone is taped to my chest with thick tape. Photos are then taken for publicity once I'm suited up. I'm told to look rugged, and then strong and thoughtful, but still happy 'because I might be meeting my future wife'. We're all told to not talk to each other so our first meeting looks more authentic on camera. The producers are busy as fuck though, running around making sure everything is being cued for filming, so they don't really have too much time for us. A bunch of the guys end up chatting. After my time with Mav I prefer not to chat – which either makes me look like I'm sticking to the rules, or that I'm an asshole. I do recognise Ruben but no one else is there from our casting. Ruben and I shake hands and smile.

"Hey man, I didn't see you on the plane," I say.

"I had to come to Sydney the week before for work, so

I arrived early." Ruben smiles. I find out he's not just a heavy machinery mechanic, but he runs his own business and travels a lot. By the sounds of it a pretty successful business. It makes me like him more that he stayed quiet about that at the auditions. We are interrupted by one of the producers. He's doing another mic check. Everyone seems pretty ladsy aside from a few creeps they've brought in. I'm unsure if they are going to get the drama they need for the show but I do notice that no one seems to like Ruben. I can see people rolling their eyes and smirking, talking under their breath. I'm not sure why though. I like Ruben. He had a good sense of humour when we had to do our sit-down at the very beginning. Maybe we are more similar than I realize. I wonder if I get eye-rolling?

A couple of crew members, I'm not sure what they do there's so many people, call myself and two other guys to leave the community hall and follow them. We are ushered into a white Land Rover. When we get close to the mansion we are swapped out into a limousine. There is a producer and a cameraman in the limousine. They give us some champagne. Sam, the producer, is hunched in a seat. The buttons of his shirt slightly pull apart as his chest rests on his belly. He has chubby legs and his feet barely touch the floor. A middle-aged body on a young face. All in all, he's slightly dishevelled with patchy three-day stubble on his face. He's the one-eighty, the antithesis to all of us. The cameraman is like white noise, he stays silent with a large camera in front of his face. He doesn't say anything and I think maybe it's because we are technically to pretend he's not there at all. He tells me later they were just on a tight schedule and were asked to avoid unnecessary pleasantries.

Sam asks us to talk casually among ourselves, to talk about the kind of girl we want to meet while we 'drive up the road'. The limo isn't actually moving. I feel weird in my makeup, slick suit and affected conversation, in a non-moving-pretend-moving car. The other guys don't seem to care. They have switched from authentic people to producer puppets in a second.

Thad, a 6'1" Swede, talks first. He's attractive and an obvious womaniser.

"She better be hot or I'm running." I think he licked his lips.

Liam, a true Aussie bogan, has wild blue eyes and long teeth. Not quite British teeth, but long nonetheless. "Of course she's gonna be hot. She's the most eligible woman in Oz Mate!" Liam grins.

Thad frowns, "Well she's in trouble, I mean look at me." He leans back and sweeps his arms open. He's joking but on screen it comes off as douchey. They get their drama. Good casting agents. We are all laughing at him.

I pipe up, "Am I the only one who's nervous?"

"Fuck no!" says Liam. Sam reminds him not to say 'fuck', but 'shit' is okay, and we film that bit again. Eventually they give up telling us to not swear and they bleep out those parts.

"Am I the only who feels nervous?" I repeat as instructed.

"Hell no! I'm about to shit myself. I'll probably throw up all over her dress," says Liam.

At this point the limousine actually starts moving, and the mansion comes into view. The whole night is magical looking. It's swimming with fairy lights, yellow poppies, roses and flowers, candles, cameramen and crew. It reminds me of when I was around ten and my grandmother brought out all the family jewels- garish glittering yellow, and white gold jewels piled on a glass table. I thought she had met with pirates and robbed them of their treasure. She was handing them out. It was magical. It was just before she died. The mansion is over the top. In some way though it looks better than real life. It's a well-orchestrated fantasy where nothing can go wrong.

"Holy shit, look at that mansion!" I blurt out. Sam smiles, "Can I get all of you to all talk about the mansion? Describe it?" We start on about the stairs, the columns, the size... the size... it's fucking huge. Sam says cut. We all stop talking. I feel my stomach do a small somersault. Sam lets us know that the limousine is going to move forward a few more feet and that when it comes to a stop, we are to get out slowly one by one, turn the corner and walk up the stairs to meet our lady. He explains that we'll each have about ten minutes with her. Everything is explained as if he's reading the nightly news. Then he puts on a big smile, "Come on, guys. Aren't you excited?" We all cheer on cue like ninth graders. After my past I'm never surprised at what I'll do for a few bucks and some status.

CHAPTER THREE

I'm the last one out of the limousine. I close the limo door as I step out and adjust my suit. I smile and start walking. I turn the corner, scouting out where the cameras are. I've always had steady nerves, and at this point I'm thankful. I can see the Eligible in the distance, man she's a beautiful woman. I forget why I am here and all of a sudden I want to make a good impression. She looks to be about 5'8" with a killer body, shoulder-length wavy blonde beach hair and she's wearing a low-cut, green silk gown that hugs all the best parts of her body.

Things start to feel dreamlike as if a conveyor belt or escalator is moving me towards her. My legs are not my legs. Yet, the closer I get the more familiar she starts to look. I get a crazy flash across my eyes. A memory, a nightmare. For a second I'm terrified. I think, no fucking way this can be real, but as soon as I'm a few meters away my heart starts to pound like a sledgehammer. My throat goes dry. My blood freezes. It's her.

This woman has haunted me for over five years. I have tried to rip her from my memory. She is the reason I lost everything – friends, my ex-wife Junip, everyone. The Eligible, *this* Eligible, is the reason I've become a hollow, shit of a man who is incapable of any moral relationship, of any life that feeds my soul. I have become the kind of man that spends his time drinking whisky and banging random women. A loser really, disguised as a 6'3" brown-haired, straight-jawed 31-year-old classically handsome man. She doesn't know me. She doesn't recognize me. I swallow hard pushing fear back down and smile. I instinctively run my hand through my raked back hair and climb the last step.

I am in front of her. I feel like Liam, like I'm going to throw-up. My mind is racing and I wonder if this is some elaborate joke or ploy for good TV drama. The host announcing off camera, "watch as sleazebag Henry Vedder gets fucked in the ass." His voice like a circus ring-leader. But then she smiles. A big wide open smile that makes her cheeks shine like honey, and as much as I just want to collapse and weep at her feet, I pull myself together and stand legs apart, shoulders back and pretend that this gorgeous woman is actually a beautiful and mysterious stranger.

If this meeting hadn't been filmed, I probably wouldn't have remembered the moment at all. When I watched it back, it looks like sweet humbling nerves not like my brain is scrambled, like torment is washing through me.

"You're gorgeous," I say with a smile. It's as if a cool,

calm and collected avatar has taken over my body and spoken for me.

She puts out her hand and I take it, small and delicate, and I reach over to kiss her on the cheek.

"Thank you," she smiles and cocks her head to one side, "I'm Poppy." She says this with a slight rise in her voice as if she is asking a question.

"I'm Henry. How are you?"

Her eyes open a little wider. Does she recognize my voice? My eyes? My stomach tightens and I feel little beads of sweat break out on my forehead, but then she smiles and I'm pulled back and I'm not even a 100% sure that anything even happened. Fuck, it was probably just my own paranoia.

"To be honest, I'm like super nervous." She lets out a small laugh. That's it, she was nervous. I get to relax.

"Well, if it helps, I think we all are." I want to wrap her up in a blanket and make her feel safe. "I'm totally out of my comfort zone here. I've never even used dating apps, so this is weird," I laugh.

"Thanks, that really helps." She's smiling, looking up at my lips, at my eyes. I sense her attraction to me. We talk for awhile about how weird this all is until a comfortable pause meets us.

"You seem real down to earth," she says. Again there's that slight rise in her voice.

"Sure," I smile awkwardly "I'm pretty relaxed but I'm always up for adventure." I feel my cocky confidence returning. "What about you? Do you like adventures?"

I already know all this about Poppy though. I know

that she broke her leg back-flipping from a high tree when she was eleven, because of a dare. I know that she got her scuba diving license when she was in the Galapagos three years ago. I know that she went skydiving two years ago even though she's afraid of heights. I know that she travelled the world for a few years and I know that she loves wine and books and hiking and camping. I know fucking everything.

Poppy smiles, "Yeah, I like to try things. I like things that make me scared," she giggles. "I think that's important, isn't it?" She cocks her head. I want to reach down and kiss her full on the lips. "No one sky dives because they're indifferent do they?" She doesn't wait for an answer. "I think there's something about the rush, the playing with death" she smiles "that... changes life."

I know what she means. Our conversation starts to slide together like warm milk and honey. I forget about the cameras. I'm enamoured, mesmerized by the movement of her mouth, by the sound of her voice, by her words. I shake my head to come out of the chimera because I notice the producers are waving at us to wrap it up.

I return to the 'confident' man. "I think I'd rather live a life filled with all the goodness it has to offer than to be too scared to try anything. I like to try new spices, new flavours." Fuck, I sound like a wanker.

"And what kind of spice are you, Mr. Henry?" asks Poppy. There's a slight shyness to her but there is also a confidence in her eyes, almost a darkness, a sarcasm. She's not afraid to hold my gaze. I laugh, "I realize I sound like a twat right now." I run my hand through my hair, "Talking about fucking spices. All I know is that I'm looking for someone that compliments me, and I them." And again, I believe it. I actually feel it. What have I become in the ten minutes I've been standing in front of this Goddess?

"Well, it sounds like you're here for the right reasons doesn't it?" Poppy smiles. But again I'm jolted back. And my head is racing – she can see right through me – she knows I'm a lying sack of shit, that I'm a morally depraved shell.

"I guess, I'll see you inside, Poppy." I smile and reach down and kiss her on the cheek and walk away. On the playback I see her watching my back and beaming. She tells the cameramen that I am her favourite so far. I walk inside and ask for the washroom. Once inside I lock the door, turn on the water over the sink and lean over the toilet and retch my guts out. I flush the toilet, rinse my mouth out, stand up straight and look at myself in the mirror. "Get your shit together." I let out a sigh, run my hand through my hair and open the door. The producers are waiting for me. I waffle on about how gorgeous she is, about what a great adventure I think this is going to be. The producer leans over and gives me a smile and a smack on the back. I feel as if I'm watching all of this from outside my body. It's disgusting how good of an actor I am.

The producer motions for me to go into the open large room on my left where I'm handed another glass of sparkling by a nice-looking girl and I take a seat on a silver crushed velvet sofa. There are a bunch of other guys here as well, who I didn't notice left the community centre before I did. There are still cameras on us but it feels more relaxed. I look around at the other men and none of them are good enough for Poppy. There is literally a circus performer and he keeps putting his legs over his head in a bid for the camera's attention. And he's in a damn suit. There is a guy with a skinny face and red hair with what I can only imagine is some kind of turrets. He blurts out things like "I'm going to shit in that plant" and "I'd like to bend her over that couch", gesturing to the waitress that's handing out champagne. Then there is a guy who misses his dog. No, like *really* misses his dog. He reminds me of Maverick. He won't shut up. Looking around, I wonder how some of them made it through. Fuck, there were psych assessments. Maybe it's all part of the drama – are the assessments to find us? The fucked up ones?

We are left hanging in this area for hours. There's a pool and about five or so open rooms surrounding it, the cameras swarming carefully around us. By the time Poppy comes in it's 3am and we are drunk as fuck. As soon as she walks in we all cheer, walk towards her and raise our glasses.

"I am so overwhelmed that you are all here tonight. That you took time out of your busy lives to be here with me." There's something in the way she says this, that makes you think that she has no idea how fucking beautiful she is. "And... well... let's be open to see where this adventure takes us. So, without going on too much, let's raise our glasses," everyone raises their glass, "To love!"

"To love!" we all recite in unison. In my head it feels like all of this is scripted, but I'm not quite sure. The way I feel and respond is at least real. Poppy stands for a few more moments with a frozen smile spread across her face. The cameras are swirling at her from all angles. Poppy's smile drops just a little, and she puts down her glass. She looks exhausted. Vulnerable. She tries to smile bigger. And then every guy there swarms her, takes her away for 'private' chats, tries to impress her with whatever party trick or line they have. I sit on the outer edge with a few of the other guys, who swap and change as they vie for attention. After about an hour she asks if she can take me for a chat and in doing so, ignores some of the men trying to take her hand on the way. I don't know if I'm surprised or not at all. Surely it wasn't just me that thought there was something extraordinary between us?

We sit on what could be described as a love swing. It's covered in fake flowers and vines and fairy lights. The cameras are on us and the producers watching from a distance. She pulls her dress beneath her as she sits, lady-like. "Are you okay?" I ask. She breathes out heavy, and laughs as she looks up at me. "I think you're the only person that has actually asked me that tonight." I feel bad for her. "I'm sorry, I hope that doesn't seem ungrateful? All the guys here are amazing," she smiles.

I point to circus guy. "Even that one?"

She laughs and winks, "Oh, especially that one."

I take her hand in mine, "Just take a moment to breathe and recollect. I promise not everyone here is crazy." I can't believe I'm using my lines on her. Making the other guys seem inferior. But it's so easy.

She follows my advice and closes her eyes and takes a deep breath. The producers are loving it. I can see them smiling in my peripherals. We chat for a while, relaxed, and then she leans down to her ankle. There is a little diamond pouch tied to it. Poppy pulls out a little coat pin. It's in the shape of a heart, and it's yellow, just like the poppy flowers my Mother used to grow in her garden when I was little.

"You know, I've been pulled away by all these guys tonight, and to be honest it's quite overwhelming. You're the first person I've taken away for a chat and also the first person who has allowed me to relax and breathe for a second." She takes another breath, as if reiterating her gratefulness, holding the little pin, and says, "Henry, this represents that I want to spend more time with you. Do you want to as well? Spend more time with me?"

I say yes, and she places it on me, squeezes my hand, and then I go join the rest of the guys with and without yellow heart pins, until there is only one person without a pin, and one poor sod has to say his goodbye's and walk sullenly, drunk and humiliated, out of the mansion.

CHAPTER FOUR

My father used to beat my mum. I don't like to use the word 'dad', it sounds too intimate. It sounds like a man who bounces you on his knee and plays catch with you in the yard. The kind of man who wraps his arms around your mum's waist and nuzzles into her. I prefer to think of my father as a sperm-donor. As a collection of cells. As a child it was scary as fuck sometimes. Thank god I was a good sleeper. Thank god for that dumb game-boy. Somehow it helped protect me. I missed a lot. But in the morning I would wake up to Mum sitting on the kitchen floor, staring with blood spatter around her. My tears would be silent but as soon as she saw me she would start to make everything alright. She'd stand up and say in a cheerful voice, "Oh, my sweet Henry let's get you some breakfast." And soon we would forget about it. Sometimes it was only a black-eye or new bruises edging up her arm. Imprints of my father's fingers. Lots of times I'd come home from school and she'd be cradling her face in her arms as she sat at the kitchen table, quietly sobbing, unable to face the world. Sometimes it made me angry. Her crying.

It's funny what you think is normal when you're a child. I didn't always dismiss my father the way that I do now. He was always nice to me. He never touched me. He always spoke kindly to me. I don't know – maybe that's why I never stood up to him. I was always trying to please him. I thought maybe if he loved me more he would leave her alone. If I could just please him, make him more happy or make him more interested in me he would leave her alone. He was never drunk. He never stayed out all night. He was never unfaithful. He worked the same job for years. He never even really seemed to lose his temper. Ever. He just enjoyed hitting her. I felt, or really I still feel, like a coward.

It wasn't until I was fifteen and my father had beat my mum unconscious that I intervened and called an ambulance on my new mobile, pretending to be a neighbour. I was out in the backyard pacing and panting like a scared neglected pup. I was afraid. My father was still in the house. The ambulance and the police came. They left, one with my mum and the other with my father. He got 18 months for nearly killing her. Mum spent just over four months in hospital learning to talk, walk and function all over again. I stayed with her best friend, Judy, during that time. She was never the same.

I looked after her the best I could, but I often stayed out drinking with friends. I had a hard time looking her in the eyes. Though she never made me feel like it, I felt guilty. I knew I should've done something sooner. Every story you hear as a boy is that boys protect girls. I should have protected my mum. I went to visit my father just once while he was still in prison. That was fucked too. We sat across from each other and said nothing. I think we both knew it was over. It was easy enough to erase him or at least that's what I told myself. I could almost convince myself that it gave me some sort of redemption, but whisky would remind me that I still had one foot in hell. Mum filed for divorce while he was behind bars, and after he got out he disappeared, and Mum slowly climbed out of her own hell.

She had been a math's highschool teacher, but she started doing post-grad uni, which involved a lot of long nights. After a few years she got her PHD and started teaching Economics at the University of Adelaide. I was pretty proud of her. She still dated a lot of the wrong guys, but they were at least decent to her. Some were even pretty good people, but not right for Mum. I met a shit ton of them. I was part of the show. She'd say: *'Here's my son, Henry. So handsome.'* And I'd smile and make some cheesy joke. After I married, I would drag my wife, Junip along. She never understood why I felt like I had to go to all these dinners, lunches and 'general outings' with each new man. *'Can't you just wait until she's actually dated one for longer than 3 weeks?'* she'd moan. I was too ashamed to tell Junip the truth until a few years into our marriage. I thought Junip would think I was a pussy, but she didn't. She just hugged me, and told me that none of that was my fault, even though I didn't agree. Being there for Mum helped me believe that she didn't hate me or maybe it was so that I wouldn't hate me. I don't know.

Then one day out of the blue my father Peter contacted me. I was 26. I opened the door to my life a crack. We would send the occasional text. I deleted quite a few that I wrote before sending. Some I deleted in my message Inbox after I sent them, just so I didn't have to see the words glaring at me when I opened my phone. I hated how kind I was to him after everything. Fucking spineless. I wanted to know how the fuck he could have treated my mother like he did but I'd always chicken out on asking. I just couldn't do it. It's weird, outside of him I can stand my ground if I really want to. Sometimes I'm even a bit of a dick but I don't care. I hate cowards, but with Peter... I guess it's too late to change the script. He's the man and I'm the boy. Our contact just naturally faded away.

Becoming a stockbroker wasn't a straight path for me. I usually just say I'm in financing or stocks and leave it at that. It's my way to avoid the question when asked. Surely everyone has secrets? We've all done shit. Do any of us really know each other or even ourselves? They say that there are more neurons in the brain than there are stars in the milky way, and I sure as hell don't control every fucking neuron in my brain, let alone understand them. I'm not saying it's wrong that we're all hidden behind different layered veils of shame but when we're butting up against our own secrets, it starts to feel even more shameful. I was about to get to know Poppy in a more meaningful way, if you could call being on the set of a reality TV show meaningful, and my veils felt like they were shrinking and sucking out my air.

Things always have a beginning and for me it was meeting Amos at some dudes boat party. My friend Keith had invited me. Junip was at her sister's for dinner, and it was a last minute decision to head on out and jump on board for drinks and a sunset. Work had sucked that day, and I didn't like the idea of just hanging on the couch playing online video games with let's be honest, pimply teenagers in other cities and other houses, shoving their sweaty fingers in bags of cheese-flavoured chips.

I was surprised when I got to the dock that it was the large white and wooden yacht that was tied to slip number five. It had to be worth at least 2.5 mil. Wealth I would never know. The deck was swarming with money. People of Adelaide who didn't know anything but that kind of life and for sure would step back from my story. Thankfully, I'm good at hiding my life and fitting in. I was dressed the part and being tall and handsome, as my mum would say, made it easy for me to slip into these types of events and conversations.

I was glad that Junip wasn't with me. She'd either think everyone was a douche and be planning our escape off the yacht, or possibly she'd recognise that I had a shit 9-5 IT job. She'd recall how most of her friend's and her sisters' husbands were easy six figures and be secretly scouting out a new husband.

Amos sold me the cocaine. It freed me from thinking

about Junip and what she thought about our half-assed life. Amos was the kind of guy that stood out. He was tall and reasonably muscular, a surfer type. A few people thought we were brothers. Crazy. I think it was just the height thing. The coke gave me even more confidence, and I was able to see things more clearly. Amos, though charismatic, was a bundle of anxious energy. His eyes continually darted all around the room, he laughed nervously and obsessively tapped his right heel up and down completely out of tune with the music. An ambitious junkie. Still, we talked about wealth and capitalism and how wide the divides were between the social classes in Australia, despite being disguised as a 'fair go' country. I was intrigued by him. He was fucken' odd no doubt about it, and maybe not the brightest but I was intrigued; maybe it was the brother vibe. We kept on talking.

Every idea I had ever had about an egalitarian Australia being in whatever way comprehensible, was destroyed that night. Even looking back, the ideology I convinced myself to do something horrific with, I still believe. It really is all an illusion that Australia is fair-go. Yeah, we all go to the same beach together, barrack for the same rugby teams and drink the same beer. Australia is a place where the frontman of the rock band Midnight Oil can become a Member of the House of Representatives in Parliament for God's sakes. A tradie can earn as much as a doctor given the right economic environment, and cleaning shit from toilets is considered as honourable as any other job, because you've worked for what you have. For whatever fucked up reason that makes us feel united – like we have something better going on than other countries. It's all distraction and all noise though, that we are classless and open and free. Aussies may all drink the same beer, but we certainly don't drink that beer in the same houses, at the same bars and in the same suburbs. Maybe Australian women are a bit more down-to-earth but they're still women. Women care about money and looks and social status, and that will always control their relationship decisions. Right? I was just lucky I got Junip before she knew any better. I figured this would change though as we grew up, as her Father's disapproving eye towards my little income caught her attention, as time would force her to be envious of the lifestyles that her sisters' husbands gave them, that I couldn't.

So Amos and I were on about how fucking hard it was to break into the next class, the next tier of wealth. That no matter how big Australia was, it was still small. Families knew families and unless you had the kind of dad that had friends on the course, you could knock at the door for fucking forever and it would still stay closed. The only thing that created wealth, was wealth. I grabbed us a couple of more beers and Amos starting dishing up lines for free, his heel constantly tapping.

Amos says, "Well, if no one will give you a leg up sometimes you just gotta take one. You can't wait for life to happen to you mate, you have to make it happen for you." I'm fucking nodding like a bobble-head and that's when he brings up the bank. I guess I thought he was joking, kind of. It's funny the kind of confidence you get when you snort coke. No idea seems completely outlandish.

I got home at 4am. I slid into bed next to Junip. Her hair smelt like tinned pears and sandalwood and her skin was slumber-warm. She rolled over and kissed me slow and with full lips, sleepy. My cock was instantly hard. She didn't open her eyes but still asked how my night was. I started to tell her about Amos, she started telling me about her sisters but we were doing more kissing than talking. Junip said she could taste the coke on my lips. I told her to keep tasting and said maybe she'd get high too. She climbed on top of me, her black hair running over the round mold of her breast; hiding one dark pink nipple. Her head was thrown back and my eyes followed the hollow of her neck up to her parted lips. She moaned, and it made me forget any of my inadequacies, any feelings that said I wasn't a rock star. Everything felt like it was enough at that moment. I grabbed onto her hips as she rode. I remember that being some of the best sex I've ever had. Fuck, I loved my wife.

Waking up on a drug downer and heading into work on Monday morning was when I decided I wanted more for Junip and I. I pictured us laughing at parties with cocktails in our hands and Junip lying naked on the deck of an Amels.

CHAPTER FIVE

Amos called two days later. I almost didn't pick up as it was a strange number. I had forgotten that I had given him my card.

"Hey, is this Henry?" he asked.

"Yeah," I said with some hesitation. I still wasn't sure who it was.

"Hey mate, it's Amos."

"Oh hey Amos. What's up?" I asked.

"You have some free time tonight?" he asked, "I have a business proposition I think you might be interested in." I was intrigued.

I grabbed a business card, *Henry Vedder, IT Specialist. Consultant, IT Keys,* and quickly turned it over. "Go ahead," I said and Amos gave me his address. After I hung up with Amos I sent a quick text off to Junip and gave her the heads up that I was meeting a friend after work. I finished work earlier and jumped in my old but well-serviced Toyota Corolla and headed to Amos's place.

His house was in Netherby, surrounded by cream coloured mansions stacked like rows of cereal boxes. The lawns were all trimmed to prim perfection with gardens boasting the best horticulturists. Every house had a long driveway with large cloistered wooden or steel doors that kept the world stuffed outside. Amos's house was the shittiest on the street, possibly the only house that hadn't been knocked down and replaced, or at the very least renovated. It was a single-story stone house with a grimy red tiled roof, and long weeds creeping out from under the cracked and worn out red concrete path. It looked like it would be more comfortable in North Adelaide or East Adelaide, but certainly not here in the South. The front door looked like an axe had been taken to it. Maybe it had. There were chunks of wood and paint missing, and when I knocked more flakes of paint fell off.

Inside, the house looked like somebody's grandmother lived there. Doilies that once made up the centerpiece of the dining room table were stuffed with dust and beer cans in a corner of the room, framed cross-stitchings were hanging everywhere. The couches were old and the 'fancy' one in the 'formal' living room was still covered in a yellowing plastic. Ritualistic-looking cigarette burns creating a polka-dot effect along the sofa arms.

"Hey man, sorry about the house," Amos said as he grabbed a couple of beers from the fridge. "This used to be my Grans. It was a rental but when she died the other old people got kicked out and I inherited it. I don't really hang here, my permanent home is in Sydney, but I like it here for a getaway, y'know. Adelaide, I mean."

Fuck this dude had a lot of money, I thought to myself. *Coke is a good business. Maybe he wanted me to help him sell?* Amos handed me a beer.

"It's a break from the lady," Amos continued chatting, "Plus, I didn't want her up in our business so I thought it was better to meet here than get you to Sydney." His heel was doing its never ending incessant tapping and his eyes were darting around. I took a swig of beer.

"That's okay. What's on your mind?" I asked. I was starting to feel nervous. Maybe I was just becoming infected with his energy.

"I found a bank." His eyes squinted. I must have looked like I was going to drop. I certainly felt queasy as fuck. Amos laughed. "Hey man, it's cool... I have contacts. I have a plan. Let me at least lay it out to you."

He had large paper plans of a specific bank, ideas to register us unrecognizable, a getaway plan. He watched my reaction with keen eyes, as he told me the plan with rehearsed care. I didn't say anything for a long while. I just swigged the beer he had given me, looked over the plans.

I'd like to say there is more to the story about my decision to go ahead with it all, than a few moments of thought. When I look back, I almost can't believe it was me. I look at Henry Vedder at twenty-six as some kind of string-puppet, or lapdog, or SIM character. Someone in Sweeney Todd's hellish den, fighting to not have his fingers turned into pies. I'm a cartoon character in The Twisted Tales of Felix The Cat. I'm an oddball in a Quinton Tarantino film. Who was I? Who am I?

"Yeah mate, let's fucking look into this." There was a clinking of beers, and an exchange of nervous electricity. The will and the way coasted through the both of us from that point and didn't leave until it was over.

Driving home I kept shaking my head from side to side. *What the fuck have I done? There's still time to back out. No! Fucking do it you coward. Do you think Junip wants to be married to some half-assed IT fuck? Come on mate, fuck it. I didn't build this system so that schmucks like me can't get ahead.* I cranked up the car stereo and started picturing Junip lying naked on the deck of our Amels, sun beating down, sucking on her nipples, my tongue running along the lips of her wet pussy. I imagined her moans, how happy she'd be with me and the life I'd given her. Happy wife, happy life, that was the saying right?

Amos and I worked on the plan for barely two weeks. We never texted or spoke on the phone about anything except meeting up for beers after work. We always met at that shit house. The bank Amos chose was in Sydney, as apparently he had a friend of a friend that could get us some pictures and plans, an architect of some kind. I didn't really want to know the full story because as they say, *the less you know, the better.*

We drove to Sydney with our phones left in Adelaide, so if it came down to it we could prove we were there. Amos seemed to think the police could geo-track our phones. The drive was tiresome and terrifying. There was way too much time to think. Fourteen hours or so with no stops aside from an occasional piss on the side of the road, with fucking Amos fidgeting next to me and snorting coke like the coke-head he was.

My heart was hammering at my chest when we stopped half way. I rubbed a little coke on my gums. I wondered if I was just like Amos after all. I was sitting in my car in the parking lot of a burger drive-thru. It was 4:30 pm. I sucked a large gulp of coke out of a waxed cardboard cup. My throat was dry as fuck. I called the Chasnell Bank. I can't even remember if a man or woman answered the phone

"Hi there, this is Pete Tackett, Human Resource Manager from Machen's PR. I need to set up an appointment to speak with the Manager and Assistant Manager regarding a somewhat serious accusation one of their employees has made. My apologies for the short notice but tomorrow morning before the start of the business day would be ideal." I was transferred to the Assistant Manager, Poppy. Yes, *that* fucking Poppy. She sounded worried and concerned and said that her and the Manager would be able to meet with me at 7:30am. I hung up and swung my car door open and gulped at the air.

I ran my hand through my hair and by the time I closed the car door the cockiness was creeping in and I smacked the steering wheel and cranked the music. *Fuck YES! Let's do this!* And I drove away.

Getting a gun in Australia is harder than you might think. Not like the good old US where I think anyone over the age of 5 can walk into a Walmart and walk out fully loaded. We scouted out the underbelly of the dark web to try to find handguns but between prices and risks we opted out of the idea. I remembered my father had his dad's old rifle, but it was too large and fuck I didn't feel like reaching out to that bastard. Not sure I could find him, anyway. In the end we opted for fake guns we found at a vintage costume store. We paid cash. There was never a plan to hurt anyone, and we had both agreed that if it came to that we would just bolt and get the fuck out of there.

Amos and I dressed in suits. We used an old pros-thetics kit of Juniper's rendering our faces unrecognis-able, which had taken a shitload of practice in that dirty Adelaide house. I wore dark-coloured eye contacts. Amos had covered his hand tattoos with thick makeup. With our gelled wig hair, high-end cologne and polished shoes we fit right into the sidewalk traffic. Amos said it felt like we were in some kind of Mission Impossible scene, but I just felt like we were heading to some fucked-up Halloween party. If anyone had gotten a good look at our faces, they'd see that we were just incompetent fakes. For all we knew, Robert and Poppy had figured out that my phone call wasn't actually from Machen's.

We were each swinging a briefcase stuffed with Wool-worths' shopping bags for the money, duct tape, gloves and two fake guns. Amos was chomping on some gum and I was whistling. Amos knocked on the door of the Chasnell Bank and the bank Manager, Robert, came and unlocked the door. When we turned to face him we pulled out the guns and were already pushing our way in.

Robert literally shat himself. Literally. I doubt he had

ever seen a gun before. Shit, I've never seen a gun before, save my grandfather's rifle, and these weren't really guns, but how the hell was he supposed to know that? "Ah man, you smell like a fucking toddler" Amos said as he held a gun to his head.

Sitting at a desk, about ten meters away was a rather plain looking woman. She had no makeup on, a plain long navy skirt, an oversized work blouse and flat shoes. Yet, when I got a bit closer, she was actually quite pretty. Hiding behind work attire was a young woman with pulled back dark blonde hair, piercing emerald green eyes, and just the right smattering of freckles across a small and defined nose. She was stern and resolute and still. Her name tag said Poppy.

"Get up!" said Amos. He ushered Robert and Poppy into a conference room. "Sit down." Amos stood behind them and I sat down across from both of them. I placed my gun on the table and said, in a voice I tried to disguise with an English accent, "We don't want anyone to get hurt here. We know that the bank has insurance, and I'm advising you in this situation to put your safety first, so let's do that?" I was speaking slowly and sternly. "All we want is for you to open the safe, we'll load our bags and get out of your way. We will have to tie you up, but your employees will find you soon enough, and soon life will be back to normal. So, let's not fuck this up." I reached for my gun. "Like I said we don't want to hurt anyone."

I had practiced that speech nine thousand times. Direct. To the point. Simple.

They both nodded. Easy.

"Get up!" Amos waved his fake gun in their direction. "Let's get to that safe," he said. They both stood up and shuffled out the room and down the hallway towards the back of the bank. Amos was walking behind and occasionally jabbing Robert in the back with this gun.

Poppy and Robert both had separate parts of the code needed to open the safe. It was standard banking procedure. It was used as a safety measure to prevent internal theft. Once the safe was open Amos said, "Okay, you two come with me." He led Poppy and Robert away to tie them up. I stepped in the safe and started to load money into our black and green Woolworths' shopping bags. Amos took Robert into one room and taped him to a chair. He then led Poppy to another room. We didn't want them talking.

I had nearly finished loading the bags and Amos still wasn't back. I had a sudden pinch of panic that something must be wrong. I left the bags of cash in the safe and went to find Amos. I found Robert wrapped in duct tape, sniveling. The front of his pants were soaked. Poor guy smelled like shit and piss. The next room I walked past was empty. When I hit the third room, I was repelled back.

Poppy was bent over a conference table, her skirt jacked up, her knickers at her knees. Amos was standing behind her, his pants at his ankles.

"What the fuck are you doing?" I yelled. Amos didn't even flinch. He looked at me over his shoulder with his eyes grinning. I wanted to hit him to death with the fake metal gun I was holding. "Just having a little fun, mate" he said.

An anger and deep-seated shame washed over me. I didn't know Poppy. I didn't know Amos. I didn't know what to do. Did I fear for my life? The guy was obviously absolutely insane. Any intervention could mean I'd be killed or end up in jail, right? I'd end up embarrassing my family, and I'd lose Junip and I'd lose my life. It wasn't worth it and fuck – the act had already been done – what could I do anyway? What purpose would it serve apart from making myself feel better?

So I said, "fucking DNA you jackass." He stepped back, his gun in his right hand and reached down for his pants. Poppy looked back at me and stared in my eyes. Her fear and terror stabbed through me.

"I'm using a condom, and wearing gloves," said Amos. *Fucking serious? He prepared for this?* And did he really think that would get rid of all the DNA? Amos starts squirting anti-bacterial gel that's on the bank table all over Poppy like some fuckwit dumbass criminal. "Pull your knickers back up, bitch." She obeyed, and he grinned. He grabbed Poppy by the arm and shoved her into a chair. He handed me his gun and then proceeded to wrap duct tape around her ankles and the chairs legs. He pulled her arms behind the chair and duct taped them together. I stood there like a zombie – the impact of what I was involved in running cold through my blood. I felt like I was seventeen again, deciding what to do about my Father – except this time I was the criminal too. Poppy continued to stare at me. I looked away.

Amos turned to me and grabbed the gun out of my hand. "Quit acting like a pussy," he said.

"There's fucking cameras everywhere. You fucking cocksucker," I yelled at him as we headed out the room. Poppy started to cry. Amos turned back and punched her in the face. I gasped. He pulled her hair back and whispered something in her ear. Blood was dripping from her nose. *This guy's a fucking psychopath,* I thought to myself. Amos pushed past me in the doorway, "Are we done?" he asked and started heading towards the safe. I just wanted to get the fuck out of there.

We gathered up the bags in the safe. We were silent. Amos was calm.

"How much?" he asked.

"Six hundred K," I answered, "Give or take."

We walked back down the hallway. I glanced once more at Robert, still sniveling and hunched over. Then I saw Poppy again. She was sitting frozen, dry tears and a small trickle of blood just below her nose. Fuck she was young, maybe twenty-two or twenty-three.

We walked out of there with six hundred K in green and black Woolworths' bags, sharp suits, slicked hair and shiny shoes. Literally walked, briefcases in our hands. It was 8am. We looked like every other working drone out on the street. After a few blocks where we were certain there'd be no security cameras, we hung a left and hopped into my little Corolla and drove away through the back streets. I dropped Amos off at some mansion with his share, and drove the lonely drive back to Adelaide on my own, considering whether or not to swerve into a truck.

That was five years ago. Three hundred thousand dollars each and a nightmare. No one remembers seeing two guys in suits at 8am in the morning because there were lots of guys in suits at 8am. The police were pretty useless, and it's probably because this kind of stuff doesn't happen very often in Australia. I have no idea if Amos was ever approached because we cut ties just as planned straight after.

For a week or so afterwards, every sound of a siren, every sight of a Police Officer, made the blood drain and then push all the way through my body and back up into my brain like a syringe. I wasn't a hardened criminal, I wasn't used to this shit.

A few days after I got home, Junip sat at the breakfast table with her daily newspaper, reading the front page news about my crime. She spoke about how awful it was – that any human would do something so awful to other human beings, make them so scared for their lives – all for a bit of money. At the time I felt she saw straight through me. I honestly wondered whether she was asking me a question, not stating something simply from the paper. I didn't know what to do or what to say, I just shoved my toast and coffee into my mouth as if I hadn't heard what she had said at all. I nodded, tried to look at her without feeling like a monster and said, "yes, isn't it terrible."

Really, the first year after the robbery was hell. The money meant fuck all. I started drinking more. Junip noticed how withdrawn I was. I couldn't even get it up for the first three months and after that it was all motion and no feeling. I was a floater, an astronaut, suspended in a visceral space inside my head. Junip would try to anchor me, to pry me back. She'd lift my head from my hands and kiss my fingers. She'd beg me to tell her what was wrong. She'd try to initiate oral, most of the time I would remain flaccid. I'd go down on her out of guilt not desire. Eventually she stopped trying. I was relieved.

I stopped going to work. I just called in sick all the time. Eventually I was fired. I lied to Junip and told her I had started my own IT company. I went so far as to get an ABN and then I just made up fake jobs. Didn't even legally set up my own company until three months later. I deposited small amounts of money into my bank account. It's a miracle the Australian Tax Office never got onto me before I got a cunning accountant that did my dirty work. If Junip was home I'd get dressed, give her a kiss and then go sit in the park and play games on my phone. If Junip was at work, I'd stay in bed.

One day, just a week after the robbery, when Junip wasn't home, I googled the Chasnell Bank. On their site I searched for Poppy. There was a picture of her, smiling into a camera. Her light brown hair pulled back into a neat, professional bun, smiling red lips, and her standing there in her oversized blouse and long navy skirt looking young and innocent. Poppy Aver. Under her name was the title; 'Acting Assistant Bank Manager'. A week later her picture and her name were gone.

At the same time, articles with more detail started appearing all over the net. There were pictures taken from the security cameras of Amos and I in our plastic-faced disguises, wearing gloves, our bodies completely covered, unrecognizable. Two thugs waving guns. I felt disconnected from it all – from the images of us holding guns in the air and the blurred faces of our victims. It wasn't me. It couldn't be me. It was some sort of strange macabre comic version of me. I started to rationalize and justify that I had been lured and hypnotized by a strange psychopath. It was the only way I could keep breathing.

There was a long article where the CEO of all the Chasnell Banks was ensuring the public that new security protocols had been put in place at all branches. There was a media gag order on victim identities. Another article mentioned that the two employees involved in the robbery were filing a class action lawsuit against Chasnell and that there had been an out of court settlement that also involved a confidentiality agreement. Oh god, I hope Poppy received a shit ton of money for what she went through, for what I and that fucking asshole Amos put her through.

Every day I kept feeling worse. I was really fucking tired. My arms felt like two-by-fours dangling from my body. My feet felt like they were encased in cement shoes that shuffled along, but for Junip I tried. I knew enough to know I was depressed as fuck and that it was killing her. I'd put on this hollow wax smile, and this stupid cheery voice and I'd make us breakfast while I was just praying for her to leave.

"How about eggs and avocado on toast?" I would ask. "I picked up some of your favourite sourdough from Perryman's" My smile was plastered across my face like some creepy clown doll. "Or there's homemade granola?" I was like a wind-up monkey on top of a tin box. Junip would say yes just to please me. I'd pour out coffee, black for me and white for her, kidding myself that this was somehow normal because it was and it wasn't. It was so far from normal that I would often break down and sob like some sort of snivelling five-year-old after Junip had left for work. It started to become harder and harder to ask her about her day and to keep up the facade of us. I was disintegrating into a grey shell riddled with guilt and remorse. If I made it to a social event, say dinner with her sisters, I'd barely speak. I felt like I was choking on sulphur and shame. The truth of who I was, was filthy and suffocating and all consuming.

I hit a week of not getting out of bed. Junip came into our room. "I think you should see a doctor" she said.

"Sure," I mumbled. Junip set up the appointment. I was given Venlafaxine. It helped, but it was a long road and guilt doesn't wash away with a long red capsule. However, it did get me back out of bed and into a new wobbly and bizarre stability. I started to launder more of the stolen money through my IT business. Junip hooked me up with her sister's husband, Roger. He was a bit of a dick but out of a favour to our wives he gave me the basics on buying and selling stocks. Money started coming in for us and this made Junip happy, well happy for me, rather than a happy for us. I still couldn't deal with sex but at least now I could blame it on the Venlafaxine. From time to time we'd give it the old college try. Junip would fake an orgasm and sometimes I would cum but it was more of a bodily function than a feeling. Our relationship was hanging on by a thread. I saw the way she looked at me, that she felt sorry for me. I had turned into a lazy, skinny runt of a man with no explanation as to why, and she didn't know what to do with me. A useless prick, incapable of conversation, let alone sex.

Yet, the money started to ease my unease. To be able to give my wife a better place to live, nicer furniture, stuff, whatever she wanted, all helped to make me feel like a man. But one day at breakfast Junip said that none of this meant anything to her. I felt like I had been kicked in the balls.

"What the fuck do you want?" I asked.

"I want you," she pleaded.

"You fucking have me." I was confused. "What the fuck? I'm working my ass off, finally fucking making something of myself and what – that's not enough?"

"We don't connect. We don't talk. I feel like I'm living with a stranger." She was crying. It made me even angrier.

"You're always fucking attacking me." I knew what I was saying was bullshit but I couldn't stop.

Junip got up from the table, picked up her bag and coat and walked out.

"Fuck you!" I yelled as the door closed behind her. *There's no pleasing her. For Christ's sake I'm beating myself senseless giving her anything she wants. And what does she fucking want? To keep me in a goddamn cage. Does she want the IT schmuck she married? Fuck that shit. He doesn't exist. I did all this for us. For fucking us.*

. . .

Junip went to stay with her sister for a while. Didn't even take any of her clothes. I suppose Claire had more than enough money and clothes and whatever for Junip, she didn't need me. She came home about a fortnight after that fight and said she couldn't do it anymore. I didn't fight her. I knew she wanted me to beg for her, to tell her that I loved her, that I couldn't live without her, but I couldn't do it. I didn't feel it. I didn't really feel anything. Her eldest sister came over to help her pack up her shit. Claire looked at me like I was a douchebag. I knew I was. I was relieved when they left. At least the fucking facade and pretending were over.

I'm not an idiot. In the midst of everything I knew I was wrong. They say that pride comes before a fall, but the problem was that I didn't recognise my own goddamn vanity before I cascaded head-first into the darkness. It can be so innocuous can't it? This idea that we are redeemable, that we deserve what we want just because we want it, as if the clear-sighted confidence we possess is enough reason to think our motives are pure. Looking back, I know I used my wife as a scapegoat, and that I tried to believe my crimes were because of her. I wanted to believe that I was committing some kind of selfless act to better her life, and that it had nothing to do with me at all. Fucking stupid, but there was no way I was going to admit it to myself or to Junip at the time.

Not having to please Junip gave me a lot of free time. At first I let the house turn into a bachelor pad. I had my mates over all the time and we'd drink, snort coke and play poker. I stopped taking the Venlafaxine. Booze and drugs were working much better. I got a cleaning lady to clean up the shit and then one night, about three months after Junip left, I brought some random chick home and fucked her in our bed. It felt so fucking weird being inside someone else, her smell, her tits, everything was different. After that, there was a slew of nameless, faceless women. I had the kind of voice that could charm the pants off of anyone. I felt like a fucking king.

I had so much time that I even started to learn French, being the swanky fuckwit that I am. I had this cute-ass little tutor who I fucked. I impressed a lot of women with my *parlaying* until I started dating Martine, who was actually French. She'd laugh at my Aussie accent and make fun of the way I jumbled words and phrases around. I'd grab her by the waist and slap her on the ass. She had bright brown eyes and smooth, dark skin. My type of girl. We hung out for four months. I was almost fluent by the time she left. Life was looking good. A year after my separation, I'd learned a language, had a nice passive income coming in and more important - my cock was hard again.

I could almost say I was happy, fully distracted at least, and that was good enough for me. Then one day I ran smack into Amos.

He must have spent all of his half of the cash on drugs. Fuck, he was a skinny fleecy-haired bloke. I barely recognized him. His skin was the colour of a concrete block and his face was cracking like a clay plate drying in the sun. There were thick lines smeared into his cheeks and around his eyes and mouth. He looked small and old, like Keith Richards.

"Hey man, good to see you," he clasped my hand and drew me towards him.

"Amos," I said drawing away.

"You're looking good mate," he said. I wish I could have said the same but thankfully he just started yammering about investments and real estate and some other such shit, still tapping his heel-up and down-up and down. I watched him squirming and trying desperately to impress me. I wanted to spit in his face.

"That's sounds great Amos," I said. "Sorry man, but I've got a meeting." We shook hands, and I ran. He tried calling me a few times after that but I never picked up. I didn't need a reminder of the dank cave of depression and divorce, and my spineless association with that mother fucking psychopath. Life was just starting to get good again.

I still googled Poppy, about once a month for five years. There was a time when she was absent from any social media – a total blackout for about eight months. I wondered if she was lying in bed trying to make sense of her life like I had, trying to make sense of what had happened to her. I even wondered if she had offed herself. I pushed that last thought away. Then one day she popped up on Instagram, Poppy Aver – 'traveller'.

I was relieved. She had been traveling through South America, learning Spanish and hiking and surfing. There were pictures of her with a tall, lean and muscular guy who had those big round black eyes that girls swoon over and a friendly smile. I figured out he was a Chilean named Gabriel. They looked happy in her photographs. Her hair was lighter from the sun and in pics of the two of them she would be leaning into him looking up into his eyes and he would be smiling down at her. I searched around and found his Instagram – 'Lawyer, Surfer, Lover'. His page was covered with surfing pictures and pictures of him cooking food. I started to let myself believe that maybe what happened to her had actually shaken her up enough and helped her. Don't they say out of everything bad something good happens? What doesn't kill you makes you stronger and all that shit?

Then after a year or so all traces of him were deleted from her profile. Another love gone south. I knew all about that. She came back to Australia and lived in Victoria. Soon pictures of a vineyard started popping up. It was hers, about an hour out of Melbourne. Good on her. There were pictures of Poppy in gumboots in the winter, her small hands reaching for the vines just as the sun smoothed the morning with its light. There were pictures of her drinking wine with friends on open air patios and at wooden bar tables all over Melbourne. She was beautiful, her long hair loose and now blonde, falling around her shoulders, little freckles dotting her nose. She looked happy. My guilt was washing away every time I saw her smile. I wasn't creeping her. I didn't obsess. Once a month – just once a month – I would let myself sit down and spend a few minutes checking in on Poppy, making sure she was happy. Making myself feel okay.

CHAPTER SIX

Being in a house full of men sucks. The fact that we were in a mansion helps but not a whole lot. There were five bedrooms, each with two sets of bunks. I shared my room with three guys and it felt like boarding school all over again. Not really the glamour the show presents on TV. I'm one of those neat and tidy guys. The only time I had ever been messy in my life was right after Junip left when I was a walking-talking zombie. The other guys were messy as fuck. The room smelt like sweat and Old Spice – 'Pure Sport or Champion Swagger'. We spent our down-time working out, drinking protein shakes, playing tennis and swimming in the pool. Sounds fun, I know, but it was like being in prison, okay, maybe an upscale white collar prison. There were security guards all around the perimeter of the estate and we'd often be kept indoors because of drones and planes overhead. It was the paparazzi doing their job. We weren't allowed to leave, and we had to write our grocery lists down on a notepad for one of the 'minders' to go and pick-up. It was super controlled. A few of the guys knew how to cook thankfully, so there was always some good food to be had.

The morning after the first cocktail party, Neil the host of 'The Eligibles' arrives at the house. He's wearing white boat pants and a short sleeve pale blue Ralph Lauren cotton golf shirt. He has on a pair of Cole Haan loafers and a perfect spray tan. He is perpetually grinning an overpaid, over-white smile. On camera it all looks like a surprise but in reality the sound guys have been mic-ing us up and the film crew has been checking lights and angles and getting all their gear in place for the past few hours. We're all a bit slow moving and hung-over from the night before but all the commotion is exciting too. Sam is with us, all his clothes look frumpy and loose on his short chubby body.

"Okay guys, I want half of you outside lounging on the patio furniture and I want the other half of you hanging in the kitchen. I don't give a shit who is where, just split it up," he says. He's holding a clipboard and talking into a wire that hangs from his ear piece.

"When Neil arrives look excited and whoever is hanging back in the kitchen start walking out casually on my cue. Everybody clear?" we all nod.

"What time is Neil arriving?" I ask.

"10am sharp!" says Sam. We all hustle around or hustle as best we can in our exhaustion and get ready before positioning ourselves casually inside and out.

When Neil arrives everyone transforms into acting mode. We cheer and the guys from the kitchen start walking out slow and smiling and get in on the cheer. When Neil pulls out a date card, we all clap and look overly excited. They do three takes of that and we have to keep up the same level of enthusiasm while the film crew do close-ups and walk-ins. I feel like a dolphin doing tricks or a monkey dancing on the side of the road. I guess it's true we're animals first and humans second.

"Okay on this next take Neil, I want you to hand the date card to Kurt. Kurt before you read the card I want you to ask the guys if they think it's a single or group date. Guys pipe up whatever you feel like. Then Kurt read the card slow and steady and guys make sure you're all looking at Kurt," says Sam. "We'll probably do a couple of takes of this too just to get some different angles in. Remember there will be a clue so get in on the guessing. And then finally Kurt you'll read out the name or names. Cool?" We all nod. "Again we'll do all of this a few times."

Trust me, reality TV isn't as much fun as the finished product makes it out to be. There's a shit ton of standing around and a lot of this tedious redo stuff. I got a chance to hang and chat with Kurt a bit last night. Nice dude. He's a little shorter than me, maybe 5'11' or 6'. He's surfy looking with a big smile, tanned skin and blonde curly hair.

We all pretty much guess it's a single date and we're right. And the clue is, "Let's get dizzy in love." We start guessing theme park or something with heights. Someone yells out 'helicopter'. And the guy who wins the date? No, not me, Ruben, good old Ruben. A few of the guys let out little grunts and some are complaining that they can't believe Poppy picked Ruben as he seems so disingenuous. They film this a few times doing 'pickups' so that they can get the guys comments on film.

The next day while Ruben is gone we all hang out and do 'actualisations'. What this means is they have us break off into groups and give us specific topics to discuss while they film it. Again, it's all supposed to look natural and relaxed. I'm still a bit freaked out about it being Poppy but if she has any idea that she knows who I am she sure as hell isn't letting on. This canned shit is about all I can handle. I'm actually looking forward to hanging with the guys and having fake conversation.

"What were your first impressions of Poppy?" Should I say: *A rather plain looking assistant bank manager that my sidekick psychopath raped while we were robbing the bank?* Instead I say "I think she seems like the real deal. Super nice smile and she makes you feel relaxed." We get other topics too: How do you feel about Ruben getting the first date? How much do you want a single date? Who do feel the most threatened by in the house?

Rueben is gone all day. The morning is taken up with the 'actualisation' conversations. Then there is some free time. With no contact to the outside world, I finish reading the book I picked up in the airport. It was pretty good, a John Grisham, The Rooster Bar. It's all about a bunch of law school students in on the losing end of a scam. Sounds like my life. Well not the law school part but the losing end of a scam. I shave, do a mini work out and cook a bunch of BBQ pork ribs for the guys.

Sam has been in and out all day and in between all this

we are plucked out one by one for a more in depth interview. They dive into my personal life in a way that makes me fidget in my seat.

"Okay, let's begin," says Sam. "And remember when I ask you a question you need to include the question in your answer. Got it, mate?"

"Got it, include the question in the answer." I smile at Sam.

"Ever married?"

"Yes, I got married when I was nineteen." Sam's eyes widen, even though I'm certain he already knows this.

"Wow, that's young," he says.

"Yeah, I was very young when I got married. Don't regret it all though. Even though it didn't work out."

"Why didn't your marriage work out?" asks Sam. He cocks his head, tries to look genuine. I fidget in my seat. I clear my throat before answering.

"My marriage failed because we slowly started to become different people." *True*, I say to myself, *I became a carcass and Junip couldn't handle it*. "We wanted different things. My wife was an amazing woman and I still have great respect for her." Some days I wanted it all to go back to Junip and I but I didn't say that. Instead I stuck to the superficiality of all this. I can tell Sam finds my answers boring. He's grimacing and tapping at his iPad, trying to think of a way to get me to say what he needs me to.

"Does having a failed marriage make you scared of marriage, for the second time?" Sam asks.

"Not really…"

Sam interrupted me."Remember to put the question in

your answer."

"Oh, sorry about that man... I think that having a failed marriage so young has made me understand and know what I want more than ever. Rather than being scared of marriage I think it is a beautiful thing and I hope to have it again someday." *I'm turning into a fucking robot,* I think to myself.

"What do you think of Poppy?" Sam smiles.

"I think Poppy is gorgeous!" She is. "I definitely felt some kind of chemistry between us when we first met." I get a mental flash of her eyes when she turned around in that bank boardroom and I feel sick. "Whether that's just a sexual thing or it's something deeper. I don't know yet. We'll have to wait and see." I flash a big smile. I can see Sam's energy peak a little.

"You're saying you feel sexual energy with Poppy..?" he asks.

"I definitely felt a sexual energy with Poppy. There were sparks. How could you not? She's gorgeous. I also had the feeling it was reciprocated." I keep smiling. "At least I hope so."

"Is there anything in particular that she did that made you feel reciprocation?" He's fishing. He wants me to say something douchey but I can't muster the strength to do it. Instead I shrug. Sam moves on, he doesn't push.

"Not many of the guys like Ruben, but you two seem to get along well. Why do you think that is?"

"I know that many of the guys don't like Ruben. I think he's a little misunderstood. He's got a pretty sarcastic sense of humour, but he's a decent guy. However, now that he's got the first date, I don't think that will help his case. I think some of the guys might just be intimidated by him."

"You're not intimidated?"

"I don't get intimidated very often and especially not by Ruben. He's my mate." I smile. "Maybe if I start to get a bit more invested in Poppy and if she seems keen on him, then yeah, maybe I'll feel that twinge of jealousy. It's crazy though that some of the guys are already feeling that."

"Ben seems a little put out by Ruben. Maybe a little more than the other guys. What's your take on that?" asks Sam.

"Ben's jealousy of Ruben is kind of creepy." Ben is a little shorter than most of the guys here. He has straight short black hair and an angular, symmetrical face. It's like he was carved with all sharp angles. Chiseled in stone. I think he has good innings to get far in this 'game'. "He's only just met Poppy. He needs to chill a bit." I laugh. So I give him what he wants, in the end. Rat on Ben.

"Alright." says Sam. "I think we have enough to work with here. That was great, Henry."

Sam was one of the good producers. And when I say good, I just mean he wasn't as ruthless as some of the others. It was like he was after the bare minimum, he got the job done. Jocelyn, on the other hand was a fucking dirty politician, the villain in a good movie, the manipulator, the motherfucker of all reality assholes. So I guess you could say she was good at her job.

She was of medium height, average weight – the kind of woman that didn't work out or eat well but still managed to maintain a reasonable figure, maybe mid-thirties. She'd wear a little black eyeliner that seemed to match her raspy voice and laugh. You'd catch her smoking at the side of the house with the camera crew. Everyone always seemed impressed by her and I guess that was her power. You wanted to please Jocelyn because she always seemed like she didn't give a fuck unless you were interesting enough.

For the first couple of episodes everyone's producers interchanged – there were four of them. In the end I figured maybe the producers were finding their people – different personalities required different kinds of manipulation. Apparently, Sam wasn't my kind of manipulator and Jocelyn was.

When we'd interview Jocelyn would mount herself on a black swivel chair, black hair messy and out, skin and breath smelling of tobacco, those dark eyes glaring at me. She'd tap at her paper notes with nail polished fingernails half chipped off, even though every other producer had tech for interviews.

She'd ask me questions about the other guys.

"What do you think of Ruben?"

If I'd be nice or diplomatic, she'd smirk or yawn. "For fucks sake Henry, are you Kevin Rudd? Did you apply for a seat in Parliament? Do you think anyone cares if you think Ruben is 'cool'? Tell me what you think of the guy. Stop being a fucking pussy, I know you're not a pussy." She'd take a big deep breath in and roll her eyes at the cameramen as if I was wasting her time, wasting her day, and something in me couldn't help but comply.

"Ruben thinks he's got it in the bag. He's used to getting any woman he wants and I don't think he understands that this situation is a little... different. He's a cocky little fuck, isn't he?"

Jocelyn would laugh at all my descriptions of the guys and slap her knee, "Honestly, I totally agree with you," she'd say to just about anything controversial I said.

I'd go back to the house after the interview and the guys would ask me how it went and I'd feel the standard cowardice guilt of my existence scourge through me. "Yeah it was good mate, just trying to give them what they want, you know how it is."

When Ruben returns from the first date of the season we are all in the kitchen. We let out a big cheer as he pulls out a large poppy flower from his sleeve cuff, which he will wear on his coat at the next cocktail party, pinning him as 'safe'. He's got big grin going.

"It was awesome, guys," he says. "They had a Cessna 172 that they took us up in. The pilot was crazy. We were spinning upside down and he would do airdrops so we could catch some G-force. Afterwards, we went on a pretty romantic sunset picnic by the river." Ruben winks.

"Did you guys make-out?" Interrupts Ben.

"We may have had a sneaky snog," says Ruben, still grinning. Ben shakes his head, grunts.

"Tongue or no tongue?" Someone pipes up from the back.

Ruben laughs. "Is there such a thing as kissing without tongue?" We all chuckle. Someone at the back makes throwing up noises, one guy leaves. I'm finding this all so weird. Here we are listening to and cheering for our mate about a girl we are all going to be dating. Dating on TV. This world is a bizarre place.

The days start to meld one into the other. Then a day comes where I'm out on a group date with eight of the other guys. They give us the heads up that the theme for the date is 'water adventure'. It's meant to all relate to her life in travel, and they'll be using the date as a photo shoot concept for a magazine. The stylists give us boardies and different coloured linen shirts. During the group date I am picked out to do a one-on-one photo with Poppy while the others pose in groups. The guys are a bit miffed. I'm fucking nervous, but also excited. Poppy has the kind of energy that you want to get close to.

Juan, the security guy on set starts running through the scenario.

"Henry and Poppy can I get you two to come over here for a second." He separates us from the group. "Okay safety first. We've tested this a gazillion times. If you do as we say there is not much risk involved. We are going to have you jump from the roof of this house into the pool below."

"Oh my god, no way." Poppy says with a nervous laugh.

"It will be okay." I reassure her. "They wouldn't have us do anything that would cause us injury. Could you imagine the lawsuits?" I smile down at her.

"Okay if you say so," she laughs, and looks up at me with her head tilted to one side. She has her hands clasped and raised in close to her chest as if she is giving a little prayer.

"He's right, Poppy," Juan chimes in. He then goes through how they want us to jump and how not to jump and to only jump when we are ready. I can see Poppy chewing at the inside of her lip. "We will be with you the whole time." Juan says to reassure Poppy.

"It's just I'm a wee bit scared of heights," she says.

"I'm here." I give her a hug and then take hold of her hand. "Let's just pretend everyone is naked." I laugh.

Poppy laughs too. "I think that's just for public speaking isn't it? Not for jumping off the bloody roof of a house."

I laugh, "Well there's some nice looking guys over there. And then there's Sam our chubby little Producer. I bet he has a nice set of tits." I'm doing my best to win her over. Poppy slaps my arm playfully.

"Okay, just picture me naked," and I do a little ballerina twirl which makes her laugh. I can't believe I am saying or doing any of this. Every time I am around Poppy it feels like an out-of-body experience. We climb up and out onto the roof. Poppy clings to me for a second and closes her eyes. Then holding my hand we walk to the edge. Then she retreats back and into my arms again.

"Okay… okay… okay," she says, and we walk again to the edge and again retreat. "Oh, fuck it." she says, and finally we run hand in hand and jump from the roof. Poppy is laughing and screaming as we hit the water. There's a great big splash and then we resurface. She has the best grin on her face and swims over towards me. I scoop her up in my arms and carry her up out the pool. I feel like Tarzan. Like a man's man. It's the best I've felt in fucking years.

We repeat the jump three more times. Poppy is loving it. She runs back towards the house holding my hand and dragging me along. I go so far as to scoop her up again and carry her up to the roof. She wraps her arms around my neck. I sense the other guys are feeling threatened but I don't give a rats ass because this is way too much fun. I feel pretty certain she has no idea who I really am.

"One...two....three...jump!" Poppy yells and we go again.

There are more cocktail parties and yellow poppy coat pins, and more deflated hearts and hurt egos as some of the guys are chipped away and sent home. There are more group dates, where no one really gets to say too much, and there are days off that are boring as hell. The days we are filming last anywhere from twelve to fourteen hours. They are a combination of exciting, boring and exhausting. Finally, there are only ten guys left, and I get picked for a single date. Again, nerves kick in but I want to be near her. It's a conflicted feeling. And I'm excited to get out of the house and away from the other guys. It will be nice to be alone with Poppy. Okay, alone save for the camera crew, producers, sound guys, lighting experts, gaffers and gophers and a million other people running around. I'm starting to wonder if this is some kind of weird twist of fate and Poppy and I are actually meant to be together. It's all just a bit too weird to be true. Maybe this is how I get to save her?

CHAPTER SEVEN

The sun is setting and the sky above the ocean is a great big lolly of lilacs and yellows, lines of reds and purples cut by fat crinkled clouds. I probably wouldn't notice this shit if Poppy wasn't standing in front of it – it's as if she's made it herself and yet she's completely unaware of how perfect she is. Poppy is an outward breath of warm air in my very cold universe, and I can't help but want to be in the way of it. She stands there with a scrunched smile, that yellow dress, those cute shoes and little freckles dotting her nose, looking at me as if I'm God's gift. She even makes horse-riding and the idea of a picnic seem less effeminate, less banal, less like something I'd scoff at. We laugh together as I adjust to the whole horse-riding thing, bouncing up and down on the horse like something from a kids school play. She's holding her stomach and laughing at me as I try to maintain my balance, get the rhythm of it all. My balls are fucking aching with the up and down jig of the whole thing. I laugh too even though I'm thinking of wiping that grin off her face with my lips, my tongue. The film crew is swirling all around us like fireflies, filming from every direction. Drones are near and ahead of us, flying sky-high. Once the whole ordeal is over, thank God, we hold hands and walk towards the picnic, set up on a grassed area above the ocean sands.

"So, what do you do for work Mr. Henry?" Poppy asks. Sam the producer walks over with the sound guy to adjust her microphone. "Oh, sorry about that," she laughs.

"So, what do you do for work Mr. Henry?" she asks once they leave, in a voice that is slightly louder.

"I work in stocks and bonds. I own a small company." I feel proud even though I know it has all gone belly up. I feel good around her. "What do you do?" I ask.

"Well you probably know that I run a winery now – that's pretty recent. Before that I was travelling a fair bit. And before that – I uh, used to work in a bank." I feel my back stiffen and I wonder if she's caught me looking anxious.

"Oh no, you looked shocked?" It's posed more as a question. She's sipping a glass of white wine.

I start pedaling, "Well I am." I let out a little laugh. "You don't seem like the bank type at all. To go from working in a bank to travelling to this," I'm babbling but I can't stop, "it seems like some kind of life transformation." *What the fuck am I doing? Opening up a fucking minefield is what I'm doing,* I say to myself.

She looks away from me and smiles out at the sunset and takes another sip of wine.

"Maybe you're right," she says in a voice that seems miles away.

We reach the picnic that the crew has set up for us. There's a cream and pink striped picnic blanket laid out. A wicker basket with champagne, scones, cream, jams and berries placed inside. I get down on my knees and hold out my hand to help Poppy down. The crew has adjusted themselves in a circle around us. Somehow things still feel intimate and I'm surprised that I am able to tune the crowds out.

"Was it some kind of trauma?" I ask. *What the fuck am I doing? Can someone tape my mouth shut?*

She frowns and adjusts the skirt of her dress and looks away brushing sand off the blanket.

"Now, why would you say that?" she turns and looks me directly in the eyes. I shrug and look away. I'm blowing it. *Remember, you're not here for love*, I silently remind myself but it feels more like a reprimand.

"Maybe I just got tired of the monotony of it all," says Poppy without missing a beat. If she suspects anything she is certainly not letting on. "The day in day out routine. It was boring," she laughs. "And my boss was always breathing down my neck. I felt like I was on a treadmill, you know? Just going round and round. I wanted to escape the walls and to have no walls. I realized I don't need much to be happy. I realized that working in finance is not me. Which of course I'd hate you to take offense to – I mean, I didn't like it, but I'm sure it fits you well." Poppy looks up at me, sincerely, but I do feel a bit of offense twinging at my chest. I lift my collar up to let some air in and smile. Is she calling me boring?

"Are you saying you don't care about money?" *Chill the fuck out Henry*, I say again to myself.

"Of course I care about money. I think it's a discredit to the billions of people in the world that are starving to say 'oh yeah I don't care about money'. Money is what buys us food and shelter. And I do like pretty things," she smooths out her dress. "I just think that for me working like that wasn't right. I'm too free spirited, maybe."

She takes a few berries and slowly chews them. I feel bad. There's a silence, so I try to fill it. "I remember at school studying Maslow's Hierarchy of Needs," I say. "The food chain in terms of the ability to self-realise and all that. We're so lucky to be born into such privilege – Australia, the land of go-gett'em." I love how I can just change my ideologies based on who I'm talking to. Trying to impress Poppy at any expense. "We get to know who we are and what we want. Whereas others have to stick to more survival-based lifestyles. I guess we don't all think about our advantageous reality in context to the rest of the world do we? Not often anyway."

Poppy swallows and clears her throat. "Excuse me. I'm sorry," she brushes her hands on her dress. "I don't know? I think you are a lot more clever than I am."

I'm not a hundred percent sure on that, I think to myself. There's something in her eyes that seems to say other-wise. It's as if she looking straight through me but her voice is so captivating and I'm lost inside the sound of it and forget everything else.

"Maybe?" she continues, "Maybe our self-realisation is relative to our position in life and I don't know… maybe that's okay. What do you think Mr. Henry?"

Poppy swallows and clears her throat, she picks at the grass around the blanket. "Seems almost stupid though doesn't it?" she says. "Sometimes I feel oh-so-clever for understanding Maslow, but does it really mean anything? Do you think it makes us smarter or better? It's just like those people that have a firm grip on the state of the world by reading foreign affairs and current political agendas. Those upper-class people, or university students, or whoever, that discuss human and environmental issues with their other clever friends or colleagues. Does 'knowing' really help anyone? When these 'clever' people still consume at the rate of anyone else in a developed country? When they only donate to charity by buying tickets to prestigious events where they spend more on what they look like, on vanity essentially, than donation? Why do we feel like we're more important or worldly for our personal research, than those who just watch meaningless bullshit and binge on Netflix? Neither makes a change do they? Maybe we have to be easy on ourselves, when the ego comes in, and remember that everything is relative rather than acting self-important. Remember that we are all just doing the best we can. And unless you're making actual, literal, sustainable change then you're a flog for announcing small charity acts so egotistically on social networks." Poppy sounds a little angry, or is it just passionate? *She let her smarts shine through there*, I think to myself. *Why is she trying to hide it?*

I don't say much but a bunch of paraphrased versions of what she's said. I'm a loser with nothing new to say. I just feel guilt. Part of my journey, part of my 'self-realization' was at her expense. I got money. She got hurt. Does she think I have a big ego? Am I one of the charitable fuckwits she's talking about? I think I see a streak of anger pass through her eyes when we both realize that really I'm just regurgitating her sentiments, but then she laughs, tries to make me feel better.

"It's not real, any of this." She sweeps her hands around. "At least right now... us... we all have masks that we hide behind don't you think? You have one. I have one. Maybe we need them to protect ourselves? I think it's hard to show our real selves. But, I guess that's what I'm here for too," she smiles, looks up at me and adds, "Hopefully we can help each other remove those masks. Maybe that's what love is? When you can love someone without the masquerade." My mind is racing and I feel my palms sweating. She knows. She has to know. She's talking about the robbery. Masks, fuck she's playing with me. Or is she? I quickly try to redeem myself by turning on the charm and settling the dizzy in my head.

"I'm pretty sure Maslow's is out of date, anyway. Prehistoric bullshit." I laugh. I think this is what she wants to hear but I'm not sure, so I just tell her she's very mysterious and cock my head and smile at her. *Just keep smiling Henry.*

"There's a lot going on in that pretty mind," I say. I sound patronizing, but she's confusing me and I can't think of anything else to say.

Sam interrupts us. "What you're doing is great guys. Really great, but we don't have a lot of time left here. The sun is about to set and we are going to lose the light." Any tension that might have existed between us is gone. "Let's get to some of more serious questions. As in not about the world's quintessential problems, but love." Poppy smiles and fans out her dress. We know what the producer needs for the show.

I clear my throat. "So, you've spent a lot of time travelling. Do you still miss that or do you see yourself being able to settle down?" I ask.

"As in having a hubby, kids, a house, a white picket fence?" she asks.

"I guess so," I say.

"Yes, that's my goal, as domestic as it might sound," Poppy laughs. "With travelling, it's a lot of temporary relationships. They're great, don't get me wrong, but it's a different kind of journey. There's a saying on the road, 'never cross a border with someone,'" she smiles. "Now, I own a vineyard and it's pretty isolated. The circle of people I work with and interact with is small. That's why I'm here. To push myself out of my comfort zone and to get to know some amazing people." She smiles up at me. "And you? Do you want to settle down one day?"

"For sure. I want to get married again." Thank God I told her about the marriage early in the game. I don't think they'll air any of this. My story with Junip doesn't have the drama and intrigue they need. She seemed unfazed about my marriage, although if anything, maybe intrigued by my ex-wife at times. "I'm not sure about the white picket fence though. Maybe, we could be a bit more original with that one?" I smirk.

Poppy laughs. "A red picket fence? Or a white brick wall?" We're laughing. Then we look at each other and everything goes silent. I lean over and lightly lift her chin and kiss her. She tastes like blueberries.

Am I a monster?

Well, something seems to be going right for me or at least it seems that way. I had some doubts about my first date with Poppy, but now every week, at the cocktail party, Poppy and I are sneaking off, out of site from the cameras and the other guys, and stealing a brief but intense snog. She tags me with one of those yellow coat pins. She tells me that a yellow poppy flower represents success, and that's what she hopes for our relationship. If the other guys ever found out, I'd be fucked. When we are with the group mingling around and chatting, and all the boys are trying to give their last-ditch attempt to save themselves from having naked coats and broken pride. I feel like a bit of a peacock who has no need to flaunt his feathers. I feel safe.

Today there's no cocktail party though. It's a Tuesday and we're all hanging back at the house. There are still cameras around though. Jocelyn is here and even still, things are chill. I'm sitting out back with a few of the guys when Ruben heads out tossing a football in the air. "Anybody up for a little gentleman's game of Rugby?" he smiles at us. Sam is his producer. I know he's been asked to do this.

"Sure. I'm in." Ben jumps up. I catch what I think is the hint of a smirk on his face. A few of the other guys get up.

"Sure why the hell not," I say. Ruben and I and a couple of the other guys make up one team, and Ben and the rest of the lads start heading to the other end of the yard.

"Hey maybe we'll be the Vikings?" hollers Ruben. "And you guys can be the Pussies!" he laughs.

"Fuck you," says Ben. Jocelyn calls Ben over, and we have to wait for him. It looks like they're having an argument, but when he comes back, he seems in okay spirits.

"How about shirts and no shirts?" I say.

"Sounds good," someone hollers back. "We'll go no shirts."

It feels good to be outside burning off some energy. The guys are all laughing and joking. Sweat is pouring off our backs. Our side is down by a couple of points, when I make an awesome throw to Ruben, who leaps in the air and catches it like he's cradling a baby. He starts running across the yard on a clean break, when all of a sudden Ben comes out of nowhere, and tackles him to the ground. I catch Ben with his hand on the back of Ruben's head and it looks like he's grinding his face into the ground. Ruben throws him off and starts to get up. "What the fuck you dick?" I hear him say. Ben leaps at him, full fucking fury and starts swinging, but there aren't any hits. Me and the other guys run over and yank Ben away. Ruben is laughing which makes Ben angrier.

"Hey, hey this is supposed to be a friendly game!" I say. Ben is glaring like a caged animal, his nostrils flaring.

Then Ruben laughs again, "All good mate. I think the Pussies just got their panties in a knot."

Ben spits on the ground and yells out, "Who are you calling a pussy fuck-wit?"

Ruben walks away while Ben is shaking off the guys who are holding him. Jocelyn is grinning.

It's not aired on-screen like this. There are trailers for weeks of this 'altercation'. The preview even includes a police siren and one of the more sensitive guys crying from another episode.

"Why don't I get the BBQ going?" Someone pipes up and we all abandon the game. I walk towards the house with Ruben.

"What the fuck was that?" I ask.

"Fucked if I know," Ruben says. "The guys had it in for me since we got here. Probably has a small dick." He laughs and slaps me on the back. "No big deal," he says.

"Typical the cameras were around to catch all the drama," I say. We both laugh. I start thinking that I sure as shit better make sure Poppy and I don't get caught snogging or Ben will fucking kill me. Then I start to wonder if Ruben and Poppy are also stealing away for some sexytime and Ben knows about it. Talk about drama and to think I thought this was going to be boring.

In other news it's possible that all these interviews have bought out too much desire for honesty and truth. Jocelyn in my ear constantly – *'What is it you like about Poppy? Do you think it's possible you don't feel good enough for her? Is that why you're holding back? How do you envision your future with Poppy? Because she's certainly told me how she envisions her future with you Henry'.* I'm with all these men that speak so fucking highly of her, all these crew members that seem to love her, and I can't help but be drawn into the romance – then when I'm alone, the reality of it all comes flooding in. I don't know if I like myself or if I can live with this fucking dank secret. I think on it over and over again, about telling her the truth, and I know if it happens, it will be on a whim, like the 26-year-old Henry, clinking that glass against Amos', a 'fuck, why not'.

There are only six of us left in the running by the time I get my second date. Everyone slaps me on the back good-naturedly, but I can tell they want to punch me in the balls.

We're at the beach. We went jet skiing first. I loved Poppy squeezed up against me with her hands holding onto my waist. There were some pretty good waves, and we caught some air a couple of times. God it felt great to be out on the water with her. We got waved back to shore and then we walk hand in hand off the beach and towards the cars so that we can drive to the next location. I feel lucky and fucking grateful being in the presence of such a gorgeous woman. Too much man-time is never good.

"What scares you?" She asks me, as we walk along. Is it a producer-induced question? It seems direct, if not a little ambiguous, but I play along.

"What, you think a big, masculine man like me gets scared?" I joke. I flex my muscles and she laughs. Then I sober up on the humour and continue for the cameras. "No, I think what scares me most is not achieving anything noteworthy in my life." I can see Poppy knit her eyebrows together and really think about what I've just said.

"Why do you think that is? Do you have big aspirations?" Poppy is frowning and looking up at me, there's a kindness in her voice.

"I know I've told you I've been married before, " I clear my throat. "A woman I respect but of course I am not in love with anymore, just so you know." Poppy nods as I continue. "I just remember when we were happy, feeling like I had done something great, that I had achieved something great. Yes, I have aspirations in terms of career and experiences and yada yada, but I honestly think that a noteworthy life is loving someone, and being loved." It's bloody brilliant.

"Do you worry that that can't happen for you?" asks Poppy.

"I worry that no one will be able to know me well-enough to love me for me. Like how on our first date we talked about masks, the removing of them." I surprise myself because this is the genuine truth. Surely I must be in a bad place when the truth feels strange to admit. Someone will either love me for what I'm not - this reality TV version of 'Henry', or if they know the truth of the things I've done and who that makes me, they won't love me at all.

"How could you think that Mr. Henry? You are so, so worthy of love. I mean… I'm already starting to fall in love and it hasn't even been that long." She's biting her lip and looking down and then up into my eyes. I can see the fear in her for having said something so bold. Fear? Or acting? Is this real? Is this for the cameras? Can you even fall in love this quickly?

I take her chin lightly with my fingers, and look directly at her and say, "I knew as soon as I saw you that your happiness is something to value. You are kind, and full of a strength I do not understand. I'm falling for you so hard and as scared as that makes me, I don't want it to ever end." I mean this, I feel it. Whether it's because I have no contact with the outside world, no cock-sucking Martine to fuck, no porn or access to the outside world, I don't know. And I don't care.

We kiss, and I imagine music playing over the real-life romance, but then the train of horror sears my mind, my stomach, my heart, and the anxiety I felt in those first few weeks after the crime hauls me into that same state of mind. Allowing a woman who I hurt so badly fall in love me, I feel is the worst kind of crime. I can't do this to her.

We're in the car. It's started raining. The windscreen wipers are waving at us, stretching out from Poppy and back to me like a game of tag. Apparently I'm 'it', because the moment I've been dreading is here – the moment where I can't help but spill my guts. I'm about to tag Poppy with all the responsibility the truth holds. It's the only time we've been alone without cameras, save a few quick sneaky snogs at cocktail parties. Even then, usually there's at least one camera following us around, but we're running late on time and we need to get to our next loca-tion pronto, so they've shoved us into a promo BMW and off we go. Poppy has insisted on driving.

"Poppy, I'm not who you think I am." It comes out like vomit, it feels like vomit – I feel sick.

"What? You're not Mr. Henry Vedder, thirty-one years old and hailing from Adelaide? Are you some kind of fugitive?" She thinks I'm playing a game with her, being funny.

"I'm just... I'm not good."

"Of course you are. Don't be silly," she swats me on the arm.

I shake my head from side to side and she continues, "There are different kinds of 'good' in the world Henry. I don't expect you to be some perfect person. Just be yourself. Where is all this coming from?"

I'm surprised by her reaction, she seems annoyed, angry. Her knuckles are white from gripping the wheel so tightly.

"I just want to be real with you –"

"We're on a fucking reality TV show, there's only so much 'real' you can get from that." There's something in her tone I haven't heard before, an edge, a controlled hostility.

"Why are you so mad right now?"

"Because I feel like you're about to tell me something you're going to regret."

"How could you possibly know that?"

She doesn't say anything, so I keep talking. "Don't you value truth and honesty, the whole removing of masks and all that bullshit you talk about in front of the cameras?" *Don't be a coward*, I'm thinking to myself, *don't give up on telling her.*

"Of course I do," she says. "But do you really think that people would fall in love with each other if they really, like *really* knew everything about each other? If you do you're delusional. Wise people keep the dark shit to them- selves." This is not the Poppy that the cameras are seeing. There is something slightly frightening about her.

"I don't believe that. It's not the kind of love that I want, anyway. I want you to know me, and for me to really know you. At the very least, I want you to know yourself and what your experiences actually mean."

There's no slow motion about it, no flashing lights before my eyes, all I see is a man with a big camera bolting across the road, then a steady stream of black through the rain, and I feel Poppy jump hard on the brake to stop the car from hitting the idiot. The car slides and then boom, all in the course of one second, I hear a kind-of explosion, everything goes white. I hear a loud, high pitch ringing, and then I'm out.

CHAPTER EIGHT

When I wake up I'm in the hospital and the world feels weird. It's like I'm waiting for the rest of my body to catch up with my mind, but it's not happening. Poppy is standing over me. She's holding my hand and she has been crying. The camera men and a producer are in the room, and they jump to action when they realise my eyes have opened. Poppy's moving her lips but there's no sound, and when I try to speak it sounds like an echo chamber cursing through the back of my skull. Like when you're a kid and you put your fingers in your ears, and talk or sing to try to see if you can hear yourself the same way other people hear you. I reach up to touch my face and it's sore to the touch. There're cuts with plasters over the top, one of my eyes is still half closed and swollen. My face is wet, too. Is it still bleeding? I look at my hand but there's no blood. I'm crying. I'm fucking crying and I realize it's because I can't hear, and I don't know if my words are coming out or if I'm speaking in bubbles of air.

They filmed all this so there's actual footage. I've watched it a million times. TV hosts love to drag this footage out, pinpointing it as 'the exact moment you realize you are deaf'. It's admittedly quite hard to watch because I am so genuinely and wretchedly taken aback. It's almost like my skin has been peeled back and you can see my soul. I'm looking up at Poppy with tears in my eyes, touching my face and looking at my hands and out the window. And then when I speak, I'm nonsensical, grabbing at my throat. Poppy is playing the perfect Eligible. When she realises something isn't right, she's kneeling by my side and holding one of my hands with both of hers, crying and speaking soundless words. I'm sure somebody must've yelled cut because Poppy disappeared. Maybe she was told to leave. I don't know how much that winded feeling in my gut has actually passed over time.

I don't remember much of the accident. I remember getting in the car with Poppy, and the guy running onto the road, but not much after that. I'm told that the paparazzi were pretty aggressive that day and that one of them, Marcus Thurwood who calls himself Misty, jumped out into the road. He has a reputation, and a few celebrities have restraining orders against him. I guess, Poppy slammed on the brakes to avoid hitting Misty and then the car skidded across the road before coming to a stop. It wasn't even really a serious accident except that the damn airbags went off. The front and the side ones, which caused some kind of freak damage to my head and inner ears.

Filming was put on hold while I was still lying up in a hospital bed, and an investigation was underway. It wasn't a long process as there was no foul play involved. I was surprised that Misty the paparazzi didn't get charged. I received a settlement of 700k from the show. Or was it the car company? Someone's insurance. Either way, probably pocket money for them. We shouldn't have been in the car alone and they had given us champagne beforehand. I was told to keep quiet on that last little piece of information. No problem here, I wasn't actually in the mood for chatting on account that I couldn't hear fuck all. I can't help but feel the irony in the whole thing. Poppy driving, I'm injured and now it's my turn for a lawsuit. Life is strange.

To lie in silence was a whole new experience. It was a new kind of separation from this world. It was like being at the bottom of the deep end of the swimming pool, like lying in a transparent isolation chamber. I would watch the machines lighting up and pumping with no sound. I would watch the nurses and doctors come and go. No sound. A silent movie had penetrated every fiber of my being. I was left alone inside myself. Watching the movie of my life pass through the sad screens of my eyes.

My mum had been called as the emergency contact, but she was in Italy with her new boyfriend. She wanted to come back, but I told the nurse, who was acting as our liaison, to insist that she stay. To downplay the situation, to say I was fine. That really all I was doing was sleeping. That I'd be right as rain in no time. That another week wouldn't matter. To enjoy her holiday. My mother deserved enjoyment, and I certainly wasn't going to be the cause of anymore misery in her life. Mum tried to insist, but eventually we got her on a Skype call and I put on my best smile and pantomime for her. I could see her laughing and it did the trick. Thank fuck. The thought of facing people was excruciating for me. I had banned everyone else from the room, my father who had mysteriously resurfaced, a few old friends, Poppy, and anyone else involved in the show. They had already filmed me on arrival, and when I first found out I was deaf, so they sure as hell weren't going to film me lying here trying to fucking figure out how the hell I was going to cope with this shit. This justifiable shit. This payback shit. This karmic debt. I had never told Poppy the truth, and I knew we were growing attached to each other. That she had feelings for me and I… and I…. I… was having a flash… I suddenly realized that I was going to tell Poppy everything in the car, everything. Oh my god. I was walking towards the truth and Bam!

Are we supposed to exist behind masks like Poppy had insisted? That nobody really wants to know the truth of anyone else? That we could never love if we did? That real, genuine love is almost a fantasy? Fuck, maybe she's right. Most of us can hardly face the truth inside ourselves. We are continually making up new stories about who we are or switching the stories we tell ourselves. It's like we are all some sort of out-of-sync novel that we are continually editing and rewriting. I'm a loving husband, I'm a schmucky IT guy, I'm a fucking coke snorting rockstar, I'm a snivelling little boy who can't help his mother, I'm a bank robber, I'm a bachelor who is winning the girl, I'm a deaf idiot lying in a flimsy hospital gown alone in a room. I started to weep, silently, weep. My shoulders shrugging up and down as the tears fall down the sides of my face. I have no fucking idea who I am and I'm not even sure anymore if the truth even fucking matters.

Eventually, a doctor came and sat on the side of my bed. He had a small whiteboard and a marker and we slowly started to discuss my situation. At this moment he didn't have a lot of answers for me. They had no idea when, or in what capacity I could be 'fixed'. The doctor explained that they would have to wait until any internal swelling and healing took place before they would be able to determine if there would be anything they could do. I grabbed the black marker from his hand and the white board. How long? I wrote out and started tapping the board with the marker. How long? He shrugged, took the marker and board back and wrote out: We don't know. It could be a three months… a year… I'm sorry. We will just have to be patient. He erased that and wrote again: You will have the best possible care and treatment that there is. There is always the possibility of a cochlear implant. I turned away. He patted my hand and left the room. I googled cochlear on my phone that was nearly dead. Fuck no – the possible side effects were water on the brain, face paralysis or a constant ringing in the ear. It all seemed a bit too high risk at the moment. I opted instead for the waiting game and started bargaining with the unseen forces that be that the swelling would go down. Then they'd be able to see I was healed enough for the second operation and all would be right as rain again.

I sank further and further into my own silent space. I was told my father had called. I didn't care. I was told Poppy stopped by. I didn't care. Junip had called. I didn't care.

The nurses kept coming. They kept opening the curtains and letting the sun in. They would ignore my requests to keep the room dark. They changed the water in the flowers that were sprinkled around the room. They took any dead flowers away. They smiled and silently buzzed around the room. One of the nurses, Janice, would wiggle my toes and force me to look at her.

Finally I ate some toast.

I was moved to another ward. It was like a hotel. It was a long-term care facility. They were keeping me close by so they could monitor my progress, the show insisted, and I didn't really care where I was. Janice came with me. She was an older short plump Italian lady. The kind you pictured pulling lots of little Luigis and Isabella's towards her large bosoms and squishing them to death. She was always smiling and wiggling my toes. Finally, I started to crawl out of my space. When I motioned for the whiteboard and marker, she told me to talk.

"Speak Henry, speak. You have a good voice," she said this slowly moving her mouth wide. I was trying to read her lips. I couldn't or could I? I knew what she was saying.

I used my voice. "Can…" it felt cracked and stiff in my throat. My voice hadn't been used in a while, not since doing my absolute best for Mum, when I was trying to convince her I was well enough for her to not bother coming home. I smiled, slightly embarrassed. Janice beamed and brought her hand to her chest. She encouraged me to go on with her eyes.

"Can… you bring me my computer?" It felt so strange to talk. I could still hear my own voice but not in exactly the same way. I don't know how to describe it. I learned that it was because it had been programmed into my brain. That if I had been born deaf I wouldn't hear it and over time if I remained deaf it might fade away. It's funny. I don't think we really pay attention to our own voices. We babble on and on without giving it a second thought, but now that I couldn't hear I became so aware of its existence.

Janice hugged me to her chest. I felt safe and proud.

With my computer I was able to reconnect to the world but on my own terms. I had signed some insurance papers a while back and I checked my bank account. Seven hundred thousand dollars was sitting there on top of the little I had left. That felt good. At least I didn't have to worry about money anymore, for a while. I typed in 'How to Lip Read.' There was a whole organization dedicated to the art of lip reading. I wasn't ready to click on the link. I kept scrolling until I found a YouTube video and started there. I watched about thirty seconds and slammed my computer screen shut. *Fuck! Fuck! Fuck!*

The next day I started again. I learnt that the phoneme is the smallest detectable unit of sound that is used to distinguish one word from another word. I learnt that English has about forty-four of these little bastards. Then I learnt that for lip reading, the number of visually distinctive units, visemes, are a shitload smaller. You can't see a lot phonemes because they are sounds made with the throat and mouth so you basically can't see them. Then there were homophones, kind of like phonemes but not. Homophones are words that look similar when you're lip reading, but they contain different phonemes, the ones that are hard to see, so what it basically boils down to is – you fuck up a lot. The best one can do is ask others to get a little dramatic, big mouths and hand gestures – but not too dramatic, that makes it harder. It's all context. Fuck's you up if someone is a bit OCD and switches topics all the time. But fuck me if I was going to stay in this hole of silence.

Janice was awesome. She would sit with me at night and tell me stories about her family. She was from Northern Italy, but her Mum and Dad had come to Australia in the sixties. She was just a baby. Unemployment was high in Italy at the time and her dad had a cousin Luiji (ha!) who was working construction in Adelaide. The city was booming. Janice would use big sweeping hand gestures and repeat words slowly, but not slow enough to make me feel like an idiot. "Con.....struck...tion." And she'd pretend she was laying bricks. She made it fun. I felt safe with her, my pride wasn't too affected in her presence. And she kept reassuring me that my voice was "so beautiful, so handsome. Use your voice, Henry." She would repeat over and over to me until my confidence grew. After a little over a week, Janice and I were conversing like old mates. Janice snuck in a bottle of Malbec to celebrate and we drank it together. A few glasses in and her hand gestures and pantomiming grew bigger. I was laughing, and I could see her giggling, and for a moment I forgot I couldn't hear, and then it all came crashing back, like a tidal wave of silence. I wept like a boy. My shoulders heaving up and down. I hadn't cried this hard since I was six years old and had witnessed, for the first time, my father beating my mother. Janice held me in her arms and rocked me back and forth.

The next day, one of the producers came to see me. It was much harder to understand her. I had gotten used to Janice and her big mouth, slow words and sweeping gestures. This woman rattled on with tiny thin lips that barely moved. Then she started speaking so slow it was all just big open gaps and wide valleys. We had to resort to the marker and whiteboard. Basically, she came to tell me I was sacked from the show. No surprise. And that they had already resumed filming. The show must go on. I figured that was it for Poppy and I, at least for this chapter. She'd never be gone from my mind. I found it strange the irony of the situations that had intertwined us for the past five years. Poppy, an only child with a single Mother, just like me. Humble beginnings to something resembling success. The twisting rigmarole of Poppy and Henry, like two old oak trees planted too close to one another, all their roots tangled and bound with no hope of escape. The money helped, but I still knew it wasn't worth it.

They let me out of the hospital soon after that. I still needed regular check-ups to see where the progression in my healing was at, but I was safe to be on my own. Walking out those doors and leaving Janice behind and stepping into a large and silent world was scary. But, I had my big boy pants on and most of my social circle didn't know anything, partly because of my contract to keep quiet, and also because I was still ashamed. It would take a while to get used to. I gave Janice a great big bear hug. She let go first and gave me a pat on the back. "You've got this Henry," she said. "You're a handsome, strong and brave, man," she smiled up at me. I could feel my eyes start to sting. I gave Janice a big bear hug, she kissed both my cheeks, and I walked back into the world.

I took a flight to Adelaide, and Junip my ex-wife, had come to pick me up. Janice had arranged it. We have known each other for so long, almost our whole lives. We pretty much drove in silence. No irony intended. At a traffic light, Junip tapped me on the arm and mouthed, "I picked you up a few groceries".

"Thanks." I mouthed back. I turned away and stared out the window. I wish I could've given her more. More gratitude than the moody-teenager act I had going on, but it was taking all my strength not to cry, and so I couldn't look at her or speak. I was certain if I did it would bring on the wail of all wails, and I couldn't let Junip see that.

I hadn't been to my house in months. I told Junip I needed to be alone. My house felt small and strange after being on the set of The Eligibles. I opened a few windows to let some air in. Things smelt stale. I started to unpack my shit and noticed I had a few texts from Amos. Fuck. I ignored them and gathered up the mail and flyers that had been shoved under the door. I found more notes from Amos. "Henry, where the fuck are you?" "Henry we need to talk" "Henry, come to the house." They were barely legible, scrawled on the back of receipts, religious pamphlets or ripped up bits of cardboard. The work of a psychopath. I hadn't heard from Amos in almost four years. The last thing I wanted was to see that motherfucker.

I put the groceries away that Junip had picked up. She had grabbed me a six pack of Corona. I cracked a bottle and then sat down at my kitchen table and flipped open my computer. I brought up my bank account and stared at the balance for a while. *Shit* that was a wee chunk of change. I closed the lid of my computer and wandered around my apartment. My record player, my dusty old record player, it dawned on me then that I couldn't hear music. Jesus Christ. I wandered to the bedroom, my bed was still unmade, I started to think about women. I could feel my eyes start to sting again. "FUCK" I yelled and whipped the bottle at the wall. It shattered everywhere. I heard nothing. "Fuck! Fuck! Fuck!" I cried again, silently on my own, sitting on the edge of my bed, my face in my hands.

Every day there were new reminders of my new reality. The rain, I couldn't hear. The notes slipped under the door from the postman reminding me to pick up parcels because I never heard the fucking door. The quiet of cooking, there was no cracking of an egg, no sizzle of oil, no hum of the refrigerator. Nothing. I became aware of the largeness of silence. The vastness. The fog. The all-encompassing blanket of no noise. It was slowly wearing me down. I shut the blinds, blocking out the days and the people and just let myself sink.

Drinking helped or at least I thought it did. I drank a lot. I drank whisky on the rocks and then when I ran out of whisky, I drank vodka and when I ran out of vodka, I drank gin, and when I ran out of gin, I raided my wine cellar and drank every fucking bottle of wine I had down there. In the morning I woke up, and I smoked weed. I rarely ate. Sometimes I'd chew on some frozen cookie dough and if I was really ambitious, I'd have toast. I took my toast straight and dry. After about nine or ten days the fruit and vegetables Junip had bought me were old, and I ran out of almost everything else, but as luck would have it I found some coke I had stashed in the back of the kitchen junk drawer. I snorted that and finished off the last bottle of 2011 Craiglee Shiraz. I was a mess. I was gaunt in the face, hollow in the chest, I had a scraggly short beard, watered-down eyes and skin that had taken on the grey hue of a long hospital stay, coupled with some serious self-abuse. My phone was dead. To be honest, I didn't even know where the hell it was and fucked if I could be bothered to look for it. I slept most of the time, except for when I had jacked myself up on the coke. I had weird lucid dreams where I thought I could hear voices, nameless, faceless voices. I'd spin around the living room looking for the source, crashing into the coffee table or the sofa. I'd pass out on the floor and if I made it to bed, I'd usually end up staying there for most of the next day. I stopped taking the medication I had been on for nearly five years and it gave me strange side effects; feelings of a painless but jolting electric shock hitting my brain, dizziness, the inability to wake up in the mornings. I caught adds on the TV, silent promos of 'The Eligibles', where I'd see images of my forgotten self, looking all suave and deboner, and then a quick cut to me in the hospital. I was reduced to an ad, to click-bait.

It was Junip who eventually found the spare key, hidden under the terracotta pot that sat out on the front walk, with the remnants of a dying kangaroo paw crumpling in its bowl. She walked into the filth that was my life. Somehow, I had once again become her burden.

"Henry! Oh god, Henry," she mouthed the words slowly. I couldn't look her in the eyes. I felt light years away.

"Why were you not answering my texts?" she asked. I looked at her puzzled. I couldn't make out her words. She just smiled, a small sad smile, and went about peeling open the blinds and picking up empty bottles, and gathering up bits of dried out toast. I stayed on the couch, curled up in a ball. She came with a glass of water in her hand and stood over me, her soft dark waves falling around her face.

"Henry you need to get up!"

I could read her lips but instead I said, "Don't you

know I can't fucking hear. I can't hear you," I mumbled it out like dribble.

"Enough!" she said. "I had a long talk with Janice. I know you can read my lips." She was frowning at me. "GET...THE....FUCK...UP!" I knew if I didn't move I would lose everything. Junip didn't owe me anything. The fact that she was even here was a life line. I sat up. My mouth felt like paste. I reached for the water and drank the whole glass in a single gulp.

"You smell like ass," she said. I cocked my head and furrowed my brow.

"You," she said pointing at me, "smell" she pinched her nose, "like ass," she turned and pointed at her ass. I laughed and immediately started coughing. I wasn't used to making sounds.

I wanted to grab hold of her and bury my face in her neck. I wanted her to hold me in her lap and just rock me.

"I have..." Junip turned away as she was talking.

"I can't hear," I said again, my voice slightly cracking. I didn't know if I was going to be able to hold it together.

Junip faced me. "I... have... food. You... look... skinny," she sucked her cheeks in. "Take... a... shower... you... stink," she held her nose again and smiled at me. "I... will... cook."

I did what I was told. I shuffled down the hallway towards the shower. I held onto the wall as I thought I might collapse. I was hunched over, my stomach was cramping. When I looked in the mirror, I couldn't hold back the tears. They fell silently down my face as I watched a stranger staring back at me. I turned away and turned on the shower.

The water felt good. I stood with my face under the shower head and let the water run down my face. I ran my hands through my hair and then stretched them out and placed them against the wall in front of me and bowed my head. I let the water beat down my neck and back. I turned the water up even hotter so that my skin went red and I grabbed the soap and began to scrub away the pity and the pain. I was in there until the water started to turn cold. When I stepped out I cleared away a small space of condensation on the mirror and grabbed my razor. I could feel myself shift. I wasn't completely out of danger from myself but thanks to Junip I was at least moving. I went to my bedroom and grabbed clean clothes. They smelt like fresh laundry. When I walked back out to the kitchen, Junip was still standing by the stove. All the bottles had been cleared away and the blankets from the couch were gone. The house smelt like a mix of ammonia, garlic and tomato. Junip had moved over to the counter and was rolling out dough.

"What are you making?" I asked. I felt shy. Insecure.

"Can..ne..llo...ni" she said slowly, smiling at me.

Junip had an Italian mother and a Palestinian father. All the sisters had beautiful olive toned skin and dark brown hair. They were a family of gatherings and food. Junip would tell me stories of how her mother would put aprons on all the girls when they were little and they would stand on chairs, lined up against the counter, making various kinds of pasta; cannelloni, tortellini, fettuccine, and then they would help to make the sauce, cutting vegetables and garlic, and squeezing tomatoes between their hands. Junip was a great cook. Her father would also get in the kitchen and teach his girls to make mansaf and mujaddara and other fatta dishes. He was the kind of man that was called daddy. I used to be jealous of her family, but after we were married, I shared in the happiness that it brought to her. I realized how much I missed her food, their food. Right now I realized I was starving.

"You've... been... drinking... a lot?" Junip asks making gestures with her hands.

"Yes," I say. "I was."

"When... was... the... last... time... you... drank?" she asks.

"Sorry?" I ask. It was still hard to read lips and always understand.

"When... was... the... last... time... you... drank?"

"I think... about three days ago," I say. I don't know whether to be embarrassed or not.

Junip doesn't say anything after that. She has opened a bottle of red wine and she gets my Venlafaxine off the window ledge and hands me a pill and a glass. I'm not sure these are supposed to go together. I do as I'm told. I already like that she's not trying to stop my drinking, that she understands it at least. I notice that she has an engagement ring on her finger. It's not big and gaudy but small and real, and pretty. You can tell it means something. I feel a pang of jealousy, but I also feel relieved and happy for her. I am glad she's not dependent on me anymore. I couldn't take it if I was the one still letting her down. She dings her glass against mine and says, "Cheers."

"Cheers," I say back and smile. She turns back towards the stove and stirs the sauce.

I sit down at the kitchen table. I still feel unsteady on my feet. "Why are you helping me? You don't have to. I'm not your responsibility, Junip," I say.

"Henry," she turns and looks at me. "I know, but I've known you since we were kids," she motions the height of a small child with her hand. The other hand is still stirring the sauce. "I will always care about you Henry. We're like family. I will always love you. Just not in that way. I'm happy Henry," she says. I'm getting use to the rhythm of her mouth and the way it moves and I don't have to ask her to repeat herself or speed up or slow down. We've got a good rhythm.

"I don't deserve this," I say.

She laughs. "You weren't a bad husband, Henry. With what you went through you could have been worse, much worse." She is referring to my father. She still doesn't know about the bank robbery, and Amos and all that other shit. "We were young. It just didn't work. Everybody has been a shit at some point in their life, no?" she takes a sip of wine.

"I guess," I say. "Everybody but you." I smile at her. It feels good to have a conversation, even a silent one. It almost feels as if everything is normal.

Junip laughs and shakes her head. "I highly doubt that. People who don't realize that they've made mistakes don't understand life. Sometimes, I think I understand life more than I'd like to." She turns back to the stove. I can't even imagine what Junip could have possibly done wrong, like bank robbery wrong. I take another sip of wine. The Venlafaxine is starting to take effect. I feel calmer than I have felt in a long time. Safe, safe with my friend Junip. That feels weird to say, 'friend' but I'd take Junip for a friend any day than have no Junip at all.

"Some make more mistakes than others," I say. I want to tell her everything. I want to lift this burden up and out of myself.

"Sure," says Junip "there're freaks out there, but people like us, we all have our secrets." I stop looking at her after she says 'freaks'.

"I'm just one big mistake," I say. Junip laughs but I can't hear her. "Sometimes I wish I would have just died in that car." She turns and looks at me. Her face looks angry. She's pointing the wooden spoon at me. It's dripping tomato sauce on the kitchen floor.

"Shut…. the… fuck… up…. Henry!… The…. fuck…. up!" I know her voice is probably raised. I can see her eyes going moist. "If you don't stop feeling sorry for yourself, I'm going to leave and you can figure this shit out on your own." I feel anger rising in me. I feel like my father.

"For fuck sakes Junip!" I yell. "I can't fucking hear! Do you get that? Like really?" I know I'm being a dick but I can't help myself. I want her to feel as bad as I feel. "Fucking nothing! I can't even hear this! Any of it! I never fucking asked you to come over anyway. So fucking leave if you want." I see her soften. The edges of her mouth turn down. She comes over to me.

"I'm sorry, Henry. You're right. I don't know how you feel. How this feels. It's just... it's just you can't stay feeling sorry for yourself. You have to live." She's crying now. I feel like a schmuck. My god, I'm lucky to have her here.

"I'm sorry," I say. "Thanks for being here. I'm starving," I say to steer the conversation back to neutral ground. Junip gives me a playful smack on the side of the head and goes back to the stove. She turns the sauce off. In my best moment of sobriety, this self-victimisation does start to look pretty fucking pathetic. I know she's right. I'm being a loser. I take the glass of wine in my hand, Malbec, she remembers. My hand is shaking. I take a sip and it makes my tongue contract to have something in my mouth, and my body shakes it off. It's like eating a lemon for the first time.

Junip and I stay in our neutral zone. She doesn't ask about the show and how I ended up there. She doesn't ask about the accident. I don't ask about her fiancé. I don't ask who he is or what he does or how long they have been together, or how he is better than me. We keep the conversation safe.

"So I have almost finished my degree," she says.

"You're at university?" I say, genuinely surprised.

"Yes," she laughs. " I did my Bachelor of Nursing. Now I'm doing my Masters in Mental Health Nursing. So, if you need some help," she's smiling.

"Wow!" I say. "That's awesome." I start to reflect on what I've done. Not much. I started to learn French so I could pick up chicks. And I partied. And I went on TV. And I went deaf.

"What have you been up to these last five years, Henry?" she asks.

"I was studying French for a while," I say. "C'était pour impressionner les dames mais je n'ai pas continué."

"Wow!" says Junip. "That's good. What did you say?"

"Oh nothing," I feel proud. I've even impressed myself. "I said, to impress the ladies, but I didn't keep it up. I dated a French girl for a while who made fun of my accent."

"Well, that's not very nice," says Junip, but she's smiling, there's a ping of sarcasm to her voice. I realise how much I've missed that. "What else have you been doing?"

I tell her about a water slide I built with some of my mates. "It was massive. It ran from the dunes into the ocean. We had a pump and all for it." I'm excited, like a kid showing off for his mum. "It was so freakin' fast. I went flying off it and scraped the shit out of my back." I'm actually laughing. Junip laughs with me as she puts the food out on the table. I like how she doesn't tell me I've wasted the last five years, even though, I'm sure she must think it. She's gracious and kind. I start to feel like maybe things will work out. Maybe the doctors will be able to fix my hearing. Maybe I will get my life together. Maybe I'll go back to school. Everything seems possible with Junip around. I eat like a man who hasn't eaten in weeks. The cannelloni is so fucking good.

I clear the table and load the dishes in the dishwasher.

Junip says, "I have to go, Henry. I've filled up your fridge. You should have enough food for a week or so."

"Thanks, Junip." I walk her to the door. At the door she turns to me.

"Henry," she runs her hand through her hair. "If you really need me, you can call me. But only if you really need me. You need to do this on your own. You're a good man. You deserve a good life. You need to learn how to believe that." I nod. Junip gives me a big hug and tussles my hair and she's gone.

CHAPTER NINE

Junip and I met when I was sixteen and she was fifteen. Kids, like she said. It's funny when you're sixteen you don't think you're still a kid, but when you're in your thirties looking back on it, you sure as hell realize that you were. Before Junip, I was dating a girl called Isla Ruton. She was gorgeous. Her mother was Russian and her dad was Spanish. She had this amazing little accent. She had only been in Australia since she was twelve. Before that she had been travelling with her family. Her father worked for the Spanish foreign service and she travelled on a diplomatic passport, often with private tutors, and sometimes going to 'American' schools abroad with other privileged kids. I had a scholarship that paid for most of my tuition, and my mother scrimped and saved for the rest. Isla and I used to smoke joints way out in the back field. She was always down playing her life and said it was a 'pain in the asshole' having to move and make friends all the time. I loved when she fucked up the language, especially when she was swearing.

All the guys at school had their eyes on Isla. She was fucking gorgeous, long legs, hips, good tits, big saucer brown eyes, full lips and long dark hair, and she was hot for me. I was the poor, bad boy. It made me exotic. I lost my virginity to Isla. She was way more experienced. I'd fooled around with a few girls before, but I had never experienced anything like this. She was so fucking confident that it made me relax, and we were high so that helped. We were hanging on the beach one night, making out heavy, her long brown hair messy from sand and salt, her skin tanned and taut. She was sitting on top of me kissing my eyes, my lips, my neck, my chest, my stomach, my cock. I was so fucking hard. I pulled her face back up and slid her dress up over her hips. She raised her arms high in the air and I took her dress off. She almost toppled over and we laughed. She pulled her bikini bottoms off and I pulled her back on top of me and she slid slowly down on to my cock and started to move in a slow and undulating rhythm. Her hands were on my chest and her head was thrown back; her breasts were high and round. I'll never fucking forget that moment when I became a man. Holy shit, I still get hard thinking about it.

Losing my virginity was like opening the floodgates to a whole new world. Even though I was mad-sixteen in love with Isla, and we had sex everywhere and all the time; the beach, the back field at school, the washroom at school, the girls locker room, my house, her house... I still couldn't help looking at every other girl that crossed my path. It didn't matter if they were tall or short, thin or fat, blonde hair, brown hair, they were all naked to me. I would picture fucking them – from behind, them on top, me on top, them going down, me going down – I had a constant fucking erection. My whole focus was sex, sex and more sex. And then I met Junip.

Isla and I, and a bunch of other kids, were all getting on the bus after school. Isla, myself and her new best friend Kelly, a girl from Sydney who had just recently started at our school, headed towards the back. Isla and Kelly slid into the two last seats at the back and continued talking about a beach party they were planning, and I slid into the seat in front of them next to Junip. She was a year younger, so I didn't remember ever seeing her before. She didn't even look my way. She had iPod earbuds stuck in her ears, her hands were folded in her lap and she was staring out the window. Her skin was the colour of lightly creamed coffee. I started to feel the old twitch in my trousers as I stared at her collarbone and imagined running my tongue along its ridge. Her hair was deep walnut and fell around her face. I tapped her on the shoulder.

"What are you listening to?" I smiled. She didn't say anything, she simply took one of the earbuds out and slid into my ear. Ah, Talking Heads. I was pleasantly surprised. I was starting to amass quite the collection of LPs; Pink Floyd, Nick Cave, PJ Harvey, Radiohead, The White Stripes, Thom Yorke, and Beck. I thought of myself as a bit of a connoisseur. Junip slowly turned her eyes, brilliant golden brown eyes, towards me. I smiled and nodded. "Love the Talking Heads" I started to sing along and Junip joined in – *'And you may ask yourself- how do I work this? And you may ask yourself- where is that large auto- mobile? And you may tell yourself- this is not my beautiful house. And you may tell yourself- this is not my beautiful...'* I felt a tap on my shoulder and pulled my earbud out and looked behind me. Isla was glaring at me. My cheeks flushed. I gave her a shitty look back and turned back around. I knew it was the beginning of a beginning and the end of an end. Junip had both earbuds back in and was staring out the window.

It turned out Junip's stop was before mine. She gathered her knapsack and slid out past me without saying a word. I couldn't even catch her eye. She walked up to the front of the bus and hoisted a white and pink surfboard down that had been up on an overhead rack. I slid over into her seat and stared out the window in order to catch another glimpse of her. I saw her. She was just standing there as if waiting. She smiled up at me from the side of the road, knapsack slung over one shoulder, her hand holding the surfboard that was standing beside her. I gave her a little wave as the bus pulled away. Under my breath I sang *'And I may tell myself- that is my beautiful wife'*.

Isla took it pretty hard when I broke up with her. She cried and then she got angry and swore at me, called me every name you could think of – dickhead, asshole, shitbag – I really wanted to feel bad with her but I was so fucking over the moon about Junip already that I just wanted to get away. With Junip it wasn't about just fucking her, though we did do a lot of that, it was more about discovering her, knowing her. I could just lie on the beach and watch her surf for hours. Then I'd wrap her up in a blanket and we'd lie there and stare at the stars and talk about all the things we were going to do and all the places that we would go. I wanted to take care of her forever.

The day after Junip left my house, I woke up early and ate oats and blueberries for breakfast. I went outside and walked to the local cafe to get a coffee, had Cannelloni for lunch, emailed my speech specialist, and set up an appointment for her to come over and help me with my lip reading for the following day. I made steamed vegetables and rice for dinner and went to bed early, already feeling so much better than the crash and burn I had just been on.

The next day, Nicola Francis, my speech therapist showed up around ten in the morning. She was a British woman. Blonde with a big ass. She told me she was British, as I couldn't hear an accent, although her mouth seemed to move slightly differently. She had big beautiful Chihuahua eyes and an easy disposition.

"Henry, lets... work... on... some.... of.... the.... more.... difficult.... words.... and.... phrases." It always takes me a few minutes to get used to people's mouths, and the differences in how they move when they enunciate their words. Nicola tries to get me to sign up for a support group for, 'Later in life Hearing-Impaired People.' I'm having none of it. I'm hopeful the doctors will fix me up soon and I'll be back to spinning some Nick Cave on the record player.

On the third day I venture further out into the world and head to the gym. It's a lot different navigating without sound. It's kind of like when you first start wearing your earbuds and you realize your eyes have to do a lot more work, except that there's no great soundtrack to chill out to. After a half hour at the gym I'm whipped. I head back home but I soon start a routine. I get up early, do a little of my own lip reading practicing from the videos on the USB that Nicola has left me, then I do a session with Nicola in the afternoon and then I head out to the gym.

I've swung by the grocery store and stocked up on all my fruits and veggies and stopped by the local butcher for meat. I bought a couple of bottles of wine and my favourite scotch whisky, Glenfiddich. I allow myself a glass of wine with dinner and two fingers of whisky on ice at night. I'm starting to feel good. I keep playing back Junip's last words to me: *'You need to do this on your own. You're a good man. You deserve a good life. You need to learn how to believe that, Henry.'* It plays like a record in my head. I've made some of those dumb post-it notes and stuck them on my bathroom mirror: 'You've got this!' 'You deserve a good life' 'Mistakes are lesson'. I know it's corny as shit but whatever the fuck it takes. After about a month, I text a couple of old friends, Rob and Paul, guys I've known since school days. We've always kept in touch but it's been pretty sporadic over the past few years, but they're the kind of friends where time means shit, and when you get together, it doesn't matter if it was yesterday or last year. I filled them in a bit on where I'm at but since I've been all over the TV, they knew a fair bit of the story. We hook up at a new bar that's just opened, a rooftop bar on Currie street. Instead of mouthing words slowly they start taking the mic out of me. Apparently 'deaf jokes' are a thing. I have tears streaming out my eyes and my gut is killing me from laughing so much by the time we are all walking out of there.

When I hit just three weeks of climbing out of my dungeon of self-pity and despair, I feel my libido kick in. I've always had an easy time wooing the ladies, and it seems that being temporarily deaf is a bit magnetic. Who would have thought? It's a bit brilliant, really. I get all the pleasure and none of the pain. Though some of them will mouth words so slowly to me that I want to scream 'I'm not fucking stupid.' I have to admit, that even if women are a bit talky for me, I do miss their sounds of pleasure; the moans and groans as they reach orgasm is a bit of a hard-on. I've brought home three different girls this week, and admittedly all of them have been fans of "The Eligibles", which is in week four, which means my noto-riety or fame is increasing, although I still prefer to believe it is my good looks and charisma that has me winning at the lady game.

I soon start ramping up my exercise routine at the gym. I eat a shitload of eggs, clean carbs and vegetables, and I've started on protein shakes in the morning. My 'accident' episode just aired, and the public has 'fallen in love'. The paparazzi is up my ass. They have parked themselves across from my house, they are at the gym, the beach, they're snapping like sharks whenever I'm with a woman. My new manager, Stephen Winterbottom, has put me on hold for any interviews. Until he feels we're at maximum saturation, I have to hold back. You want to make sure you are doing the 'best' interview and the network isn't pushing anything. All they want is for me to say positive things when I do agree to talk.

Finally, my first radio interview pops up, then I do a full scale editorial with a magazine, then it's talk shows, and it just keeps going from there. I'm on The Project, the Network News and pretty soon there's a half a dozen or so fake Instagram accounts under various versions of my name, and I have a shiny blue tick on Instagram. It feels weird to care. I mean I know it's D-grade celebrity shit, and I know I don't actually have any talent, and I know it'll all fade out eventually – but for whatever reason it's so easy to be sucked into thinking you're a little bit more awesome than you were before.

Fame or notoriety, or whatever you want to call it, is a fucked up game. It's a huge kaleidoscope of funnelled happiness and embarrassing missteps. Nothing is off limits. My depression still haunts me like a magician's game of cups, *'guess where the despair is in the cups in front of you, as I shuffle them to and fro'*. For the most part I feel pretty good and can go for weeks without a slide into the dark cloud. Then bam, I'll get triggered. As much as I try not to let media affect me, a couple of snide comments or shit stories in a row can definitely be a downer, particularly if I'm feeling a bit off kilter. My mates will tell me to just not look at them, but that's near impossible. The curiosity is the killer.

There is still no certainty on whether my hearing is ever going to be restored, which makes all the bullshit not even feel worth it. That's the most important thing to me, not a fucking write-up in the Daily Mail. It's a hard one to keep hopeful about sometimes. I've suffered a couple of hard setbacks where it has felt like I was tunneling down into a terrorist's den of despair. Those days I can't make it out the house. The curtains stay closed and I'm usually curled up in my bed in a fetal position, or wandering from room to room like a zombie. It can feel like you're just a piece of roadkill being picked at by faceless men with big cameras, and fickle faceless women with no minds, and agents and companies who see dollar signs in exchange for hearing loss. I'm touted around at events like some prize pony. That's when the whiskey switches to four fingers and not two.

Crawling out of the dark space is hard. I feel cold and detached and I find myself looking at people who seem at ease and happy, and I wonder if it's all fake. The women I'm bringing home have no concept of my pain. We have this raw animalistic sex where they bite at my jaw and dig their nails into my back and take me gagging into their mouths. I lick them from navel to thigh; from ear to collarbone. I bite and suck at their nipples and pussies and leave their lips raw. I fuck them without feeling like we're in some deranged porno. I'm ashamed to admit I feel nothing with them. They're dolls of distraction, of ejaculation. Right now, it seems like a necessary step, to getting out of my hell.

Then slowly I start to connect to the world again; to myself. It's not perfect, but it's better than the nameless vacant feeling of despair that I have just been through. And once again I wake up with the alarm pulsing up and down my back and I feel the light hitting my eyes and I realize that I am no longer part of this world. I do not understand it or care for it even if my Sim walks the walls of this fucked-up earth.

Next Saturday, I'm to attend some black-tie ball. I'm wearing an Armani suit, with Salvatore Ferragamo loafers, and a Yacht Master II Rolex which the show stylist picked out for me. Everything is controlled. Everything. Poppy is going to be there, and apparently, so is Ruben. He has a huge following, fans and foes alike. He's been good for the show. I sure as fuck hope I don't run into them. I'm feeling super fucking anxious for days leading up to this gig. It will be my first really 'big' staged event and this fucking perpetual world of silence is killing me. I've been snorting a fair bit of coke, and I know it's not good for my mental or physical well-being but I can't stop. On the night of the event I buy a bag. I head to the toilets, the small plastic bag of coke in my pocket. There's no-one in there, so I wipe down near the sink, and start to cut myself a large line with my credit card.

I didn't hear the swinging of the door or the music seeping through when Ruben came in. First, I jump, and then I feel ashamed, white powder all laid out, a rolled up fifty between my thumb and forefinger. We're looking at each other through the mirror for a second. Then Ruben, with hands in his pockets and a smirk across his face, mouths, "what, you're only cutting a line for yourself?"

It's funny how such a simple thing made me feel so warm – or at least a little defrosted. We snort it up just before the red carpet photo ops. He tells me about his life since the show – just what I'd expect from him really, a lot of women, a lot of publicity, events, rigmarole. Similar to me, aside from the depression, the accident, and the loss of hearing and mind. He mentions something about the show ruining his real-work life, but I'm having a hard time concentrating on his mouth and miss a bunch of what he's saying because the champagne has been flowing and I'm high as fuck. We share another line, then Rueben takes a piss and heads back out. I tell him, I'll catch up with him later, as I turn toward the urinals.

I've seen Poppy but she hasn't spotted me yet, her and Ruben are talking – they seem on good terms despite the fact that she dumped him on National TV. In a way it feels like I'm walking inside a plastic hamster ball. The separation and alienation caused by a lack of sound keeps me isolated from everything around me, and sometimes I mistake it for protection, until I turn around, and wham, Poppy is there, and a slew of fucking cameras are thrust into our faces. Poppy leans in and gives me a kiss on each cheek while the flashes descend like a seizure storm. I almost topple over and spill champagne down the back of Poppy's gown.

"Shit, I'm so sorry," I mumble. I'm well past articulating words.

"Henry, so nice to see you." I can't hear Poppy. I have no fucking idea what she has said but I see her composure, her perfect smile and I know she is saving the day for both of us. I start to feel nauseous and make a quick get-away for the men's room. I dive into the first stall and puke my fucken guts out.

I look in the mirror and I'm white as a ghost. I get the fuck out of there and hop in the first cab I can find. I give the guy my address as I slump down in the backseat hoping none of this has been caught by the event photographers, people with smartphones, or the dreaded paparazzi.

No such luck. The next day the papers and online media sites are buzzing with pictures of Poppy and me, me retching my guts out in the toilet, and me slumped down in my Armani suit in the back of a cab. My manager is pissed. I don't give a rats fucking ass. I keep the curtains closed and hide-out.

I dream that people are grasping at my mouth and trying to reach into my chest with small, clenched, greedy hands. There's a small golf ball in the back of my throat and it contains all my happiness, and they are trying to take it from me. Eventually I let them take it as I'm too tired to fight. The people are all beautiful and glamorous, and they are smiling and laughing and passing the golf ball around, and everyone takes a turn sucking on it. I feel heavy and tired and I can't move, and then I realise I am just empty skin because the crowd has taken everything else. They've taken my guts and my manhood and my emotions, and I'm just sloppy, vapid skin.

I wake up sweating and gasping. I swallow water and fall back into my nightmares.

Women I have fucked before are pulling out my teeth and letting them fall and crumble into my hands where they grow into pinecones. One of the women takes one of the pinecones and it turns into a sharp icicle, and she starts stabbing my stomach and my thighs. I watch black sludge draining out of me. Then Junip is there with her kind face, salty and wet from surfing, and she's picking up my teeth and placing them on my tongue like a priest offering the host. I close my mouth after she places a tooth, and it slips back into my gums, and I open my mouth again and she places another tooth on my tongue, and we repeat this in silence, and I start to feel whole again.

Then the dream switches and we are young, and a kitten is playing at our feet, and it is Christmas and we are sitting in front of a fireplace, and I am stroking the kitten under the chin, and the kitten is making Junip sneeze and laugh. Junip is snuggled into me and I'm just about to bend down and kiss her when I suddenly wake up. I'm not sure if this is a dream or a memory. Grief washes over me and I sob like a little boy. Silent and alone in my room.

Then, it's daylight and back to the bullshit, back to all that is required of me. I never realized when I signed up for "The Eligibles" that so much would be involved. I actually thought I would do a show and go back to my life, but now it's part of the settlement that I spend some days where I speak and pose for cameras. And they pay me for every event; keeping me happy, keeping the network happy. At least, that is what I tell myself. I'm asked repeatedly about the accident and about what it's like not to be able to hear.

I've started an affair with Nicola my hearing instructor and her and I rehearse all the glib phrasing and inspiring quotes I will use, while we get drunk on red wine that she lets drip down her chin and between her breasts. We laugh as I bend her over the kitchen table. I feel like if I thrust harder enough it will break the sound barrier and I will eventually hear her moans. I fucking miss the moans.

I feel like a fraud. A fake. This whole media circus works against all the ground I thought I was gaining with my life. It's the superficialities: the wear this product, mention this cologne, stand with this woman, this man, these children. I feel like a robot, like a shell, like a one-dimensional participant in someone else's reality. But, whose reality? The viewers? The producers? The consumers? I don't fucking know who this is for.

I continue to tout myself as some kind of hero. I have blurted out such nonsense on social media and to friends, things about loving oneself and yogic platitudes of grati-tude, that when practiced in reality, can be helpful, but at this point are simply flashcards that are blurted out as expectations for the press. It's like some sad sorry sack's Facebook page, where you know they are suffering because all they are posting are pictures of flowers with 'insightful' sayings: *"Live in the moment" "Just keep being you" "Life is only as good as your mindset."* I feel as if I have used my platform, not for good or the betterment of society, but to guide others towards a superficial and fleeting happiness. I finally decided to get the hell out of Adelaide. I'm going to lose my shit if this ride doesn't stop soon; all the travel, all the bullshit. I find a real estate agent and ask them to scout apartments for me in Sydney.

PART TWO

"Speak, I'm listening
    Baby, I'm your sweet thing
    Believe what I'm saying
    God's truth, I'm not lying

I lie steady
    Rest your head on me
    I'll smooth it nicely
    Rub it better 'till it bleeds"

-PJ Harvey "Rub 'Til It Bleeds"

CHAPTER TEN

(Poppy)

People are idiots. They think there is such a thing as love, as your 'soul-mate'. It's such bullshit. Oh he's my rock, she's my peach, he's my apple, she's my angel, he's my sponge cake that just won't fall. Hahaha. What is wrong with people!? You know what the truth is? You know what the truth looks like? Love or whatever you want to call it, is at its best and the most exciting when you're making up the whole thing, when you stay far enough removed and make up the whole person in your mind. That's why I love a language barrier; dating someone who barely has English as their second language. It's just way more fun and way more physical. I love watching their mouths move as they try to form words. I love the slow opening of temperament, opinion and habits. The kind of relationship where you communicate with sex and not words. It takes much longer for things to get boring, to go bad.

Oh, another great love – the unfulfilled. Isn't it fantastic? The what might have been, the one that got away. Those are always so romantic. When I look at married people, all I see is bored, lazy and defeated people. I just watched a film on a couple who had been married eighty years. Who the fuck wants to be married to someone for eighty years? The woman never said one nice thing about her husband through the whole film but it was made by their granddaughter, so they had nice music playing and she narrated some sappy dialogue over their lives to make it all seem romantic. The husband had been a general in the army and had to have his breakfast at exactly 7am and fruit at exactly 11am. Imagine living with that?

If you do decide to go long-term, for whatever your reasons might be, I don't judge, I would suggest you treat it like a Netflix mini-series. Don't get all real and predictable. You'll have yourself and your audience yawning in no time. And by audience I mean your loved one. You need to maintain that mystery and you'll have him or her falling all over themselves trying to figure you out. For me at least, the character I create for someone forms by exploring intuition. I watch them and listen. I reflect on their culture, conscience, fears and circumstances. I watch the emotional significance in the small inflections of my lover. Read their body language, what does and doesn't turn them on. Then I make the stars of their 'dream girl' slowly constellate into a universe, a person. 'Me'.

I can feel you all judging, but think about it, we all do this in some way don't we? We become different people in different social scenes. It's a survival instinct. No one can say that their work personality is the same as with a good friend. That's why we have different friends for different purposes, and why our lifestyles and actions change so much from relationship to relationship. I just take owner-ship of that reality, take advantage of it. Accept the script laid out to me. Figure out the character they've already written and then become that. It's easy. It reminds me of 'The Eligibles.' The ultimate dream girl. The one that everyone wants and wants to be. The unattainable, but is she? Now that's my game. It's all acting. And like I said, isn't that what we are all doing anyway?

When I first heard Henry's voice, I have to admit it took me a moment to connect the dots. There was some-thing familiar, and I was a getting a flash, a déjà vu, but I couldn't quite grasp the scene or fill in any of the details. I dismissed it and thought he was just this statuesque, sophisticated, well-spoken, narcissistic man, who maybe I wanted to date. Well maybe not date, but definitely fuck. I watched him walk down the stairs to join the other bach-elors all eagerly awaiting my attention and I admired his back and broad shoulders and the animal magnetism of his stance.

It wasn't until I had arranged for our 'second date' that I started to feel like this Mr. Henry knew me a bit too well. And to top it off he was treating me like some sort of victim, or a delicate flower at best. I was used to playing the latter role for men. It is a common fantasy about women – we were scared and cold and easily offended and needed protection. Then all of a sudden it hit me.

This Henry was… *the Henry*… the one Amos told me about. The one we used. Shit, I hadn't thought about him in years. This is too funny, so surreal. What a small world?

I had met Amos when I was twenty and he was twenty-one. A little before I got good at the game. It was when I still had 'soft emotions'. He was the kind of guy that always had a slightly pissed off expression coupled with gym honed abs, thighs and biceps. But I think it was his 'I-don't-give-a-fuck' pout and attitude when he spoke to women that first charmed the pants off me. He was born into a privilege I could hardly comprehend, but he squandered and pissed on it in such a way as to make me even more hot for him. I had no idea where his parents fit into the picture, and that certainly made me happy – it was hard enough dealing with my own Mum. It was like the world was a fucking gold maze he had created for himself. He hung out with a lot of other rich people, probably because he dealt them drugs, and partly because they all grew up together. It was a fun study. I went to some really epic parties, on yachts and in houses that were, shit, twenty times the size of the house I grew up in. I ate at the best restaurants and learned a lot about food and wine.

Growing up I lived with just my mum. She was poor and proud. Irish stock. She had never had the chance, or maybe the inclination, for much of an education. It had always been just the two of us. I went to a government school, in a shit neighbourhood in the Hills, and wore second-hand uniforms, and I even once spent two months in year ten keeping my sport shoes together with duct tape because there was no way we could afford new ones, until I thought of a plan. I just nicked Rachael Blain's shoes. She was a cunty little rich bitch or at least what we considered rich. I was so tired of her showing off all the time. She thought she was so cool because she was going out with this guy Martin who was captain of the Rugby team. I had already had sex with Marty and honestly I thought he had a small dick and he was certainly an asshole for fucking me while he was with Rachael. The funny part was Rachael actually thought we were friends. I was pretty good at acting even at a young age. She was the first person I really started studying. I would watch how she spoke or acted or how she laughed or pretended to cry and I would do the same. It was fun to learn how to play someone else. I scuffed up Rach's shoes a bit and traded out the laces so there was no way she would know they were hers. It would have taken Mum weeks to squirrel away bits of money to buy me new shoes.

What Mum lacked in finances she tried to make up for in love. It was a bit of a clingy desperate love though. I think she was lonely, and she 'needed' me more than she should have. She wanted to be best friends and hang out all the time. It was too much for me. We were too different, she was so annoyingly emotional. I worked really hard at making sure I was in control of my emotions rather than them being in control of me. I think it was a natural reaction to the type of Mum I had. Mum was somehow content and happy with what she had. I was like, not a chance in hell was I going to be sticking around here. I wanted to experience life, not just have it happen to me. I worked my ass off in school and ended up going to university a year earlier than my peers to study business and finance. I wasn't super smart, but I was determined. I wanted to climb my way up the ladder and become the CEO of a bank or something. I was not going to live in the ghetto my whole life.

I was working, studying and dating. I was pretty non-committal as far as men went. I did have a six month affair with this philosophy professor Robert Mahoney, who worked at the university. Mahoney was around fifty – hot fifty. Tall and fit and greying in all the right places – but it was his intellect, confidence and the way he'd look at me as if looking into a universe, that really turned me on. He rented this tiny little studio apartment for me and I would let him come over and go down on me, and then I would send him home. It was so much fun to be the one who was in control, especially with a man that wasn't used to being submissive. Then Robert said he left his wife for me.

I never shouted, but I did raise my voice, saying "don't ever say that. It's not fair. How do you think that will make me feel? You left your wife because you decided to leave your wife." I'd let my voice tremble a little and Robert would get all apologetic. He knew I was right. Nobody does anything for anybody, really. It's all about how we want to be perceived, or who we believe we are. That's what determines how we act.

The Professor started to toughen up after a month or two after he realised I wasn't like the other young sluts he'd bedded in the past, and it was then he started to teach me a lot about philosophy and what good literature can bring to the mind. I liked those old, thick, hard books, the ones that looked like they had been written and read by important people. He'd bring them over and we'd read them aloud in the apartment bathtub, choking on bubbles and expensive champagne. Other times Mahoney would wash my hair while I yammered on about this and that. I'd talk about how fucked up the divide between law and morality was, and then on the other hand how I didn't fully understand social acceptance and morality as tied principles. He'd ask me a lot of questions about my worldview, and listen with grey, knotted eyebrows. Once I'd had enough of talking, he'd fuck me raw with my wet hair tightly wrapped between his fists and fingers, and the water spilling out over the edge in small tidal waves. The sex was okay. His cock was fat and long but never fully hard. I wasn't sure if it was the age thing. Once I spiked his drink with viagra and we went at it for hours. He was so impressed with himself. So I kept doing it whenever I was really horny. I'm sure he thought it was me that brought him into some kind of personal sexual revolution. I figured I could always use that as ammunition to damage his ego if things went sour.

After a while our affair did go a bit awry. I realised I was starting to become some kind of social experiment. And worse, a fucking cliche. I'm ashamed I didn't realise it earlier. He'd attempt to convince me to act on all the impulses I had. "When I talk about acting on your impulses Poppy, I'm talking about expressing your free will. I see how afraid you are. You want to fit in, you want to control how people see you, and so you jerk around the perimeter of the freedom zones."

"I don't think I care as much as you're saying Professor. Look around, who am I trying to impress? Who am I acting for?" I hated being told what to do. *Who the fuck did he think he was?*

"You acted for your mother, you acted for your school friends, and now you're acting for me."

Instead of getting angry I tried to laugh about it, sink my head half way down into the bathtub water so just my eyes were showing, blow bubbles. He'd just keep talking, his arms up around the neck of the bath, white foam stuck to his chest hair, until I'd give in and talk. It was as if he was saying, *now it's my turn to dominate.* "Poppy. Listen. Viktor E. Frankl once said, 'between stimuli and response there is a space. In that space is our power to choose our response. In our response lies our growth and freedom.'"

I hated playing his fucked-up professor-student game, but at the same time I didn't mind his study and the version of 'me' that Mahoney was trying to create. I liked the conversations and disagreements. I felt like one of those Chinese wooden puzzle boxes. He'd try to synthesize the knowledge and information I'd render him in on to elucidate the clues, but be left with an impossible puzzle. A mystery that not even the most renowned puzzle prodigy solver could figure out.

"Who the fuck is Viktor? And why would I give a shit what some presumably dead, old dude said back in the day?" I'd scoff. "I'm pretty sure what this 'Viktor' meant by what he said is that we need to be able to control our impulses, not let them lead us down the rabbit hole. Do I look like an Alice? Do I look drug-fucked? Do I look like some disjointed art-major who's idiotic enough to believe society will let me do whatever the fuck I want without consequences? Are you serious? I'm not some dumb slut you can manipulate for a story in your philosophy classes like the others." It was as if he didn't hear the insults, or perhaps he just didn't care.

"You're the one that talks about freedom Poppy, not me. If you deny your impulses for too long, no matter what that impulse is, it will become an oppressor." He'd be massaging my feet, pressing his thumbs against my heels and the sides of my toes. Cracking each toe knuckle with a stretch upward.

"Come on Mahoney. If we all gave in to every 'desire' we're just ruining freedoms in our future. That's how criminals end up in prison, right? On a smaller scale, look at you. You cheated on and left your wife as an act of fulfilling your innate desires – me, and now if your impulse is to fuck her, you can't. If I wanted to push over some toddler in the street which I want to do quite often, I might have to do community service as legal recompense, which again takes away my freewill. Where does freewill start and where does it finish? There are lines, and those lines are distorted and grey. We navigate around them, or sit in the middle, and sometimes cross over completely, but choosing one side or the other seems like chains to me."

Mahoney smiles, as if I have told him exactly what he wants to hear, exactly what he's been saying all along. "Ah, and see, there is the answer. Just don't let society *know* where your moral crossovers are. Be smart about it. Navigate the grey lines yourself. Learn how to keep your secrets."

Looking back, I wonder if he had more influence over me than I even thought at the time, or if he was merely a prophet predicting the future. After a while the professor got boring. I stopped spiking his drinks with viagra and watched the embarrassment flame his disposition when we'd try to have sex. It was fun watching his demise. His flaccid cock, his social experiments, his weird obsession with my 'impulses' slowly disintegrating. So I stopped being available and went to live with Mum again. He took it hard. They are always so weak, but eventually he disappeared from my life and from the university. I could have coined the term ghosting.

About six months before graduating I completed a month-long placement at Chasnells bank and was offered a paid position in the finance department with promises of a quick promotion once I graduated. I was already making more money than my Mum. I was good at fitting in. I was easily liked. I was good at knowing what to say and how to say it. Aside from that I was just generally good at my job and management saw that.

Then along came Amos, with his ripped abs and camel coloured boat pants that hung off his hips at the exact right angle to show the leading 'V' that pointed to sex heaven. I became focused. I started to study him, to figure out what he liked and what he wanted. We hooked up pretty quick. And I soon learned more. He had dropped out of university and was making a killing dealing coke. I was okay with doing a bump or two, here or there. Sometimes it made sex a lot more fun. Soon enough I was pretty much living at his place in Manly, a hefty social distance from the Hills where I grew up. He also owned another place in Adelaide that his grandmother had left him, but we never went there.

Hanging with Amos and his friends made me very aware of my 'humble' beginnings. The shit ton of work I had put into my education and my life, how I never had a father and only a hardworking, but hung-up mother, who couldn't seem to turn it around if her life depended on it. I was pretty damn proud of myself. Amos knew where I came from and what life had been like for me. He didn't give a shit. Maybe, he really didn't give a shit about much, but I didn't care. I was finally going to the 'right' parties and learning more about life than I ever had before. His friends had a bit of that frat-boy-white-guy-self-entitled shit going on. One night, his mate Rob punched this guy right in the face outside a bar because he accidently bumped into him, and Rob started going off on what a 'low-life' piece of shit the guy was and how the hell he thought he could hang in our neighbourhood. I looked at the guy, blood coming out of his nose, and thought he probably had more privilege than me. Fuck, if this is what Amos's friends thought, I sure as hell didn't want them to find out where I was from. Amos gave me a wink and bent over and whispered in my ear, "Rob's a dick," and then kissed me on my neck. I forgot all about the guy with the broken nose and snuggled in closer to Amos as we walked away. I knew Amos liked playing protector, and I liked playing the role of the poor upset damsel.

Even though Amos didn't seem to care where I was from, he would tell his friends that I went to some elite boarding school in Sweden because he knew I was embarrassed of my childhood reality. We made it a game. I can't even remember the name but I liked playing the troubled little rich girl. I was slightly aloof with everyone as inside I felt like I was better than most of them. I was smart, was almost finished uni, and I had worked my ass off to be where I was. Mummy and daddy hadn't just handed me the keys to a car when I turned sixteen and handed over a trust fund to burn through in my twenties. It came off as some sort of cool and I was often envied by the girls, and most of the guys had made a pass at me at one time or another. I was certainly smart enough to know how to dance in conversation and avoid having the spotlight on me when I was chatting with any of the Amos's friends' girlfriends. It was always easy enough to pretend I knew all the designers. The local ones and the international. After a while I didn't have a choice to how much I knew – I was dragged along to hundreds of fashion shows in Sydney. It was so wanky. Everyone would pretend they knew shitloads about art and then get drunk on champagne and high on charlie.

I didn't give a fuck about fashion but it was a really fun game to play. I think that people are often fooled by the needless, tedious controversy of 'friends'. It becomes a kind of addiction. That's why I've never really had many girlfriends. I let them come in and out like food. Consume and dump. I find there is too much snide deviance in female friendships anyway, although I'd never admit that out loud.

The guys were easier to hang with as all they ever really wanted was to talk about themselves. I would just pretend that whatever they were saying was super funny or interesting. Then I'd give them a little, just a little talk, to show I wasn't just a pretty face. I'd say something insightful or different, political even, and they'd basically just bow at my feet in awe. Guys are dumb, so dumb. It was super fun knowing I could trick everyone. People are stupid.

I was soon living full-time at Amos's and I think he really liked the permanent girlfriend/wife thing. Slowly, the sex started to go from the really hot up against the wall banging to tender in bed love making. It was horrible. He'd talk the whole time, not dirty, but things like *"I'm so happy you're mine" "I want us to stay together forever" "I want to marry you."* I had thought that this was what I wanted but when I got it, it made me want to throw up. I started to pull away. I still played the part in public, hanging off his arm at parties and drinking champagne and laughing, and I loved that I had a credit card and Amos was always throwing cash at me. I could go shopping for whatever I liked. I would stash some of the leftover cash away. I was always planning ahead. That's what smart girls do.

Then things changed. Amos was snorting more coke than he was selling. He was starting to lose a lot of weight, and soon enough the credit card dried up. I could barely look at him. The train had stopped, and I was sure as hell getting off. I had just graduated from uni with a degree in Economics and Finance, and like I said, I had managed to squirrel away money, while Amos was raking it in. I still had the job at the bank, so I ran. I moved temporarily into a little studio apartment closer to work, near the financial district, and in my downtime I started scouting out new jobs. No way was I staying with a coked-out loser. I was better than that. I was good to go.

Unfortunately, it was at that happy crossroad, the one I'd usually jump across without fear, that the shit hit the fan. I was pregnant. Eighteen weeks. Fucking halfway to hell. I had had two false periods and then I had missed a couple. I didn't think too much of it as we were barely having sex and I've always had irregular periods. I talked to the doctor about an abortion but I was already passed the cut-off date. I had been drinking and doing coke while I was pregnant, but I didn't say anything to the doctor. They get all judgey and shit and I didn't fucking know I had been pregnant. It wasn't my fault. I got in touch with Amos. I figured he had a 'right to know' and I also thought I needed a plan and maybe he could be part of it. He was ecstatic, overjoyed like some newly rescued puppy. Delusional. I was the woman. I was the one whose life was going to stop, and I had barely just started living. I had crawled out of my ghetto and was on the brink of having it all and now... I wept for three days. I was so angry at myself. I knew better, a lot better. And I had worked so fucking hard. I had started missing the occa-sional pill or maybe two in a row when Amos and I stopped having regular sex. It was so far off my radar. I was thinking more about an exit plan and my new life than popping a little round pill. Fucking stupid.

It was so strange to have this life growing inside me that I couldn't stop, that I had no control over. For the longest time I was completely unaware of it. I never had morning sickness, and I was barely showing despite being so far along. During the day, I could sometimes even forget all about it. At night I would try to will it away but my body just kept feeding it, expanding. It started moving around, an insolent child having a tantrum in my womb. It would kick my ribs and start doing somersaults the moment I laid down to sleep. I didn't like it and I didn't want it.

I didn't tell my mother, I just avoided her. I could tell she was hurt that I didn't come to see her, but I made excuses about how busy work was, and that I was lining up interviews for better jobs, and I'd be there next week, I promise. Then next week would come and the next and the next. I started getting bigger and bigger. At first I wore empire waist dresses, and that worked. Then I think it started to just look like I was putting on a bit of weight. The kind of weight where you think someone might be pregnant but you don't want to ask them because it could be really embarrassing.

Amos became a changed man. He was so into it. I moved back in with him. He had begged, and I didn't have the strength or willpower to resist. I was also thinking that maybe I could convince him that we could give it up for adoption if I had more time with him. You know, better parents, better life, we could have fun, blah blah blah. It was when he started painting the nursery and a bassinet showed up and a pram that I knew my fight was over. We found out it was a girl. I was so angry that she was coming to ruin my life. Amos bought cute little baby girl dresses and blankets and bibs that I would barely glance at. He was the one reading baby books on how to burp and what different cries might meant and who knows what else – I tried not to listen. He stopped snorting coke. His frat-boy mates disappeared because I told him if he told anyone I was fat I'd cut his balls off. He'd lay with his head in my lap at night and talk to my stomach. Fuck. I started to think that maybe he could stay home and look after the baby and I could get on with my career and then when I had a good job or a new guy I could just vanish. At least Amos would have something going for him, something *good* in his life. Maybe his parents would even let him back into their lives if they knew they had a grandchild.

She came at sunset. I've never experienced so much pain, so much stinging electricity coursing through my womb and my body in waves. I tried not to scream. I wouldn't let Amos hold my hands through my agony and hot tears. She came out silent, silent as darkness. The midwife wrapped her warm and wet body in a thin yellow blanket and placed her on my chest. She was twenty-nine weeks old. I swear she propped herself up on one wobbly wet elbow and looked me square in the eye. The midwife assured me that that wasn't possible as she had died two days before. Intrauterine fetal death. I still wasn't a hundred percent sure. She looked sad. I knew it was my fault. I didn't want her, and I had willed her to die. I had drunk and smoked and partied. And then when I knew she existed, I hadn't loved her.

Amos was crying, his big mouth upside down and gooey with saliva and sweat and tears. He took her from me when she started to get cold and had the nurse take photos with him holding her and standing next to me. My eyes were as empty as morning blackboards. I was stiff and spent. Any guilt was safely tucked in next to my sweat stained body and the hospital sheets. The midwives assumed I was in shock and were very nice to me. I slept for eighteen hours. Then I woke up and started planning.

Amos and I continued living together after I returned from the hospital. It was like living with a zombie. He cooked and cleaned but he walked around like a flatline. I had been given a week off from work. I told them I had to have an operation and got a doctors certificate to prove it. The week was more than enough. I was itching to get out of the apartment and away from Amos and I needed money. Thankfully I received some good news when I got back to work. They had missed me, and I was offered a promotion to an Acting Assistant Bank Manager while the boss was, ironically, on maternity leave. It helped, but it was still slow going. I remembered when I thought it was a big deal to get a job in a bank. Now, I was looking to be able to get the hell out of working all together. Those girls I met through Amos were not working for a living and I wanted what they had. Who wouldn't? Why did all the hard work and pride matter? Who actually fucking cared? Amos wasn't contributing anything aside from the place, and since it was his apartment, I couldn't really tell him to fuck off. I felt like a rat in a cage, going around and around on one of those hamster wheels. I felt like I was going to be stuck in a shit life just like my Mother, well maybe a bit better, but shit none the less.

My body was still recovering. I had the pudgy stomach of a woman who had just given birth. The linea nigra, the dark line up my guts, was starting to fade but was still etched in like charcoal on paper. I started working out and eating better. I wanted all these scars, all these memories, to be gone from my mind and my body as quickly as possible. Until that happened, every time I had a shower or a bath or got changed in front of a mirror, I'd look down and see guilt and pain. The vulnerability was killing me, and I needed some power.

I was the one who came up with the whole scam, the robbery, the insurance, Amos' latchey, the whole works. I could make Amos do anything. I told him to head out to some parties away from Sydney, grab a bit of blow and to start scouting for an ambitious gullible schmuck. Fuck they were a dime a dozen. I didn't want to know who it was that he found in Adelaide, what his name was or how he met him. And I sure as shit didn't want him to know anything about me. I knew if things went south, Amos would never turn on me, and the anonymity with the other dude would ensure my safety. It was fucking brilliant. I had minimal risk and all the gain, and two fucking blokes doing my dirty work for me. I was starting to feel like I was back on my game.

Finally, the day came, and it was brilliant. They came in and literally scared the shit out of the bank manager. It was probably the shit prosthetics job they did on their faces, which almost scared the shit out of me too. It was hard not to laugh, but at least the disguise worked. The guy that Amos recruited was in the back loading up bags of cash and Amos tied the manager up in one room and took me to another. I told him to treat me rough, a little rape fantasy, and to smack me around a bit, but in front of the other dude so that the whole thing looked more authentic, and it would also help to distance me from the whole thing. I have to admit it was smoking hot. He had me bent over a conference table and had put a condom on. He was about to bang me hard as opposed to that sickly sweet love making he used to do at home in the past. It was the first time we were going to have sex since, well, since whatever. The thought of getting caught was totally turning me on as well, and sure enough the Joe that Amos recruited walked in and started yelling at Amos before he even penetrated.

"What the fuck are you doing?" he looked shocked as shit. "Nobody is supposed to get hurt you fuck!" he screamed, "And your fucking DNA will be everywhere!"

It was brilliant. Amos treated me like a piece of shit and shoved me into a chair and taped me up. I was so fucking hot for him. But then he turned back and smacked me across the face. I thought that was a bit too far. Maybe it was for losing the baby. It felt real. He then whispered in my ear, "Is that how you fucking like it bitch?" and I felt a rage like no other. When I saw Amos later at the apartment after a day of rape kits, lawyers, police investigations and a shitload of crying, I find Amos so jacked up on coke that he was dancing around like a rabbit.

"Baby... baby... did you see Henry's face?" his foot was tapping and his leg was going a million miles an hour. He was cracking up "Henry, was shit scared man. Fuck you were hot." He grabbed me by the waist.

"Calm, down Amos." I said. "And shut up. I told you I didn't want to know fuck all about the guy you got involved and we need to be calm. This shit isn't over."

Amos just smiled. I turn away and start counting the cash on the small dining room table, and then I feel hot, needy breathing behind me and I turn around and he's on one knee with that stupid, pathetic grin on his face, and a ring box open to reveal the ugliest ring I've ever seen in my life. He probably stole it. Well I sure as fuck hoped he did because I'd have been even angrier if he used any of our money to buy the piece of shit. The ring literally looked like one of those candy prizes you get out of game vending machines. It had a gaudy pink diamond in the centre, with tawdry blue stones around it. I had no intention of marrying Amos but I say yes anyway, to keep him off my back until my plan is in play. I knew I had to get the hell out of that apartment and away from Amos.

The next few days were taken up with doctors appointments, the bank's lawyers and then my lawyer, detectives, police, psychologists, HR, and meetings and meetings and meetings. They wanted everything on internal records but they didn't want it out in the public. I even had to do a lie detector test to ensure it wasn't an inside job, and I passed with flying colours. Maybe it was because I was actually so angry, or so naturally cold, or so determined for a good life. I didn't even break a sweat. Mahoney would've been proud. After all he was the one that taught me how to control my vitals in any stressful situation. Here I was, acting on my impulses and coming out with a win. I really put myself in character when they asked all the rape questions too. The guy doing the test even cried, watching my body respond.

I settled for 1.2 million dollars in damages. I couldn't fucking believe it. I was set. I never expected that much cash. It soon got out to the public and was all over the news. Thank God my name was kept private. They never caught the guys who did it and the bank hushed it up pretty fast. They wanted, they needed, to save their reputation. Nobody wants to bank at a place that isn't secure. I let Amos keep his take from the robbery, I gave my Mum a couple hundred thousand, I left the ring on the bedside table, said adios amigos, and took off for the open road.

CHAPTER ELEVEN

I spent three years travelling. I lived in the now. There was no past and there was no future. For the first six months I was in Vietnam, Cambodia, Thailand and Indonesia. It was one long grand party. I had the perfect relationships with no strings and no expectations. I spent the next six months in South Africa. I had a mad affair with a commercial real estate broker, which was all yachts and champagne. Back to the good life. He started to go all soft on me, exactly how Amos had, so I ran the fuck out of there and headed to Central and South America. I took a different route this time and became the 'regular' back-packer. I stayed in hostels, got high, did the Inca trail, dived the Galapagos and had a shit ton of random flings with other travellers from all over the world. I had a weakness though for the Spanish language and *me encantan los guapos hombres españoles.*

I ended up camping out in Chile for a while learning

to surf and that's when I met Gabriel. He was at university finishing up his law degree and I was the shiny new exotic treat. He came from a wealthy family and had good manners, and all his friends were fun and pretty cute too. It was perfect. I invented a story for him and he invented a story for me. Two myths banging our brains out. I was getting to hang with some of his local crew and I would take him out with some of the fast friends I made at the hostel. We'd smoke weed, snort coke, and often eat a rock of MDMA and come home and rip each other's clothes off before the door to his house was even closed.

I still fantasise about the sex. Being up against the wall. Gabriel reaching under my legs and pushing me up by my ass until I'm high enough to slide my legs around his shoulders and neck. Him sliding his tongue from ass to clit and sucking on my lips until the wet is sliding down his chin. I'd fuck him on top while he pinched my nipples and grasped at my breasts, and then he'd flip me over and with a single movement fuck me from behind. His hand reached around and played with my clit as he pulled me back to meet his thrusts. There were no submissive's in this relationship.

It was insatiable.

We were together for nearly a year. My first *real* relationship. Well at least the first person I thought I might actually love. Gabriel gave me the space no other man had. He'd work and study and surf. I suppose everything breaks down in the end though doesn't it? I guess even in the best situation humans aren't meant to be monogamous. We're designed to love and learn and then move on. It's evolution.

Sure enough, his family didn't approve, or at least the women in his life didn't approve. I wasn't your typical traditional Chilean girl. The men were a bit more forgiving and I am sure most of them were proud of their nephew, brother, son, mate and wished that they also had a little piece of exotic ass to call their own. Gabriel loved everything about us at first, but as sure as it rains in spring, he started to resent my 'untraditional' ways. It was the slippery slope into ownership and possession. Almost every guy tries to go there. They call it protection. I call it bullshit. So what did I do? I started spending a bit more time away from him. Whenever a man is trying to control me, or pull me close, it has the opposite effect on me. All I want to do is bolt.

"Why you be so selfish," he'd say with those pouty lips and dark black eyes.

"I just need some space my sweet chili picante," I'd say, and give him a quick peck and grab my red puffer jacket, pile my hair on top of my head and sling my backpack over my shoulder and head out.

"Why you leave? You selfish. My family is right. You go sleep with men? When you come back?" It was always the same, and it was getting boring.

Being alone for me are some of the happiest moments of my life. It was calm and connected, a powerful happy. I didn't have to perform a script for anyone. I would rent a dune buggy, grab some provisions, and drive along the beach until I found a deserted stretch of sand and dunes, where I was shielded on all three sides with only the ocean out in front. I would strip down naked and collect dead wood and build a fire. I would get out my small gear of camping pans and fry up fresh fish and grill pineapple and sweet peppers over the open flames. I'd rip off chunks of marraqueta and dip it in fresh melted, salted butter and I'd open a bottle of really good Bodegas Re Velador-a white Pinot Noir.

I had grown fond of good wine from my time in Chile. I felt like a God. Like I was connected to the historical lineage of all heroic women – Draupadi, Anath, Artemis, Mami Wata. I was me. I was a warrior who was going to win.

I'd smoke a joint and stare at the sea, listening to the sounds of the waves splashing up against the rocks, in and out, over and over. The sounds of the fire would crackle and snap alongside the water. Birds were singing and chattering away to each other. The soft long grasses stretched up from parts of the sand and were swaying in the wind. The sounds at dusk would wrap me up like a warm knitted blanket. It made me think of my mum and being on her lap and the comfort I felt when I was very very young. I really felt like I could live on the beach forever. A glorious madwoman in a hand built shack, left alone to enjoy the silence and to grow old. A place where no one could hurt me, a place where I could hurt no one.

After a night or two on the beach I would return to Gabriel. We'd have this great blast of fighting and fucking where he would accuse me of all kinds of lewd acts he thought I was engaging in with other men. It was the

antithesis to what I had just experienced and jolted me back to the man-made world with a kind of shock and awe. However, it soon became apparent that the fantasies we created around each other were cracking, and dirty little lines of truth were peeking through. It was soon time to go for good.

After we split up Gabriel sent me a message to tell me he was engaged to a Carla, the daughter of a family friend. He told me that sometimes when they were making love, he would close his eyes and pretended that it was me. I hit delete.

I headed back to Australia. After three years of travelling I wanted somewhere to call home. I had burned through two hundred thousand and now had seven hundred thousand left. I found a rundown vineyard near Melbourne and convinced the bank to lend me what I needed, and I began to build a business.

I hired a viticulturist with whom I could consult regarding the vines that were already planted, mainly shiraz and cabernet sauvignon, and asked questions on what might need uprooting and replanting. His reports were good. He suggested with a little pruning and vineyard management we could probably secure a decent yield for next harvest. So, I hired a vineyard manager and a winemaker. They brought on a small team of initial support staff and I took on the role as marketing manager. I called the Vineyard, Tenacious Winery. The vines, the word, the meaning, all reminded me of my determination and singularity, of what I had overcome and transcended. The gnarly and knotted vines with their deep roots had clung to their existence, so it seemed fitting. I turned it into a working farm and renovated the house. I soon had chickens and fresh eggs. I thought about bringing cows in but my vineyard manager suggested that supporting a local dairy farmer would bring a sense of community to the place. I liked the idea. We purchased all our milk from a farmer down the road and I outfitted the old farmhouse with a commercial kitchen and I brought in a young and ambitious cheese-maker called Jen, who had trained at Fifth Town Cheese in a small community in Canada. The place had closed and Jen was now travelling. I liked the idea of providing a temporary haven to others who were on the road. Jen taught me some basics, and I gave her a place to crash. We soon had other travellers and volunteers working out in the vineyard with Steve the vineyard manager. Jen and Steve started hanging out a fair bit, and soon enough Tenacious Winery's first love affair was under full swing. The place had a nice vibe and I could trust them. Once we got our first small batch out I spent more time travelling, to Melbourne and Sydney, to promote the wines. It was great. I had a more simple and solitary life out in the country, where I'd have my hair thrown up, and usually a pair of wellingtons on and old jeans. And then I had all the city had to offer with designer clothes and parties. For once in my life I wasn't interested in men or sex. I could go months on end without it. Occasionally, I reminisced about Gabriel and our mind blowing fuck sessions, but I was glad to be out of that and happy with where I was. Happy being alone. Happy being a business owner. Happy being busy.

I did spend that time to think a lot about my relationships with men. How there was a distance, and how it seemed that men were only capable of knowing me through a fantasy that they had already created in their head. It was a bit sad but a bit freeing at the same time. I had known at an early age that I wasn't going to be like my mother or anyone else for that matter. That I didn't fit in with my upbringing, with its daily drudgery of work, and its endless cycle of living pay cheque to pay cheque. The poor pride of the working class, who had nothing to hold onto but a beer and some bitterness. I was transforming, and not just playing the role of a rich girl, but actually *being* it – was fun. The only place I felt connected, felt whole, felt content was at the vineyard when I would walk among the vines at sunset by myself. And for now that was enough.

I started using social media more heavily as a means to promote the winery. The winery was doing well and with that my status was increasing. It was a bit too easy to convince people that I was powerful, smart, beautiful and good. The followers, the likes, the constant affirmation in photo comments. And it was also a bit too easy to forget that I was ashamed of my upbringing and my past. Too easy to forget about my shitty relationship with a drug dealer and a stillborn baby. Too easy to forget that I had conned two men into robbing a bank where I worked, and that from that, came the means for my travel and for my business. Then it became a bit too easy to convince myself that it was my hard work, my spirit and my tenacity that had made me who I am. I regretted nothing and was slowly starting to believe a version of myself that was transforming. But isn't this what we all do? We become versions of ourselves. Some of us are just more aware and a bit better at it than others. And it always feels good to be good at something don't you think?

I went to visit my mum. I hadn't seen her since I told her I won the lottery and had given her the cheque for two hundred thousand dollars. That was just before I had left for all my travels. She looked fantastic. She had a great little apartment in the city. Her hair was cut in a really flattering layered cut that framed her face. She had gone for some cosmetic touch-ups – a little Botox and filler, and a slight lift and augmentation to her breasts. She was all flowing and glowing in light linen clothes, gold jewelry and sandals. She looked like my older sister, not my mother. When I told her she giggled. She was still simple and humble and sweet, and she had a new man, Michael, who although a little on the short round and hairy side, adored her and showered her with lots of attention, presents and holidays. I loved who she had become. I think I was genuinely happy for her.

It must have been about two years after purchasing and running Tenacious, that I was approached by a producer for 'The Eligibles', and asked if I would consider auditioning as the next Eligible. It wasn't something I had ever thought about doing but once I was in front of the camera, I found it so easy to give them what they wanted. I could cry or laugh on demand, and I had the perfect story. A beautiful young woman works hard through university, travels the world, starts a successful business, and has everything: Except love. It couldn't have been written any better.

CHAPTER TWELVE

The idea of being thrust into the spotlight with its hair and makeup, paparazzi and invites was gloriously intoxicating. It was like bathing in a soaker tub with a bevy of handsome men to wash your arms and legs and bring you champagne and caviar. It was the antithesis to my solitary beach burning parties of calm and inner self-connection, or my late night walks in the vineyard. It was a different kind of drug. The perfect distraction to vanquish my pitiful childhood, erase my Amos' days, and lift me up to a throne of glitter, glamour, diversions and noise. And in that noise, the beautiful busy, distracting and attractive noise, I would be able to play, to be the easy and the accommodating *Eligible*.

The reality wasn't really the fairytale I expected, admittedly. There were a lot of long days and it was hard to deal with so many men's expectations, stories and emotions. But I loved it. I thrived on it. I was good at it. The flirtatious and fun girl of your dreams. The ultimate object of desirability, who can date multiple men at once because, well – 'they knew what they were signing up for'. There's no conflict. I was on my game.

On the first night of official filming I was fitted out in a custom-made emerald green silk gown. It draped and clung perfectly to my body alone. My blonde hair was tousled and swept around my shoulders. It was magical. Cinderella had nothing on me. I stood at the top of a grand staircase outside a huge and magnificent house. Limousines pulled up unloading gorgeous, beautiful men that I would get to pick from. Individually, they climbed the stairs and introduced themselves. There was a huge cluster of behind-the-scenes people who would swirl around from all different angles, dusting my face, adjusting my dress, and choreographing the ebb and flow of this strange and distant reality that I was starring in. The men started to blend together. They became unmemorable in their syncopated similarities. All gorgeous, six-foot, chiseled, athletic men creating a slightly out of sync reality. However, there were a few stands-outs. One super bendy circus performer was placed in a glass box in front of me from which he slowly stretched himself out to meet me. There was this other guy who I think was honestly and truly in love, like in love-love with his dog. And then there was this crazy erratic guy who told me I looked like sex on legs. He had a shirt with him with his face on it that said: 'Sex is the best kind of breakfast.' My guess is he had a small dick.

In terms of perking any kind of romantic interest or sexual desire (are they not the same?) there were only three. First, Ben with his lips that I watched the whole time he spoke. There was a sweetness to his energy that I wanted to slam against a wall. Then there was Ruben. Ruben was beyond gorgeous and carried himself with a sass and swagger that reminded me of Gabriel and our love-making. He was pinned as a villain and something about that is always attractive. Then there was Henry – humble, confident, sexy, funny Henry, who didn't look at me but through me. I felt exposed and vulnerable in a way that I wasn't used to. I was intrigued.

I got back to my room after a long day of shooting. We filmed until it started to get light, and couldn't keep going. Exhausted. I started to think about life and this idea of so much multiple love, so much liberation and freedom. I find it confusing. How was it even possible to know if you were in love? What did any of that even mean? What the fuck is love? The idea of limiting myself to 'the one' seemed ridiculous and unrealistic.

It was distracting, abandoning the noise of attention from all that had just happened, to the solitude of my room. It felt like I was literally stepping from one world into another. There was no grace of transition. I sat on the bed and played reruns in my head of the gathering inside the mansion, the endless meeting of all the men. I was required to always have champagne in my hand, a smile on my face, and to circulate the room without spending too much time with anyone man. I felt like all the men were competing for my attention, telling me stories of their triumphs or talents, and I was required to seal clap for them, like a circus animal sitting on the side of the pool. It was like being on an endless roundabout or ferris wheel, spinning and spinning. And now, silence. Strange overwhelming, strangling silence. I didn't have the sunset walks through the vineyard to decompress anymore and I couldn't go camp on a beach or spend long nights by my vineyard fireplace. So, instead, I'd walk around the border of the property, security keeping a watchful eye on me, keeping me safe.

When I started to grow boobs at thirteen, I thought a lot about my skin; this thick collection of cells that separated me from the world, that kept my blood tucked up inside, that kept my darkest thoughts and urges safely covered. I'd prick my finger with my Mother's sewing needles just so I could watch the inner me come out of its shell, as if my blood was an alien that needed to breathe. I started to notice the difference between my skin, my appearance, and the others at school as soon as puberty kicked in. Little knobs of puss freckled the other kids ruddy faces, their young flesh stretched like pigs hide over fat legs and bellies, ears stuck out and lips sucked in and noses curled too far up. Girls cried in bathrooms about their fat knees and acne and whatever else and shouted at me if I'd try to help or resonate with them.

Maybe I wouldn't have noticed or cared if the girls hadn't hated me so much when I'd try to be nice, and if the boys didn't bother trying to flick my skirt up when I was walking through the halls. But I did notice, and I did care. At first it was resentment and horror, becoming a woman, the monthly blood and the surge of hormones and the constant scrutiny as my body became of innocuous interest to my peers.

I thought, don't all of us humans, ugly or pretty, have to come face to face with the fact that we are souls living in vestibules of decay – bleeding and shitting and sweating until we die? We take mouth-watering food onto our tongues and then turn it into shit. We shit out of a hole that is really close to another hole that brings us great pleasure. We smell perfume through the same nostrils that hurl snot. Bodies are confusing and mysterious when you're growing up, and it made it even more confusing that mine was deemed too attractive to feel anything other than happiness. I remember the Pastor at our church patting me on the head and saying, "What a curse your face is. What a troublesome curse." And I started to really believe it.

After a couple of lonely years I began to learn that my beauty was a power, and so I started to wield it to my needs instead of being frustrated by the loneliness. I realised that my skin was kind of like a con artist attached to all my flesh and organs. See, without being aware of it, an attractive person is hoodwinking everyone into thinking they're worth more than other people. It's exactly why the murder of a hot person gets more press than an ugly person. It's as if their body is more of a waste being dead, all that beauty decaying away in the ground is a loss to the world. How fucked up is humanity? I suppose in the knowledge that humanity is vain, and will never stop worshipping facial symmetry, I ended up taking advantage of the fact. And here I am, again taking advantage.

I take Ruben, the villain, on the first date. I really think the other guys are just jealous of his attitude and his looks. I'm fascinated. With Ruben, I match his bravado with my own. It's a more subtle feminine version that I know how to play. I tilt my head but I still meet his gaze. I smile but my eyes squint like I'm hunting. We are taken up in a small Cessna and the pilot does some airdrops and spins us upside down. It's exhilarating. I grab Ruben's hand, as if I'm slightly frightened and laugh. When we land, he lifts me out the plane. We are driven back to the grounds of the mansion and led out back to a secluded couch that I dub "the kissing couch". Ruben laughs but the producer edits it out. He starts to tell me the story of how his Mum died in a car accident when he was fourteen and I'm not sure why he's telling me. It's overly sad and inti-mate for a 'reality' show. A bit of a downer, really. Everyone is crying. Maybe that's his shtick. He woos women with woe, and afterwards they want to soothe and rescue him. I let myself be swept up in the drama of it all and I cry. I guess the audience will love it – the fact that the potential villain is actually a soft family guy. He's probably setting himself up the be the next Eligible. We feed each other strawberries and eventually Ruben leans in for a kiss. There's a mini make-out session with crew and cameramen around. I like the thought of everyone watching me. The kiss is good. There's a syncopation to our play. We nibble, pull back and plunge in at the right moments, teasing and surrendering. I love a good kisser. And to think all of Australia will be watching. It's intoxicating.

For the most part, the crew play the game with me, we all pretend together. The producers need me to be sweet, to be falling in love, to be kind and gracious. They don't let me escape from my role for even a second, except for Jocelyn. Jocelyn says it like it is. She's not even my producer, but she likes to know what's going on in my head, so she can create strategies to really get the good stuff, the drama. Sometimes, she comes over to the back of my private residence, and we smoke a cigarette so she can get ideas.

I have my own room across the garden from the main mansion where all the guys are. A Granny Flat you could say, except it's huge. A mini mansion just for me, without cameras and film crew and desperate men following me around like puppies. I have a security guard at the front at all times, mainly to make sure none of the desperate's try to get unwanted extra time with me. Greg, the security guard will always turn a blind eye if I ask him to though.

I have Ben back here sometimes on the rare occasion the house is dark and silent. He sneaks off and we fuck. I guess he thinks because of that I'll choose him in the end. He's a bit smug about it on group dates, but I've had one of the other guys here before too, Levi. I think that's what his name was? A broad-shouldered, tanned hippie-looking guy. He wasn't great in the sack so I cut him from the show.

It just kind of happened with Ben. At least the first time. It was night and I couldn't sleep, so I was sat in the garden with a bottle of red, a rug pulled around me, enjoying the fairy light display on the little bridge over the pond right at the back. It's quite beautiful when you forget that it's all fabricated for the show. I felt like I was alone. In my sacred space. I started to think about how far I'd come, and then there was Ben, standing there, hands in his pockets. "You can't sleep either?" he asked. I was secretly pissed he had stolen my me-time, but he looked so cute, his hair all ruffled and that warm-sleepy look about him. He was wearing trackies and UGG boots. I swear I could see the outline of his cock hanging to the left.

I smiled at him, patted the rug next to me, and he sat down.

"Anything on your mind?" he asked.

I was hugging my knees to my chest, my chin was on my knees. I turn to look at him. I try to look thoughtful. "I grew up pretty poor. I'm looking around at all this," I sigh and spread my arms wide. "I'm looking around and thinking that I don't deserve this. How did I get so lucky?"

Ben shakes his head, takes my hand. "You deserve every beautiful thing in the world."

We talk for a while. I tell him about my Mother, how hard it was for her. I'm actually honest about that. I know everyone will find out anyway – my face will be all over the media. He talks about how he's also self-made – humble beginnings to success. We even talk a bit of philosophy. He's quite clever. By the end of the conversation I realise how physically close we are, how I may finally be able to kiss those lips of his. We kiss and it's hot. Like, movie-hot. I'm almost sad the cameras aren't here to witness it. The kiss gets a bit hot and heavy, but I can see the security guard patrolling the edge of the boundaries staring at us.

"Do you want to come to mine for some wine?" I ask. And that's where the whole thing starts. Two or so months of occasional fucking. But seriously, as if I could choose a 'life-partner' without knowing what they're like in bed? Is Australia delusional?

I tell Jocelyn that Ben and I have kissed, without including any of the other explicit details. We're always thinking of ways to get guys to do what we want them to. She tells Ben in one of her interviews that I really like Ruben, but that she doesn't think Ruben is genuine. Then she gets the boys to organize a footy game. It's genius. Simple, but genius. The boys hustle, fight, and create the spectacle needed for high ratings. Then Ben comes to me at a cocktail party for a 'private chat' to rat out on Ruben. It's fickle but fun. I don't just like the way they fight over me (what woman doesn't like that from time to time) but I like the way Jocelyn can wield them into humiliating themselves on National television with just a few convincing words.

Jocelyn acknowledges her power and acknowledges mine too, uses it for a purpose – even if it is just for entertaining the masses. Over time I come to respect her in some very small way. However after two months of filming, it's obvious she's getting a little too comfortable.

Maybe I've let my Eligibles character get a little too loose in her presence, maybe I've been helping her do her job too well, and she thinks we are the same. She turns into some kind of Professor Mahoney reincarnate, who thinks she knows me and has me in the bag, who thinks she can manipulate me.

"You know why we are good at all this? Because we know what people want. If you can figure out what people want, what the public wants, you can have a lot of power," she says.

I hate the way Jocelyn says 'we'. It's just another way to deceive someone, make them feel like you're banded together, that you're both part of something. I play dumb. "What people want? Like how everyone is looking for love?"

I can tell she can't figure out if I'm being sarcastic or not.

"No, I mean to make the audience want more than the shitty little lives they have. Make them feel old and unattractive and boring. You make them feel like that and then wham! You can give them that small glimmer of hope, you can force them into dreaming of transcending that ugliness. The idiots think that if they are more like the people we show on screens, the princes and princesses we present with all the makeup and editing and forced romance, then maybe they'll be happy. It's like Stockholm Syndrome through a TV screen and we are the Masters, Editors, Kings." She used that fucking word again, 'we'. Jocelyn puffs away, shoulders hunched over, neck arched back as she blows smoke into the cool air. I wonder if she's testing me, seeing if I'll break out of the character I've been given.

"I don't know if that's true," I say. "I think you should give the audience more credit. Surely people know that this isn't completely real, even if many of the emotions are. There's so much out there that makes fun of Reality TV culture."

"They make fun of it because they can't be part of it. It makes them feel better about their lives." I can see she's getting annoyed at me. That maybe she thought I'd open up and agree with her. I'll never open up to anyone let alone Jocelyn, with her sad life and sad addictions to manipulation and cigarettes and loneliness. I know I can't trust Jocelyn, she's the kind of woman who likes revenge.

"And is this you, Jocelyn? Are you saying you want to go on the show? Are you saying you want to be in my position?" I know this will piss her off, kick her smack in the guts. To make it worse, I have an innocent but daring look plastered on my face. I lean over to pat her hand and she swats it away. I can feel her seething, she's trying to work out how to redeem herself. It's really entertaining.

"No, fuck off. *I'm God.* I tell my mignons what to want, I tell them who they want to be, I make the fucking calls here." I can feel her spidery anger and spidery peripherals stretching out past the smoke. I reach out for a second smoke and Jocelyn raises her eyebrows, smiles, lights it up. She thinks I'm making peace. I drop the innocent attitude for a minute. "Jocelyn. Reality TV creates cultures, and social culture creates sales. I get it. I get what you're saying. I get the manipulation and I get that you get off on it. I can't pretend that I don't like the attention or that maybe there are ulterior motives for my being here. But in saying all that – it *has* to be real for me, doesn't it? I'm expected to stay with one of these guys. That's the real shit. There're the distractions and all the glitter, but this is my fucking life Jocelyn. Who do I like? Who am I attracted to? Who suits my lifestyle? You think I actually want to spend my life alone?"

"You really want to end up with one of these idiots?" Jocelyn is spitting out the words, she's losing respect for me the further the conversation goes on.

"I don't know yet. But I hope so." The lies slide off my tongue like milk. I can't let this woman untangle what I'm creating. I can't trust her.

"I think the whole show is idiotic. I actually thought your position on it was real Poppy, but I'm obviously wrong."

"For god's sake Jocelyn. This whole show – whether you – or people like you and I, created it, it would still be there in some capacity wouldn't it? We're suckers for fucked-up avocations of 'reality'. Look at history. The Gladiators in ancient Rome, or public punishments all over the world just for entertainment – beheadings and hangings and electric chairs. Even pornography with its violent and strange concepts. That shit is created for plea-sure. Fuck, your standard theatre performances from caveman days until now, they're all riddled with little socio-cultural or socio-political insignias, aren't they? At least The Eligibles is about love, not violence, despite its archaic gender roles. We are all looking the next best thing, we all want love, we all want distraction from the pain of our lives. And I'm okay with giving people that hope or dream of a better life. Because if simple-minded people can believe things can be better than yesterday, that's something to live for. The show gives hope. For love, for fame, for a new start – whatever your jam is. Isn't that an improvement from past entertainment? Don't you think small steps are better than no steps at all?"

"The problem is that they're dreams Poppy, not reality. The problem is you're part of the problem, even if you don't know it."

"There are always problems in change. And in the meantime what's wrong with distraction? We're all the same. You included, even though you think you're a step higher. A world of fucked up people looking for amusement because secretly we all hate ourselves." I don't know if that's true. I don't hate myself, at least. I just do what I need to in order to get ahead. I presume from the conversation though that Jocelyn doesn't like herself at all and that's why she's trying to justify her job. I've used her key idiotic word 'we', to make her feel more normal. It's my charitable action of the day. The best I can do.

There's silence in the cool air of the night, I can feel Jocelyn thinking. I can feel she's about to say something important and I want to cut her off, but she speaks before I can stop her.

"Do you think I'm cruel?" She asks, holding her breath at the end of the question. I sigh and don't say anything. I can feel her shivering in the silence, because of her vulnerability or the cold, I don't know. Why is she asking me? Why is someone like this opening themselves up to me? For God's sake, I suggested she wanted to *be me* earlier in the conversation. Why would she let herself be so vulnerable? I don't want to deal with her shit. The silence starts to get painful but I let it clap and ring out like a cymbal between us.

"Never mind," she says when she realizes I'm just not going to say anything at all. As if I don't want to offend her with the truth, with saying, "yes, I think you're fucking cruel."

I feel her anger rise up, and her voice becomes strained. "At least I know we're as cruel as each other you fucking bitch. Don't think I don't see myself in you." Her outburst shocks me a little but I try to remain neutral. Just another idiot that doesn't like to be called out on their shit. Jocelyn puts out her cigarette a little too close to my thigh, and I don't say anything. I just lean back and wipe off the small bits of ash that have blown onto my dress. She walks away and I feel glad she's out of my life.

Some dates are definite no's. They're just not interesting enough to play with. Others I'm not a hundred percent certain I want to toss out right away. And then, not surprisingly there is Ben, Ruben, and Henry, and surprisingly another one has come out of the works – Carlo, who was a blow-in on Episode Five to create some jeopardy.

I am given a fair bit of freedom while I play this game but the producers do make 'suggestions' – '*Look we'd really like you to keep Jerry on a little while longer*' or they say '*how about we give you an earpiece so you can remember people's names'* or *'we'd like you to take this guy for a chat.'* It's almost fun being told what to do, because I know they're a little scared of me. For fucks sake, I want to make as good a show as them for ratings, they should know that.

Back in my room after every date, I pour myself a glass of wine. I take stock of how I feel. How was my performance? Was I convincing? Does the audience likes me? I hope so. I'm so curious to see how everything will play out – if they'll edit the show the way I've played it to be edited. I can't be too demanding, I can only be smart enough to get it to play my way.

I find it curious and intriguing how people confuse 'reality tv' with reality. It's so fucked up. It's like the men who have 'real dolls' and have treated them like their wives or girlfriends. I watched this film once called "Love Me, Love My Dolls" – it was crazy. This man was crying his eyes out because his doll had to go back to the factory for some touch-ups and they were going to be separated. And the syncher, he lived with his parents. What is wrong with people? Another guy would plan elaborate picnics and do photoshoots with his dolls reading or sipping wine, then later frame the photos. I guess he was creating his family album. It's almost the reverse on The Eligibles. It's like I'm real but trying to conform to some sort of doll, but I get to transform that doll to whoever I am interacting with, or to whatever the producers suggest, or whatever I come up with. I think I did a great job with Ruben. I really hope everyone likes it.

I ask my minder for my phone. We're not allowed to have them while filming, but they let me use it for business. I shoot a text off to Steve, my vineyard manager to see how everything is going out at Tenacious. I've given him and Jen basic management of the property. I know they will make sure everything gets done. I might sound like a controlling bitch, but I'm not a micromanager when it comes to business. We have what people would call a good friendship, but that's only because I had the awareness and intuition to give jobs to people I knew I'd trust. Plus, I always make sure they're happy with regular pay rises, words of encouragements and gifts. I'm a good boss.

I get a ding back, and Steve tells me not to worry, all is good. Works done. It's so awesome having this kind of wealth. The best part is time. My time is my time. Stuff is great to a point but things become boring after a while. Don't get me wrong I like my indulgences. It certainly helps with 'keeping up appearances'. Botox isn't free. But losing stuff would be way easier than losing the freedom wealth brings. The ability to chill and explore. If I hadn't had been able to get Amos and his crony to pull off that bank heist I would have just been like everyone else. I heard Jay Z made all his money selling coke and nobody seems bothered by that. I'm golden but I'm super exhausted. It's been a crazy day and the days are only going to get crazier. I feel like I'm addicted to this kind of distraction. I lay back on the bed and sigh. I could get used to this.

As much as I found it funny when I realised who Henry was, it was also a bit of a shock. I really had to think hard about how I was going to play it. It was like a lightbulb had burst inside my head, the thin glass shattering around the edges of my skull. We were sitting at a picnic and he was talking, and wham! It came to me. This was the Henry that Amos had conned into doing the bank robbery with him. I had to keep staring out at the ocean. I wanted to turn and tell him to shut-up and not to keep worrying about me. It explained a lot. It explained his digging and truth seeking. It explained why it felt that he could see right through me. I had thought he was a stranger, and he had kept looking at me like he could see me, as if he knew me. I thought that maybe we were equals. That maybe he was like me. I found myself completely drawn in like a moth to a flame. But now that I knew the truth, that he did know a version of me and worse, that he felt sorry for me, I was slightly repulsed by him. I had to push the thought away and snap back to reality, or at least this reality of picnic blankets and camera crews. I reached down and ate a few blueberries. When I looked back up at Henry, he leaned in for a kiss. And cut the scene was over. I made it through.

CHAPTER THIRTEEN

Henry and I have another date. We find ourselves alone in the car, really alone. It feels strange not to have a producer or handler in the backseat or a camera attached to the dash filming all our actions and conversations. It's as if we are teenagers that have escaped from overly strict and protective parents. I just want to pull the car over, let the rain shield us from the outside world and crawl on top of him and start fucking. A hard angry fuck for all the bullshit that has been going on. For his sucky need to 'protect' me. For his search for truth. For his making out with me and groping my ass when he thinks he watched me get raped. That's how I want to fuck him. But the crew is all around us. We have this one little bubble, this fish bowl of moving private space. The cars in front and behind carry the team of people and equipment that will be needed to record our third date. So instead of fucking him, I keep my eyes on the road and my hands on the wheel.

We had had a good day. And I had started thinking, maybe this connection of lies and half-truths and weird synchronicity, and that we both ended up, years later, on the same tv show, and it was 'The Eligibles' to boot, had to be more than just a coincidence. It was just too weird. I'd find myself assessing him from a distance. He is handsome. And like I said, he is an ace kisser. And he had some cash since he had invested his gains from the robbery into a business. He would fit with my outside world as long as he didn't get too needy or too dependent. We already had a good story going about each other or at least he did about me. And now, with this – someone should write a story about our lives. That's how unbelievable it was.

But then I got this weird feeling in the pit of my stomach and I look over at Henry, and he's just staring at me from the passenger seat and I can tell that he is about to tell me. Oh shit. He's about to tell me his 'truth'. His 'I watched you get raped and cry truth.' Oh my god, I don't want him to do that. I think I might have fucked up. Henry had caught me checking him out, looking him up and down and figuring out how he could fit into my life. I had said that I was falling in love with him. I know, me. I don't believe in love. What I wanted to say was if you stay chill, if we keep these lies and this facade, I will probably want to keep fucking you, at least for a while, and you look the part and could fit in to the world that I am creating. And it came out as, "I think I might be falling in love with you". The producers loved it. And now he wanted to fuck it all up.

I looked back at the road and just up ahead less than a

hundred yards away was a guy with a camera slung around his neck. Paparazzi. He was running out into the road. I hit the gas and cranked the steering wheel to the right at the same time. It was the only thing I could think to do. It looked like I was deliberately trying to avoid hitting the guy and it saved Henry from blurting out his truth and perhaps hearing one that really would have fucked him up.

The road was wet and we skid across the lanes and hit a tree and my head slammed forward, my air bag ripping out like the starting engine of a motorcycle. Henry's front and side air bag banged out next. We were trapped in clouds of white. Separated. Then the air bags slowly deflated and I could breathe again. I turned to look at Henry. A producer had whipped open his door. Henry was slumped sideways, blood was coming out of his ears and he was unconscious. I stared in a sort of curious disbelief. I didn't know if he was dead. I thought there is no way he can be dead. I am fine. But it feels like everything has slowed down, as if the sound has disappeared and everything has become extremely focused and clear. The colours are brighter and then sound comes back and everything speeds up again. The producer is yelling, "I've got a pulse!" My door is flung open. "Poppy is okay," somebody yells. Walkie-talkies are crackling. People are on cell phones. The paparazzi guy is making his gold until one of the crew rips his camera off his neck and yanks out his SD card. Someone has taken me from the car and I am sitting on a large rock at the side of the road. We are out in the country. Away from the city. Someone is holding an umbrella over me. We can hear the ambulance before we can see it.

The ambulance crew puts a brace around Henry's neck and they gently guide him from the car and on to a stretcher. Someone is finding a vein and they are hooking up bags that drip things up to his arm. I am put into a different ambulance. I keep telling them I am fine but they want to run some tests. They check my pulse, my blood pressure. I have to follow a light with my eyes. They ask me questions: *Where are you from? What is your full name? What show are you on? What day of the week is it? What year?'* I am able to answer all their questions and I can follow the light and my pulse is okay. They finally let the crew drive me back to the hotel. Henry is sirened away.

I barely remember getting to my room. I remember I took a doxylamine tablet and went to sleep. In the morning a producer came to my door.

"Henry is okay. He's alive obviously, but he is unconscious. We won't know more until later," he says.

It's so weird. I start to think about how I didn't love my unborn baby, and I was able to will her dead, about how I wanted Amos to get me money and he did, and now I start thinking about how I wanted to silence Henry and now he's unconscious. His whole world is gone. I think I must be connected to some force bigger than myself. That I am more powerful than I even I thought. That there is something strange and sinister about who I am, but it's something so very, very powerful.

"Thanks for letting me know." I reach out and hold the

producers arm. "Can I go and see him?" I ask, tears welling up in my eyes. I don't miss a beat.

"Not right now, I'm afraid." And then he adds, "we need you to get dressed and come downstairs".

I feel my mouth dry up and my stomach do a flip.

"Oh of course. Give me ten minutes just to get dressed," I say.

"Take your time." He smiles at me and turns away.

When I go to lift my t-shirt off I feel stiff and my chest hurts. There's a thick dark bruise running diagonally across my chest where the seat belt had gripped me in place. It's going to look like hell when it starts to yellow. There will be no bikinis for a while. I touch it gingerly. The handlers have already been in the room and have laid out a blue ribbed t-shirt, black jeans and a camel-coloured cashmere sweater for me to wear. I throw my hair up on top of my head and put the clothes on. I dab some concealer under my eyes, and I'm ready.

A detective, the show's safety officer, the show's lawyer, and Bobbi the show's executive producer are all sitting in the hotel lounge when I come down. It kind of reminds me of when I went through the investigations at the bank, except this time I might really be in trouble. Again, my mouth goes dry. I smile and walk over towards them, they all stand and we shake hands. Juan, the show's Safety Officer gives me a sympathetic smile. "I'm so sorry this has happened to you," he says. I swallow, incredulous. I feel my eyes going moist. I've always been good at crying on demand. "I was in the car behind you," Juan continues

"I saw it all happen. Thank god you swerved or you might have hit that guy."

"Damn Paparazzi!" pipes up Sandra Cromack the shows lawyer.

"There's no way she would have been able to break in time. The guy jumped right out in front of her." Juan is talking to the lawyer and the detective now. Doing all my dirty work. "If she hadn't of reacted the way she did I think we would most definitely been in a far worse situation." I realize that the show is covering their asses. I'm in the clear.

"Do you mind if we sit down," I say. "I'm afraid I'm still a little shaken up and I have a terrible bruise across the front of my body." I smile and cast my eyes down and make as if I'm wiping away a small tear from my left eye. I take a seat in one of the plush navy blue lounge chairs. The gentlemen and Ms. Cromack all follow suit. The detective has just been scribbling notes in his pocket book and has not asked me anything directly. He's young and seems a bit nervous. It's being in the presence of a beautiful woman, I'm sure. He would be putty in my hands.

"In terms of legalities," Ms. Cromack starts, "I won't go into all the details, just know that you and Henry were the victims, Misty the Paparazzi is no longer allowed anywhere near yourself, Henry or the show. We have not filed charges against him, only instated the restraining order. He should count himself lucky. We are however, seeking financial damages because of the airbags. Henry is the one who will receive compensation as both of his deployed simultaneously which resulted in his injuries.

I'm afraid, Poppy, bruising is typical with this type of accident." She leaned over and squeezed my hand.

"Oh, I totally understand," I say. "I was not even thinking about any kind of compensation. I just hope Henry is okay? Do they know what is wrong with him? I really liked, liked... like him," I say.

"We're still not sure," says Bobbi. "He is still unconscious."

A couple of hotel staff come over and place fresh coffee, creams and an assortment of pastries on the coffee table in the center of us all. "Would anyone care for coffee?" one of the girls ask. We all look at each other. Bobbi says "It's okay we'll pour it ourselves."

"Enjoy," the staff says and walks away.

"We will stop filming for now," pipes up Bobbi as she leans over and starts to pour out coffee. "Do you take milk?" she asks me.

"Just black," I reply.

Bobbi hands me a coffee and continues, "We are hoping to be up and running again in a week. That will give you enough time I hope to heal." Everyone smiles at me, even the shy detective. It is the first time he has looked directly at me. I smile and take a sip of my coffee. "Henry won't be able to continue, unless things move along a lot quicker for him but we are not anticipating his return. Therefore, we are working on how to tell the audience." Bobbi takes a sip of her coffee. "I realize this is a lot to take in Poppy. Are you okay if I continue?" she asks.

"Oh, yes, please do," I smile, trying to look as if I'm

acting strong.

Bobbi has set it up for me to be in the hospital room for today. There have been some positive changes in Henry's vitals and they are anticipating that he should wake up soon. After the lobby, I was sent back to my room, hair and makeup came in, as well as wardrobe and I was prepped for the shoot on 'location'. As I walk down the hospital corridor there is a camera behind me and one in front. The man in front has a simple gimbal attached to a small camera and I am guessing the big-guns are already set up and waiting in Henry's room. I walk slowly and with a solemn expression. I think I am doing a great job. I am hoping that it makes the viewers cry when they get a chance to watch this. It is what they will want. I enter Henry's room and burst into tears. All of it is captured on film. I dry my eyes with the back of my hands and walk over to the side of his bed and take his hand in mine. Henry is still unconscious.

I have spent nearly seven hours in this damn hospital room. I've only been allowed to use the washroom. They want to make sure they capture the moment when Henry wakes up and I am sitting beside him, holding his hand. They've had the shows caterers make up a lunch for us of various assorted sandwiches, little bags of crisps and some homemade cookies. I start to feel tired, it's so boring, so I take a nap on the small leather couch. I'm careful not to mess up my hair and sweep it out the way before I lie down. Someone places a small thin blanket over me. It's also a good way to escape all the idle chit chat going on and to stop this one camera man from continually trying to hit on me. Seven hours is a long time to spend in a room waiting for someone to wake up, and we really have no idea when that will be. I've not been lying down for long before I hear someone say, "I think he's starting to wake up."

Bobbi comes over and gently nudges me, "Poppy... Poppy." I open my eyes. "Can we get you to sit beside Henry. We think he is waking up."

I rush over to Henry's side. Makeup and hair come over and fluff me up. Here we go, and action. I am holding his hand. I've brought it up to my cheek. Henry slowly opens his eyes. He looks confused. "Oh Henry," I say as I reach for his face and gently caress his cheek. "Henry, it's me Poppy." He looks scared and confused.

The camera men are swirling around us. It is being filmed from all angles. They will edit later to get the best effect. Henry is looking around the room and then again back at me. He looks terrified. His eyes are darting everywhere.

"Something is wrong," I scream. "Somebody DO something!" Henry is lifting himself up onto his elbows. He's staring at me. I get a flash of my dead child. He starts to talk, but it's all mumbled and makes no sense. He puts his hands over his ears. He yells. The doctors rush in and I'm pulled away.

"What's wrong?" I ask. "What's going on?"

One of the nurses turns to me and says, "We think he could be deaf? They will need to run some tests. He will sleep now. There is not much we can do at this point." The cameras have been turned off. Deaf. Shit. A deaf guy is not going to fit into my life. I'm going to have to figure out how to untangle from him without looking like a villain. I don't think though, that people would really expect me to sacrifice my life for a deaf guy. Besides, we just met on the show. It will work out. My little panic attack goes away.

After we filmed the scene in the hospital Henry refused any visitors. I was relieved. It was a good way for me to start distancing myself from him again. He could keep his secrets and I could keep mine.

During the week that the show is on the shelf I'm busy with interviews. Some are formal ones with the detective and the lawyers again. It's the same story: '*I saw the guy jump out into the road. I panicked and I guess I yanked the steering wheel too hard... the road was wet... how's Henry?... I don't remember much after that... I'm sorry... yes my shoulder is still sore.*'

I just want to get back to filming. I do a few interviews as publicity for the show where at least I get to act a bit more. I cry over Henry but respect his privacy. I talk about new restrictions that should be placed on the paparazzi, when really, I love them documenting my life. This accident will be great for me and great for the show. I can't help but think of the other guys: Ben, Ruben, Carlo, Peter. I wonder if one of them will fit into my life. They are all super hot and I know Ruben is a good kisser. I'll have to have a date with Ben when the show starts up again.

CHAPTER FOURTEEN

We eventually hit that part in the show where I have to meet the remaining guys' families. There are four guys left standing. Ruben, Ben, this guy Carlo, and Peter. I'm not really that into Peter but the producers wanted me to keep him around. It doesn't take long for me to realize that I abhor families. Family obligation takes so much time. Easter, Christmas, birthdays, Mothers Day, Father's Day, anniversaries of marriages and deaths and whatever other shit goes on. Even being here for a relationship show and tell is boring. It takes all the thrill away and instead puts you in this dull as fuck role of appeasing overprotective mothers and sisters. Ben's family didn't even try to hide it.

"Aren't you just here for the fame?" asked his sister Bridget. All the kids names started with B. WTF is that. So cute. Usually, I have a glib answer I roll out but I just couldn't be chuffed anymore. Though I didn't say everything I wanted to say.

"Sure, that and then some. Probably the same reasons your brother Ben is on the show," I smiled. Bridget looked me straight in the eye and smirked. Stupid cow. Why does she think people go on TV? To really and truly find love? Is she a moron? I went for fame, money, experience, the thrill, because I was asked and she wasn't. I get so tired of pretending sometimes. I wish the world was more honest. That we didn't have to play this scripted roles of goodness. I sometimes think I would have been much better suited on the boatload of criminals that came over and founded our country. I think there would have been a lot less bullshit compared to this dress rehearsal.

I let Peter and Ruben go. Poor Ruben, I feel like we had a history, but Carlo keeps me moist thinking about Gabriel and wondering if we could share the same awesome sex. Now I take Ben and Carlo to meet my mother and Michael, who is now her husband. They had a quick city hall ceremony, just the two of them, and then ran off to Bali for a two-week honeymoon. I was pretty stoked I didn't have to do the daughter-mother shit with pre-wedding and wedding stuff. Although, I let her believe I'm a little offended. She cried, and I hugged her, and then I said not to worry because I'm really happy for her, and all I want is her happiness.

Her marriage has also freed her up from wanting too much attention from me, which is a massive bonus. We're at Tenacious, my vineyard. Since I lack any other immediate family, in particular the requisite father who would do all the hardline questioning of the blokes, I'm required to go with a bit of a sad story. I couldn't really ask

Michael to play stepdad as we hardly know each other. I only met him after I returned from South America so that would just be ridiculous.

It's the story of struggle. I almost want to barf telling this. The poor hard working single mother. How we were like best friends rather than mother and daughter. I leave out the part about her neediness and suffocation, and willingness to accept her lot in life. I waffle on about how much she supported and loved me. I suppose there is some truth there. My mother was never cruel. She was just pathetic. I'm not sure if that's worse? She never offered any sound advice, and her aspirations for me were to get a cashier's job or a job as a secretary. If I had listened to my mother, I would never have left the Hills and I would probably be married to a sad sack with a baby on my hip.

My mother had also been a fairly religious woman. Not so much that I was dragged to church every Sunday but enough that she believed everything was god's will. The fact that we were dirt ass poor was god's will. The fact that she was never happy was god's will. And even the money I gave her and the Botox and augmentation were god's will. What a crazy safe world she lived in. There was zero responsibility. I'd rather author-up and own my life than have it be god's will.

I remember once as a little girl coming home from school and asking my mum, "do you think God is real?" She was just putting the finishing touches on a cake she had made and slid me the icing bowl as I jumped up on the kitchen bench. My legs swung back and forth underneath me as I dipped my finger in the icing bowl.

"Of course I think God is real, Pops. Why are you asking such silly questions?" she asked.

"Well do you think God is good?" I kept dipping and licking. It was chocolate butter icing, my favourite.

"Of course God is good. What is up with you girl?" my Mother had stopped what she was doing and turned to look at me with her hand on her hip. I could feel she was proud of herself, standing up for her god with her 'righteous anger'.

"Well, today at school Mrs. Inglewood asked us to pray for all the families who died in the Tsunamis and I started to think that maybe he did it. Like Noah and the flood. God admitted that he got angry and so he killed everyone, which makes him a murderer doesn't it? Maybe he's like a serial genocidist. Maybe god is into all that stuff? He thinks it's fun. Like Ted Bundy."

I had stopped dipping and was facing my mother.

"How did you learn about Ted Bundy?"

I shrugged.

"It's God's will, Poppy. It's God's will. It's not our place to question God's will. Now would you like a slice of cake?" And that was as far as we ever got.

It was at this juncture that I decided God only existed for the simple minded. It was a way for them to understand and accept the mess of this world, without having to take any responsibility. What a brilliant idea. It was after this revelation that I felt a kind of freedom. I was released from

God and subsequently released from sin. To test my theory, I started doing little small things to see if God would punish me. I stole Trevor's lunch at school and just ate all the good stuff and threw the apple and his shitty sandwich away. Nothing happened. I put a dead science frog in Lace Terroni's shoe while she was in gym class because the boy I liked, liked her instead. Lace was called Frog Feet for the rest of primary school but no wrath of God came raining down on me. My theory was proving right. When I got a bit older, my mother was sick one Sunday, and she asked if I would please deliver ten dollars to the collection plate at church. She thought it would help her get better. Instead I bought the book, "The God Delusion" with the ten dollars. Richard Dawkins was my hero. Mum soon got better, and it had nothing to do with her delusion.

I've decided the only way to live in this fucked up world is as a hedonist. I don't make any public declarations; I just feel that we are here for such a short period of time that we really should be seeking to maximize our pleasure. Why not? I'm not suggesting we get all pervy or psychopathic about it, but it makes sense to me that we should all go after what we want. And if that means sometimes we bend the rules a bit... well isn't that why rules were made... to be broken? Just like how I told Professor Mahoney humans are all about wandering along the grey lines of morality. You can't tell me that the banks didn't get to where they are right now without breaking a few rules along the way. All that Catholic guilt stuff just keeps people following along and never complaining. Nobody got hurt when I came up with the idea to rob the bank.

Actually everyone seemed to get rewarded. Well, maybe poor Henry became a little wounded on the inside.

I sometimes wonder if the God obsession was my mother's guilt. This strange idea that her prayers were pushing some kind of earth-to-heaven lever in the hope of a periodic reward from the creator, or perhaps a discounted ticket to heaven. She had hooked up with my father at a bar in Sydney. He was a tall blonde backpacker from the Netherlands and I often feel I am probably a lot more him than I am her. The relationship, at least for him was transient. For my mother, I became a permanent reminder of that 'night of sin'. I think I was dragged to church so she could amend for her transgression and she could introduce me to a couple of male authority figures. I had Jesus and God telling me how to behave and what to do until I was about ten years old. I had started the questioning at a younger age but came to full on rejection once I hit double digits. It was one act I didn't think I needed to keep up – I could call myself an atheist and still be considered normal.

I don't remember my mum ever dating while I was growing up. It's funny, I never really thought about it at the time. It was kind of like mum's don't date and teachers don't pee and God sees everything. I'm not sure how it would have made me feel or how it would have changed my life. I suppose if the guy had been nice enough and rich enough it could have been good but chances of my mum picking out a good one back then were pretty slim. I would often catch my mum staring off into space while she was folding the washing or making a cup of tea and I sometimes wondered if she was thinking about my dad. She didn't talk about him very much. I don't think she really knew too much about him. She was a million miles away, and I'd bring her back by pinching her bum or coming up and saying boo in her ear. I always startled her, and if I'd ask her what she was thinking she would just shake her head and laugh and tell me that she couldn't remember.

As I got older, I sometimes wondered if she had suffered some extreme kind of hurt, besides being disowned by her family and having a child out of wedlock with a man she barely knew. I didn't know much about her. There weren't any relatives around. She had one brother, my uncle Conor, over in England who she never talked to and who I never met. Then outside of that she had one sad simple friend June who would come over with fresh homemade cookies and plop herself on the couch beside my mum and together they would sip sherry and watch the American version of The Eligibles and laugh and make friendly bets on who would be sent off the show that week. June was nice but her and my mum were stuck in the muck if you know what I mean.

I had it pretty good with my mum, besides the being poor bit and her sometimes over clingy emotions. Mum was what you would call respectfully negligent. I didn't have a lot of rules and I didn't really need them. I always brought home good grades, and I never got caught doing anything wrong so there was really nothing for her to worry about. I think a little neglect can go along way as a parent. It made me ambitious and self-sufficient. When I meet people whose parents mollycoddled them to death, there's a suckiness there that is so unattractive. It's as if they are missing their spine.

Having the film crew come to the vineyard and into my house was a real invasion of my space. It was weirdly intimate. It was my private inner sanctuary. It was my fire on the beach, my place where I shed any of the layers I wore for the outside world. The only other people allowed in my house were Jen and Steve who look after the place while I'm away. Now, I was having to wrap myself up and mask myself in layers of an accommodating and light hearted persona to protect myself from the public seeing anything that might hint at a true reality. The place is swarming with huge cameras, small drones, sound, lights, and camera crew. A fucking army of people.

I'm glad that Michael is here as he's actually filling the father role I didn't ask or expect him to. It's actually kind of nice and I think he intuitively knew I needed it. We are sat on the couch with my Mum and Michael beside me while Michelle my producer, is interviewing us.

"Let's talk about Henry," she smiles at me.

I automatically make my eyes go moist. I picture Henry in his hospital room watching me on the TV. "I really thought I was falling in love with Henry... and then... then," I wipe my eyes with a tissue that my Mother has handed me. She has her hand on my back and is making small circles as she rubs my back. It reminds me of when I was a child and had the flu. "It's all my fault" I sob. My Mum leans in "Pops it is not your fault. It was an accident."

"Your Mum is right," says Michelle. "It wasn't your fault. Does the way you feel about Henry though, make you wonder about whether the two left are right for you?"

"I do wonder if I can get over Henry. I catch myself wondering how he is and what he's up to, and if he actually is the love of my life. Even though Ben and Carlo are so lovely." I tear up a little more.

Michelle is listening to her ear piece and then nods and says "Let's move on." We get a five minute break so I can get my make-up refreshed. That was brilliant. I've set the stage. Now, if I decide not to choose anyone at the end of the season people will think it's just because I love Henry.

The next scene we film is Carlo and Ben at the vineyard. They have come to do the meet and greet with my Mum and Michael. The film crew has set up in the vineyard and we first do a tour and tasting, out among the vines. It's great free publicity for the brand. Joanne Wang, my winemaker is there, and she's spectacular at press. Nobody expects that the reputation and quality behind Tenacious wines is all because of a tall gorgeous Taiwanese/Chinese woman. She gives so much credit to Steve, the vineyard manager, who holds up grape clusters and explains canopies and root systems to Ben and Carlo before letting Joanne talk about reductive wines and malolactic fermentation. I am sure sales will go through the roof.

I sneak both Ben and Carlo away for one-on-one's and we kiss. I love Carlo's thick luscious lips and how he slowly moves his tongue around in my mouth. They both tell me that they love me. According to the rules of The Eligibles, I am not allowed to say it back and thank god because it's not really my thing. The closest I got to 'breaking the rules' was telling Henry that I thought I was falling in love with him which was all part of a plan I had for myself.

Michael and my mum have a list of questions that have been supplied by the show, they take them away separately and take turns asking both Carlo and Ben. Ben comes off as the most sincere and kindest of the two. He's slightly nervous and humble. I'm thinking that he is also playing a role as I've met the cocky and territorial Ben. My mum, Michael and I all think the audience will be hedging their bets on him as the winner.

I have a couple of days of space before having overnight dates. I spend the first night with Ben. I'm really dragging out the sex thing with Carlo. Thinking about it keeps me hot and crazy.

Ben is so eager to please. He always has been. He's slow and sensuous. He spends a lot of time crawling down my body. Biting my neck and sucking at my nipples before going down and slowly moving his tongue around the edges of my clit. He puts a finger inside me, I arch my back, he sucks and inserts another finger, opening me up, making me wet for his cock. It's slow and easy, not really my style but I'm so hot for him that I surrender to the whole experience. My body rocks with pleasure and I don't even have to fake an orgasm. I picture Carlo watching us and I think of it all as foreplay for tomorrow night.

The next night Carlo doesn't disappoint. The tension has built up for so long between us that we both feel like we are going to explode. He pins me against the wall and holds my hands back while he kisses me and rips my shirt open. I bite his lip hard. He puts his hand around my throat. I'm wet as fuck. He pushes me over the kitchen table and rams his cock in me from behind. He grabs my hair and yanks my head back. I moan with pleasure as he holds my hips and thrusts hard. It's good but not as good as Gabriel. I think about Gabriel while Carlo is fucking me. I almost cum but he finishes too soon.

The film crew films the guys coming into my house and then they film us the next morning, all bleary-eyed and tousled hair eating breakfast but they never know what really goes on. It's the mystery and the guessing that keeps everyone intrigued and keeps the ratings climbing.

The big Eligibles finale is always the most important to the public. The highest ratings, the highest media leaks and interview proposals. I don't know how many times I've been told about the various girls nights that have been held for this event. The workplace bets. The Eligible nights for sad, single mothers – the Judy's of the world. It's a mindless game for others. A time to laugh at its patriarchal, idiotic conjectures. The funny thing is that 'they' still participate don't they, still endorse the premise of the whole show by watching it at all?

CHAPTER FIFTEEN

It's finally the night of the finale. I'm a little bit sad that it's all going to be over soon. I'm wearing a custom made gold gown and my hair is in a loose updo with swirls of gold falling down. The place is lit up with candles and fairy lights, gold globes are suspended from the ceiling. It's magical. I'm sitting outside in the garden, hibiscus and hydrangeas are arranged around a beautiful wooden two-seater swing. The first to come out is Ben. I can tell he's super nervous, and he smiles shyly at me as he walks over. He sits down and I take his hands in mine. I've been practicing this speech all day.

"Hi Ben," I say

"Hi Poppy," he leans over to give me a kiss. I offer him my cheek.

We stand there on the small X figures that production have put there for us and we hold hands, elbows at our waists. I sigh, I smile, I look down and then right into his eyes. "I think you are an amazing man with insanely admirable qualities. You have taught me a kindness I never thought possible. You are tender and interesting and full of a warmth I never thought I could find." I tear up. He is smiling at me with those kind eyes. Then I smash it all like a hammer. "But my heart is not yours." I start to cry. Not a sobby kind of cry, but I let the tears fall and I let my shoulders shake, I look down and say, "I am so sorry". His hands fall from mine. I waffle on about how great he is. That I hope we can always think of each other with fondness and warmth and that I wish him nothing but the best… blah blah blah. He breathes big, his eyes red, trying to force down the tears, and says basically a bunch of the same back. And then he walks down the beach with cameras following him. I wonder if he feels heartbroken or if he is acting. I don't know.

They cut for a makeup refresh and I even cry for the producers even though I'm not being filmed. We take a twenty minute break – that's all the sun will allow us though.

This leaves Carlo. We've snuck off and had a sex a couple of more times since the vineyard and it has always been hot and raunchy.

We start filming again and Carlo comes out. He struts across the lawn with a wide grin across his face. The thought of verbally smacking it off makes me smile back. I can almost feel the audience tingling with some kind of excitement and love. That I'll tell him what they've wanted me to. That I want to spend the rest of my life with him, that he's the man I've always wanted, that this experience has made me believe in love. But I'm not going to do that.

First, I'm going to tell him that he is passionate and strong. That when I am with him I feel full of admiration and zeal. And then I'm going to tell him that my heart doesn't belong to him either.

I can see Jocelyn with a smug smile off to the side. She's talking into her earpiece, one hand up to a wire dangling around her chest. We haven't been on great terms since the conversation where she unnecessarily verbally vomited all over my calm. I'm lucky they have to show me as 'perfect' because Jocelyn for sure would otherwise be plotting a way to embarrass me.

Carlo comes up, and I get to say the first part of my speech. And then he says abruptly. "I know you're going to dump me." Then he calls me a manipulative bitch.

I start to cry and say, "How could you say that? How could you think that?"

"You don't think I don't know you've been fucking all of us, you fucking whore?" This genuinely does make me blush; I can see all the wide eyes and gaping mouths of everyone on set. A few people are laughing, trying to cover their faces and smiles with hands. I know they'll edit that part out, but it'll still come out as a rumour and who says Carlo won't talk? I'm shaking my head and letting tears fall down. I can feel the anger rising in me, but I'm trying to remain level-headed. I think fast.

"You're disillusioned Carlo. I don't care where you got this bullshit from. I was about to tell you I loved you that I wanted to be with you. I thought we were amazing together? I just dumped Ben because I want *you*."

He's staring wide-eyed, a little shocked at my 'confession'. He glances back at Jocelyn, and I think, *Fuck you Jocelyn*. Carlo straightens, looks me directly in the eyes and says, "Do you love me?"

"Yes I love you! Good God, a minute ago I was about to scream it to the world!" Carlo covers his mouth, there are tears in his eyes. My hands are dropped to my sides. "I don't know Carlo. Is love enough? I'd never be with anyone with such a temper. I could never potentially marry someone that could call me a bitch with such anger, without even talking to me about what's wrong." I start to cry uncontrollably, my hands on my knees and I'm bent over. "You have broken my heart," I babble out.

Carlo takes me by the elbow with his hand to lift me up, his eyes piercing mine. At first I think he's going to apologise, convince me to make it work. He's realizing the producers have manipulated him and he's feeling remorse. But then he starts to squeeze me harder, those eyes piercing me like knives, and I say, 'Ow' out loud, through the sobs. One of the security guards is walking up as I say, "Please, don't Carlo." He lets go, as a security guards grabs him by the arm which he shakes off. Carlo walks off and pushes over a pot plant with his foot, and then screams, "by the way, I'm pretty sure a yellow poppy represents death not success you fucking idiot!" I actually want to laugh, but I maintain the look of hurt and shock.

As much as I know Jocelyn did this with ill intentions-to humiliate me, instead I know it's going to appear that the man I thought was the love of my life has just dumped me. Everyone can resonate with that kind of story. I'll be a hero. Everyone will feel awful for me.

The public goes nuts. There has never been an ending without the fairytale romance, with this kind of drama. It airs all over the world. My Instagram following hits the million mark, higher than any other Eligible in the history of the show. The controversy starts a media frenzy. To steer any bad press away from me with all of Carlo's claims of my 'fucking around' which is actually a breach of his contract, I drop Henry's name a couple of times in interviews and a blitz overtakes anything Carlo. "Was it Henry all along?" "Heartache and Love: The Surprise Twist". There're headlines everywhere. Women start tweeting that they admire my strength and my ballsiness for not putting up with Carlo's bullshit. I'm hailed as revolutionary overall. The heartbroken Eligible.

Carlo loses his job as a PE teacher. No one will hire him. Women are kind of scared of him. He's the National Asshole of the Week. Fuck, of the year. I feel a little bad, but still – I've always said – you can't control the situation you're in sometimes, but you *can* control how you react. The guy reacted badly, even knowing the whole of Australia was watching, so he deserves everything coming to him. Plus, I didn't know Jocelyn was going to tell him everything. He did have the chance to leave with dignity and he chose not to.

All of this publicity happens months after the actual

filming. There's about a three month lapse time between the filming of the show and the actual airing. I watch all of it at the privacy of my vineyard, occasionally travelling into Sydney for press or events. There is a big surge in the press when Episode Eight airs. This is the episode where Henry and I have the car accident. Although a great job was done in the editing, there's still a shit storm of negative press thrown at me. As if I'm responsible for Henry's hearing loss. I'm accused of not caring and of 'acting' during my interviews. I can't believe it. I didn't manufacture the airbags and of course I'm acting. That's what I am, a 'reality' star, an actor – well, at least I have to dramatize a little. Do they think I love all these guys? That I actually care? I'm amazed at how naïve people are and how they can possibly think any aspect of TV editing at least, is real. There are also those that hate Henry and think he got what he deserved, and that he was too smug and too egotistical and that maybe his hearing loss will make him 'more human'. It all makes me laugh and as they say, all press is good press. It's when they stop talking about you that you need to be worried.

I like that there's distance between Henry and I but I am a miffed that he doesn't want to see me. For sure he was falling in love with me. I wonder if connecting with Henry would be good for my public image? We could hook up for a little while and who knows if his hearing comes back, maybe for longer. I wonder if his voice is going to get all slurry and sloppy. He has such a beautiful voice. Just listening to him talk made me want to rip his clothes off.

I don't contact him though, for the sake of my pride, and Henry just keeps on staying silent. This both intrigues me and annoys me. I can't understand it. He must be in a deep depression. I'm sure he thinks there is no possible way I would ever want him and although that might be true I still want to play the game. Then about six months after the accident and a month after episode eight airs it's announced that Henry is going to be doing a radio show. I'm super excited and plan an evening alone with a great bottle of Shiraz.

Remarkably, he sounds just like Henry. He doesn't have that thick slow round and mumbled voice that often accompanies the hearing impaired. If he didn't need to interrupt the host to ask him to face him when he speaks or to repeat his question you would never know there was anything wrong with him. His voice still has that silky sexy confidence that gets me wet and he's light hearted and funny. Not what I was expecting at all.

He does talk about sinking into a depression initially after the accident but that with the help of a good team of specialists, doctors and friends he soon realized that he still had so much to be grateful for and that he is still optimistic that his hearing will return. The doctors have told him it's early days still. Then I hear my name. I knew they would ask him about me. I reach for the bottle and top up my wine as I hear Henry say. "Poppy is an amazing woman. She saved a man's life. She is in no way responsible for what has happened to me."

Ah, that is so sweet.

The host asks, "has she reached out to you since the show?"

I verbally smack myself wondering why I didn't just contact him – it doesn't make me look great does it? Although he did tell me not to contact him. There's a long pause and then Henry responds, "no, she hasn't." You can hear hurt and sadness in his voice. I'm yelling at the computer "you haven't reached out either, Mr. Henry!" And "I was told not to contact you" and "I call bullshit." I'm having so much fun.

"That's surprising since most fans believe that it was meant to be you all along," continues the host.

"Sorry I didn't quite get that, would you remind repeating yourself?"

The host talks slower, "Oh, sorry Henry. Sometimes I forget that you're deaf. You manage so well."

"Thank you Jimi. I do my best but I have a long way to go."

"I was just asking if you knew the public thinks Poppy loves you?"

"Oh wow," says Henry. "I certainly don't know anything about that."

"Bullshit" I say out loud.

"What about you, Henry? You said, I believe it was in episode six or seven that you thought you were starting to fall in love with Poppy. Has that changed or do you still see a romantic ending for the two of you?"

"Ha!" I exclaim. "Come on Henry. Let's hear it." I take a swig of wine.

"I don't know" he pauses. "To be honest, I've been so caught up in all of this craziness and learning how to navigate the world without sound that I really haven't had any time to think about love."

"Fuck you, Henry" I say to the computer but I'm laughing. I'm loving this.

"Well, that wraps up our interview with Henry Vedder from The Eligibles. Henry, thank you for meeting with us today."

"Thank you for having me" Henry says.

"One last request before we finish up."

"Sure" says Henry.

"Let's sign off with your favourite song." There's a long pause. I suddenly realize the awkwardness of the request. Henry can't hear. I never even thought about that part. Henry loved music. He had mentioned some old turntable his mum had given him and his album collection. Oh shit.

"My apologies" says the announcer.

"No no all good. Just thinking." You can hear the strain in Henry's voice. "How about some Sampha? Do you know 'Close But Not Quite'?"

"You got it Henry."

I listen to the lyrics *"Of these words I've tried to recite, They are close but not quite, Almost impossible to do, reciting the makings of you."* I take a big sip of my wine. I bet Henry chose that song for me.

The media have dug up a few of my old lovers and posted them all over the celebrity news sites, comparing them to my suitors. Gabriel is one of them, compared to Carlo, of course. They've found one of our old pictures and it makes me feel a little nostalgic every time I see it. He was better than all of them, even with the controlling behavior. At least he was able to play the part.

Aside from him there's a model, Justin, who I hooked up with a bunch of times. Great in the sack but boring as fuck. There're pictures of him topless everywhere. He's even given dumbass comments in the media, saying I was dating him at the same time as other people. I mean I was probably sleeping with one or two other guys around that time, but WE WERE NEVER DATING. These guys will do anything for a little attention.

Surprisingly, Amos isn't one of the old, dug-up boyfriends, thank God. I suppose we never went out in public past the first few months. And it was a long time ago now. I can't even remember ever getting a picture together aside from that awful day in the hospital, which I made Amos throw out, and maybe the first time we met at a dress-up party and I actually thought he was God's gift. I never told my Mum about him, or my uni or work friends. I hid at home with my fat belly and he hid at home trying to make me happy. I doubt they'd be able to find anything and if they did, how would they even contact the drug-fucked loser?

Imagine if it had come out though, and Henry found the truth – I can only laugh at the sliding doors of that whole fucked-up situation.

A few months later, through the good ol' reliable tabloids and social media, I find out Henry has moved from Adelaide to Bondi in Sydney. Every time I have to go into Sydney for an event or interview I worry about bumping into him. I even have my own rented apartment there now since I spend so much of the year at events and doing publicity. He still hasn't reached out and I don't want the awkwardness of a public meeting. I start to avoid Bondi altogether. The paparazzi is all over his ass and there's a steady flow of beach shots. He looks hot. He's looking even more muscular and lean than usual. The Daily Mail is pumping out pictures of him with various socialite blondes – other reality TV people, mainly. I think he's lapping up the fame-zone or at least it looks that way to the outside world.

With Henry back on the radar I can't help but play some simple harmless games. I wonder if he is noticing? I've made sure that when I'm at events, I'm always photographed looking gorgeous, and at home it's that casual, sexy look uploaded to Instagram. I know Henry always liked that and for sure he'd be checking my social media or the showbiz news at least. I have also upped the game a bit and wear a little charm bracelet with the letter H dangling on it. I called up a paparazzi friend of mine to take some pictures for me at the beach. There was one small mention of this in New Idea magazine and they did one of those close-up shots of my wrist with a red circle around it and the headline said "What does the H stand for on Poppy's wrist?" Of course what followed was more media commenting on it. I was asked once in an interview and I responded, "why, happiness of course!" and I winked and smiled. It's driving me crazy that he hasn't reached out. He's burrowing in me in a way that makes me uncomfortable. I find myself on a night wandering through the vineyards with a glass of wine in my hand and thinking about and questioning my life. The media circus and expectations from the show are wearing thin. Though it was fun at first to be in the spotlight and have cameras popping out and following me everywhere it's getting boring, and when it's not boring, it's frustrating. It got so bad that I had drones flying over the vineyard and I had to seek a court injunction to get them removed.

Henry seems different. I mean different from me and the surrounding people that I see at the parties and events. He doesn't seem to care about what others think. Or does he? He always has a different girl on his arm. Maybe he's as shallow and thoughtless as the rest of us. Maybe he really is basing the opinion of himself on the opinions that others have of him. Maybe that's where he's getting his self-worth? The unreliable, transient opinions of others. I wish I would stop thinking about him. What a waste of time. I need to think about myself, my life. What goal, what adventure, what or who do I want to conquer next? Seeing Henry's photo everywhere makes me wonder if maybe I am missing out on something. He's fucking with my head. *Fuck off Henry!*

PART THREE

"You bring out the devil in me
   Girl your loving has got me crazy
   You bring out the devil in me
   I sold my soul to be with you baby, baby

Take my money, leave me out in the rain
   To love you, I would have to be insane
   There's nothing, that I wouldn't do
   I'mma need your burn, I'm a devil with you"

- Purple Disco Machine "Bring Out The Devil In Me"

CHAPTER SIXTEEN

(Henry)

I bought a dog. He's awesome. A King Charles Cavalier named Clyde. He's always by my side. I've started taking up what might be considered weird hobbies for a deaf guy. I'm learning to play the guitar. I can't wait to hear it when I get my hearing back. I figure this way I don't have to listen to myself while I'm shit. I've got a visual tuner and I'm learning all the basic chords and a few songs. I can feel the vibrations of the songs and it does actually bring me a bit of joy. I'm spending a lot of time at Dan Murphy's perusing the shelves of wine. I even pick up a Tenacious, and go through just about every Malbec that Murphy's sells. I've started cooking like a mad man. I've got a pretty good repertoire of Indian, Italian and Spanish dishes under my belt. I make a great butter chicken, bolognese and paella. I've even started fucking around with my own 'fusions'. Clyde likes my cooking so I figure it can't be that bad. I tuck a napkin under his collar and we chow down together. Fuck I love that dog. I've even cooked the odd dinner for Nicola when she's been over giving me my speech lessons and she's survived.

My life is slowly starting to feel better, but it's still fucked sometimes. It seems to work in opposites. I'm either chilling in my own silent little world with Clydey boy, playing silent songs and cooking up a feast or I'm out on a bender with my mates doubling up on antidepressants, illicit pills and booze, riding some sort of time warped rollercoaster. I get so fucked sometimes that I feel like I've stepped out of time and space and that I have no identity. That I'm just a floating mass of empty space and cells that goes blah blah blah and everyone around me is also floating and we are connected in some type of liquid gaseous bubble of some giant Leviathan. Clueless blobs making sounds and waving our arms around. Look at me. Look at me. Then I'll wake up with some tall skinny blonde beside me, face down on the sheets, her ass sticking up in the air. I'll have no idea who she is or how long I have been floating in the dirty muck of humanity. Thank god Clyde seems no worse for wear. His tail simply wags to and fro. I realize I'm not a bad looking dude but being 'famous' or whatever the fuck you call being a d-grade celebrity certainly helps with bedding the women. I don't care either way about any of them. I appreciate them coming over to fuck me but I also appreciate when they go home.

Word starts to get out about what a man-whore I am.

Some of the stories are true and some I just wish were true. According to the Daily Mail I'm having orgy sessions with five or six women at a time. Fuck, my dick would fall off. It's starting to affect my bottom line though. Sponsors are pulling contracts. I had been booked in for four different contracts for fashion week, all of which would have netted me five to ten thousand a piece but they all pulled out. I feel bad for my mum who has probably seen all these articles but never says anything. I feel like an embarrassment. I look like a sad fuck. The Daily Mail has not been nice. When I'm on the benders, I don't have a fucking clue what's going on around me. It makes for the best press. It's all anyone ever sees. I'm drowning. I'm just waiting for someone to kick the chair out from underneath me so I can dangle from the noose.

I spend a fair bit of time thinking about the accident. It makes me laugh. I was just on the verge of spilling my guts, like a young boy at a confessional. As if redeeming myself, unburdening my guilt was somehow the gateway to Poppy's heart. That if she knew I was the guy who watched her get assaulted, that did nothing about it, that spent years stalking her life and now made out with her on reality TV, she'd been fucking giddy with excitement and so eager to bang me. What the fuck was wrong with me? This is insane, these lines between morality and crimes, between reality and fiction. I feel like it's all just a undulating grey blob of nonsense and I have no idea where or how I fit in and I'm a fucking grown man for crying out loud. I never thought this is what it meant to be an adult.

I haven't talked to my Mother in ages. She was travelling through Europe with her boyfriend, what the fuck is his name? I can never remember. Who cares. My mum sent me a text when she got home and I've arranged to go visit her on Friday. Whatshisname is away visiting his kids in Melbourne. She has her own little house now in Balmain. It's blue and white and has a tiny white picket fence out front. It practically screams security and happiness. When I arrive she can't stop moving around. She's putting tea on, making sandwiches, straightening up the magazines in the living room, putting laundry in the dryer. I sit there, at the dining room table like a lump on a log. Mum forgets that I can't hear and unless she's sitting across from me or standing still in front of me so that I can read her lips, I don't have a clue as to if or what she is saying. I imagine it is mainly nonsensical natter anyway, giving me the details on her friends lives that I have never met. I wonder if me coming to see her is painful. A trip into her past. I look more like my father as I get older. I always start to feel shitty, guilty, after I'm around her for more than an hour. I start to feel small and helpless. I start to feel ten.

"Mum, I'm going to head out" I say. "Mum? You have to come here if you are talking to me. I need to read your lips." My Mum comes over and smiles down at me. She exaggerates her mouth and says "Okay honey. I have some biscuits for you to take home."

As I drive home with the tupperware container of biscuits in the passenger seat next to me, I start lecturing myself. Okay, I need to get my life together. I'll stay cleaned up. I need to find something meaningful to do. Maybe I can help other people who are hearing impaired. Possibly a Charity event at least to raise money for people like me. Fuck, maybe it'll make me feel better about the whole situation at least. I'll sit down with my mum when I have my shit together and we can talk all this bullshit out that keeps a wall between us. Maybe I will talk to Poppy. Not to win her love just to get rid of all this bullshit.

Before I deal with it I'm sucked back into the vortex. I can't trust my myself and my own judgements anymore. I'm like a fat kid in a candy store, a sex addict in a brothel, a killer with a loaded gun. I can't stop myself from wanting more. More women, more sex, more booze, more pills. After a week or so I crash. I crash so fucking hard and I sleep for days. I don't leave my apartment. I barely leave my bed. Clyde whimpers beside me. Then I slowly crawl out the hole and I have a week maybe two if I'm lucky of some sort of normalcy. I take my antidepressants as directed. I cook dinner with vegetables. I drink smoothies in the morning. I go to the gym. I clean the apartment. I take Clyde to the beach. Then I end up getting bored as shit and the whole cycle starts all over again. I can't seem to hold it together for longer than two weeks. I ache for what I had with Junip. I think about Poppy and wonder if maybe she is the one. I'm scared to approach that. I don't want to fuck her up. She's had enough. She seems so together. She has fame, but she doesn't seem to go crazy with it. I'll see her in the press for a few days and then she heads back to her winery. She's figured out the balance. She has some sort of normal. I wonder if Junip and I would have had a baby if we would still be together. Maybe two or three kids. I was never satisfied though. I always felt like I was missing out and now that I've had all the sex, booze and drugs that anyone could want I still feel like I'm missing out. I don't know how to get back though. I don't even know what that means. I just want some goddamn peace.

I'm having my week of sobriety. I've decided this time that maybe I'll take some steps to reconcile the past. My first stop is Amos because those notes he left me have really got me thinking. I feel like I need to see where he's at, to try to understand how I could have let someone like him talk me into robbing a bank. Why he hurt Poppy. I haven't seen him in years. I find one of the old notes with his number on it and shoot him a text and I'm surprised when he responds. We set up a time to meet at the house where we used to meet. Maybe he lives in Adelaide permanently now. When the day arrives to fly out to meet him I'm super fucking nervous. I just want to back out. What the fuck do I think this is going to accomplish anyway? Then I talk myself back into it. This fucking merry-go-round of yes… no… yes… no goes on for two fucking hours. I finally get myself in the car and head to the airport and after the three hour flight, grab an uber to my old place. I still haven't rented out or sold the house. It reminds me too much of Junip and I just can't let those memories go yet. I chill out for a while and then rev up my old corolla, which is still sitting in the garage. It takes a few turns to get it started, and then I drive out and head to Amos' place.

I pull up to the house. The lawn is overgrown, the sidewalk has more cracks and crevices worn in over time and neglect. I bang on the front door. No one opens it. I bang again. I can feel the wooden floorboards of the front porch reverberating under my feet. BOOM BOOM BOOM. The heavy bass of loud music that I can't hear but can only feel. I try the door but it's locked. I'm tempted to leave. What was I thinking? The guy is obviously a mess still. I decide to walk around back. The backdoor is swung open wide. I holler, "HEY AMOS." I wait. I holler again. "AMOS." I wait. I decide to venture inside. I walk through the cherry-coloured kitchen. Dishes are piled high in the sink. The floorboards are reverberating, BOOM BOOM BOOM. The place stinks of stale smoke and sweat. There are empty beer cans and liquor bottles on the dining room table. I head into the lounge and I see the back of Amos's head, his hair just peeking out just above the red-sullen couch. "Hey Amos." I say but he doesn't move. Fucker is passed out cold. I walk over to face him.

He's lying stretched out diagonally on the couch back, his mouth half-open in a grin. His throat is slit from ear to ear. The blood has dripped onto the ground beside him covering a packet of chips that are scattered all over the floor. One arm is across his body, the other dangles loosely off the couch. It's ghost like in its paleness. I stagger back, by body wretches from the sight and the smell. I head for the back door and once outside I bend over and take big gulps of air. What the fuck do I do? What the fuck is this? My mind is reeling. What the fuck! Then I'm scared. Did I touch anything? Does anyone know I'm here? How long has he been dead? I carefully walk back inside. I force myself to look at him. I touch his arm, rigamortis is starting to set in. The blood has dried around his throat but sits in a sticky toffee pool on the floor. I'm guessing he's been dead for a day or two. I'm not sure. I'm not a fucking forensic scientist. I need to find his phone. I look around the living room. I can't see it anywhere. I go back to check the kitchen table. Fuck. Fuck. Fuck. My texts to him are on there. Thank God he uses prepaid throwaway phones. I don't want to be caught up in any of this. Shit. Fuck me. I'm going to have to check his body. Fuck. I go back and look down at him. I'm scanning the front of his jeans. Nothing. Then I see it. It's tucked between the side of his left leg and the back of the couch. I carefully reach over him, holding my breath the whole the time and with my index finger and thumb I slide it out. "You stupid shit-eating motherfucker" I say to his corpse. Then I notice there is something else tucked in between the side of his body and the couch. It's a shoebox that's been wedged and squished half under his body. I pull that out too and his body slumps down even further, catching my arm on the way down. It makes me want to puke. I open the box. Fuck me! Fuck me! Fuck me! I've pulled papers out of the box and they are the fucking plans of our bank robbery. They are sketches of the interior of the bank, he's drawn fucking arrows with my name on it leading to the safe. I stuff the whole box under my arm and I get the fuck out of there.

I'm driving home and I feel as if I'm on high alert. Every cell in my body is vibrating. I can't stop picturing

Amos, lying there. A corpse. No energy no life. It's so fucking strange. I've thought about my own death before and I always thought I wouldn't give a rats ass what they did with my body. It's just a thing. And it *is* just a thing, but it's *my* thing. It's the thing that has let me walk and talk and be. Fuck I'm wigged out. I always thought it would be great if my body was placed naked on the top of a mountain for birds to eat. They could feed their babies. At least it would be of some use to something. Better than being dumped in the ground or burned. But that ain't going to fucking happen. What the fuck am I thinking this shit for. I've got to get rid of Amos's phone. I have to burn that fucking shoe box. Fucking cocksucker. I bang the steering wheel. I better not get caught up in this shit. What was I thinking in the first place going to his house? Oh my god, what if I had just walked away? Oh shit. I could've been in a lot of shit. Shit, I hope I'm not in shit. The guy's a fucking loser. "You fucking deserve to be dead," I say out loud. "Good riddance Amos."

CHAPTER SEVENTEEN

Two days earlier
  (Poppy)

He lets me in the front door and I breathe in the stuffy and stale emptiness of Amos' life. The grimy walls smell of grease and stale cigarettes. The square discoloured brown and yellow linoleum at the front door is splattered with letters, paper takeaway bags and cigarette butts that have been ground down and trodden over. Everything reeks of neglect. This is the place he used to brag about? What a fucking waste of my day. Amos shuffles over the mess and I follow. A dirty crack pipe sits on the living room table, resting half in and half out of an overflowing ashtray. I feel filthy even being here. I can't believe I ever fucked this guy, lived with this guy and fuck, almost had a baby with this loser. Amos asks me to take a seat on a sweat stained light grey sofa chair which sags in the center. I perch on the edge. There's a boombox near the TV playing music that is reminiscent of the time that we were together. Is he serious? Does he think we are even in the same league? I was a naive university student from the wrong side of town when I hooked onto his fucked up ass. The chandelier is missing from the ceiling fixture and a single light bulb is screwed into a socket and spreads light around like an interrogation room. Why doesn't he open a blind or two? It is sketchy as fuck in here during the day and I couldn't imagine being here at night. The thought sends a shiver through me. Amos takes a seat on an old red couch to my left, his skinny legs parted like the Arabian sea, his lank, yellow stained fingers intertwined as his bony elbows rest on his knees.

"You know, I've always had this place" says Amos. I don't say anything. He told me this a million times. My lips are slightly pursed and my brow is drawn together. It's the face you make right before you have to take some awful tasting medicine.

"I had it when we were together, I mean," he repeats.

"I know," I say through pursed lips. "Looks great." I can't help the sarcasm. He doesn't notice, or pretends not to.

"It was my grandmother's. She died a while back. It was willed to me. Nothing anybody could do about it." His right leg is jiggling up and down.

"Lucky you," I say with a smirk. Amos lights a cigarette. I mentally note that I will have to take all my clothes I am wearing to the dry cleaners or throw them out.

"What am I doing here Amos?" I ask.

"Come on Poppy, surely it's nice to see me after all these years?" He grins exposing a half set of yellow and rotten teeth. Fucking meth head.

"Your letter sounded threatening, Amos, not nice. What am I doing here?" I ask again.

"Well, consider yourself lucky I didn't send a text. They can trace that shit, y'know." He lets out a cloud of smoke. He's trying to look tough and menacing. He looks pathetic. We both know he didn't text me because he doesn't have my number.

"Too good for me now are ya? All celebrity an' shit. Australia's most eligible slut. Remember who even brought you on the scene when you were a nobody from the Hills. Without me you'd still be a nobody. Just a dirty slut bitch." He takes another drag. What a delusional waste of space. I've always been smart and strong. He was a just a stepping stone. Any schmuck with a bit of cash would have served the same purpose.

"Just get to the point Amos" I say.

"I want my share." He looks straight at me and his leg stops jiggling. He leans over his knees with his hands.

"Share of what?" I ask.

"My share" he says again. His leg starts jiggling. "I got 300k, you got 1.2 mil. From the robbery – remember that? The way I see it that's a combined is 1.5 mil and half of that is 750k. I want my share. You owe me 450 thousand. Time to pay up."

"Fuck you" I say.

"I have proof of what you did. I bet you don't want the

magazines and newspapers writing about that, do you? Or the police finding out?" he's grinning again like a half-baked moron.

"You running low on crack, Amos?" I ask.

"Fuck you, Poppy. I'm clean. I want to reno this place and make myself some coin," he says.

"Even if you had proof, which I doubt, you would have to implicate yourself if you planned on exposing me." I say. "You're an idiot." I see a flash of anger pass across his face. I remind myself that I'm dealing with an addict and to chill out a bit.

"Calling me an idiot, again Poppy?" he asks. His eyes now look sad as if I truly hurt his feelings. I try to regain some composure, but all that comes out is a scoff.

"I did everything for you Poppy. Everything. I was clean for you. Clean for you and our baby. Then you fucking left and fucked everything up." He stubs out his cigarette and rests his head in his hands. I'm seething inside.

"I never wanted the fucking baby!" I yell. "It would have been much easier if you used fucking protection, but no, you wanted to be a dad, didn't you? Fuck you! You ruined your life, and you almost ruined mine." I can't even begin to imagine if our child would have survived and if I would have been tethered to this man for the rest of my life. The thought makes me sick.

"I robbed a fucking bank for you, bitch," he spits back.

"You're choice buddy. You came out 300k richer. Not a bad gig for a couple of hours work if you ask me" I say. "Go ahead, Amos. Go tell the police. You think they'll listen to a crackhead like you? I passed all the psych evaluations, and the lie detector tests."

"I sent a text out to Henry and I'm hanging out with him in a couple of days." He lights another cigarette. "I bet he'll be excited to hear that you were the one that planned the whole thing. And you probably fucking rammed that car on purpose, you're so fucking evil" he spits back. "All glory, all hail the Eligible Poppy Fucking Aver." He makes bowing gestures towards me.

I stand up. "No one is going to believe you, you little man. Not a chance are you fucking with my life." I head to the front door but the door knob falls off. He laughs. So I head towards the back door.

"Fuck you, you stupid bitch. I don't care what happens to me. I'm going to take you down if it's the last thing I do! You killed my baby and ruined my life. Fuck you." He's stood up. I look at him and then turn around and keep walking. He sits back down.

"You have twenty-four hours. Twenty. Four. Fucking. Hours. Bitch" he yells from the living room. I open the back door and let it swing shut so that he thinks I've left. I stand there for a moment. I feel so utterly calm, so in control. I feel as if I'm infused with a power much stronger than anything human. I feel protected and invisible. I feel intoxicated but so clear headed that it's hard to describe. I take a knife from the knife-stand in the kitchen. I stare at the cold clear metal, at my pretty reflection, and walk silently back to the living room. Amos is sitting down on the couch with his back to me. I stand behind him for a moment while he looks into blank space.

He stubs out his cigarette on the plastic armchair cover, watches it sizzle. Sinks back into the couch. He has no time to react. I reach down with a sturdy clenched hand and hold his hair in a bunch, like holding up a bag of oranges, and slit his throat from ear to ear. I'd like to say it feels like slicing butter, but I have to push harder than that. It's gritty and messy. I hear a gurgle as if his throat is gasping for breath as the blood bubbles out, his arms are kind of flailing as he reaches for his neck. Then there is silence. I walk around the couch to look at him.

"Fuck you, Amos," I say out loud. I'm about to spit on him when I remember that I don't want any of my DNA near him.

I wash my hands in the sink and then with the tea towel wrapped around my right hand I start to search the house looking for this so-called evidence. I pull open drawers and rifle through. There is nothing, anywhere. I use the tea towel to wipe down the handle of the back door and I leave. I'll burn this filthy fucking piece of rag along with my clothes and shoes when I get back to Tenacious. I know that I am not just saving myself from this low life junkie that nobody will miss, that contributes nothing good to this world, that has probably caused more pain and suffering by being here than he ever will in death, but I am also saving Henry.

CHAPTER EIGHTEEN

(Henry)

I can't even remember the route I took home but somehow I got there. I'm still in the driveway when I sift through the box. The thought of bringing it into my old house is repulsive but I don't know what else to do with it. Under the bank plans are two polaroid's. The first is of Poppy and Amos, holding a baby in a hospital. This makes no sense. What the fuck is this? Poppy is lying in the bed. The hospital sheets pulled up to her chin. Her shoulders are shoved up to ears like a pair of large dangling earrings. She is staring blankly at the lens. Her mouth is a straight line across her face. And Amos is standing next to the bed beside her. His face is twisted and stained with tears. He's holding the baby. It's wrapped in a yellow hospital blanket but there is something weird about the position of its neck. It's small... too small. What the fuck is this? Was this after the robbery? Did he rape Poppy and get her pregnant? How or why would she be with him? I think the baby is dead. My head is spinning. I flip to the next picture.

It is the two of them at some kind of party. They look young. They are dressed up in costumes. Amos is a pirate. He looks fit and healthy – bigger, wide-eyed. Poppy is dressed up as that woman who flew around the world, what the hell is her name? Amelia... Amelia something. Fuck. They knew each other? This comes hurdling at me like an avalanche of confusion. How the fuck did they know each other? Did they fucking set me up? Was the show a whole set-up? What is going on? I dig deeper.

I'm pulling out papers, 'Gone out to grab some milk and strawberries. Love Pops xx.' 'Hey Amos, I've just gone shopping with the girls - surprise me for dinner.' A heart is drawn on the page with a stick figure drawing of a girl and a boy holding hands. They both have big smiles. There are copies of insurance papers with Poppy's name on it and the banks name on it and a settlement of 1.2 million dollars. What the fuck? This has to all be a set-up. And now Amos is dead? Who the fuck killed Amos? Poppy? I keep digging. There is an engagement ring in a small blue box. It's very gaudy, large – not the kind of ring I would've thought Poppy would like. I start to feel like I'm hyperventilating. I can't catch my breath. I start to count. I start to slow my breath to my counting. When I was a boy and would get anxious, my Mum would make me count and breathe, count and breathe. I feel my breath coming back. I let out a deep guttural scream that vibrates in my gut. "FFFFUUUUUUUUCK!" and my fists pound the steering wheel. "FFFFUUUUUUUUCK!" I feel tears at the edges of my eyes. The last time I have ever felt this fucking confused, angry and helpless was when I woke up in hospital.

I shove everything back in the box and look around. There's nobody nearby. I get out the car with the box tucked under my arm and head into my old house. I bring the box into the bedroom and pour myself a good stiff shot of whisky and sit on the side of my bed. The box is beside me. I take a few good gulps and then let my head dangle. I'm trying to make sense of this. My thoughts are scrambling on top of each other. I take another long drink and top my glass up. Then I realize something. Amos wasn't raping Poppy at the bank. He was fucking his girl-friend during a robbery. Wow. All these years I've been carrying around this guilt thinking I fucked up someone's life. That fucking bitch! Was Amos about to tell me the truth? And Poppy couldn't handle it? Did they hatch this plan together? Did they have the baby after the robbery or before? Has that cunt known who I am the whole goddamn time? Has she been playing me? She would have been shocked as shit seeing me walk up those stairs the first night of the show! Fuck she's good, or was I just too fucking startled myself to realize her shock?

I play the meeting over again in my head. I remember she did seem to know me but I pushed it away as she was right back to playing the stranger. Maybe she told the producer I was her favourite because she wanted to keep an eye on me? And here I thought she was falling for me.

And I was going to tell her everything. Fucking every-thing she already knew. Did she know what I was going to say in the car? Was my accident no accident at all? Oh my god, the woman is demonic. Why did Amos want to meet me? Was he planning on getting me in on framing Poppy? Did she get there first? If she was, and she didn't find this, she must be shitting her pants. I take another gulp of whisky and look over at the box. I've got myself some collateral here. Then I say out loud "give your fucken' head a shake, Henry. You frame Poppy you go down too you moron."

I let out a laugh. I take another swig. "That crafty fucking bitch" I say. No wonder she hasn't tried to get in touch with me. Well, maybe I'll start getting in touch with her and play some games of my own. Fuck you Poppy Aver! I pick up my glass and take a large gulp and drain it. "Poppy, I'm coming after you" and I cheers the air with my empty glass.

I know that I'm going to have to play it cool. She's the kind of lady that likes a bit of the chase. I've never felt so clear headed and sober in my life. And if she's been avoiding me, I'm going to have to make it seem like a coincidence that we are bumping into each other. This means I have to get out there. I text my agent, Steve, and tell him to start booking me into events. I let him know I'm done with drugs and too much booze and bedding random women. I fly back to Sydney but leave the box tucked up under some old clothes in my wardrobe, aside from one item I have a plan for, and it'll really fuck Poppy over. Since finding the box and knowing what the fuck I need and want to do I've been driven in a way that I never have been before. Once I'm back at my apartment, I'm up early every day, I go for a run on the beach. I down a veg and protein shake, head to the gym and do a good hour there. Maybe I'll meet a mate for lunch, and then Clyde and I go for an early evening walk. I cook us up some fine food, watch Netflix and crash and the next day and next and the next it's the same routine over and over again. I look and feel better than I have in a long time.

I start popping out to events and at first I don't give a rats ass about finding Poppy. I just want my face picked up by the press. I want her to see me. In the meantime I've booked some more appointments with a speech therapist. I'm not seeing Nicola the old one since that turned into a bit of thing. My new therapist Melissa is older and not very attractive. Super nice lady and we work hard together on ensuring that my enunciation doesn't slip into the deaf man's slur. I've been for another intensive check-up with the ENT specialist, Dr. Leyland who's been with me the whole time. We've set a date for surgery. That fucks with me a bit. One minute I'm super hopeful and then next I'm scared as hell. It's a one-shot deal. If this surgery doesn't work then I'm going to need that implant, and it'll be a waiting game all over again before that can happen. I might be fucked forever, who knows. I try to stay positive. Melissa helps. She assures me that with a voice like mine I am most certainly meant to hear.

The next big event out is a club opening in Bondi that Steve my manager told me is a must attend. A ton of Reality and TV stars have been sponsored to be there. I'm certain Poppy is going. I have to admit I'm a little nervous. I almost feel like doing a line but I know that it would mess me up and I want to be aware and in control of this whole facade of a fiction that she's been spinning.

My heart nearly jumps out of my chest when I see her. She has a small braid curling around her head with little wisps curling down around her face. She's wearing a white, low-cut jumpsuit and a diamond bracelet. She is so fucking gorgeous. Beyond gorgeous. There's a bunch of people surrounding her, she's like a flame, and the rest of us are like moths that just gather around. I want to yell out 'don't get too close – she might slit your throat' but of course I don't. I take a glass of champagne from the girl that is circulating the room with a tray and start to edge my way a little closer. She hasn't seen me.

Once I get within a few feet of her outer circle, I stop and start chatting with a group of guys from other shows that I casually know. It's hard to really chat in groups as I need more of the one-on-one face-me-while-you-talk contact but it's a good diversion. I'm good at smiling and nodding when I don't have a fucking clue as to what is going on. And there is not a chance in hell I am going to approach her. I want her to work for this. A few ladies join our circle and soon enough I'm pulled out on to the dance floor. I take one last glance towards Poppy and I catch her as she quickly looks away. She's seen me. It makes my heart pound. I turn back towards the girl who is dragging me towards the floor and I smile. I catch up and put my hand around her waist and whisper, "You know I can't hear the music right? No laughing at my dancing or I might have to spank you," and I give her ear a little nibble. She smiles up at me and gives me a kiss on the cheek. "No problem," she mouths, "just follow my lead."

I'm dancing away, twirling whoever around, drawing her away and back to me, when all of a sudden it's as if the Red-fucking-Sea is parting. There are so much paparazzi and all of a sudden there she is, everyone is watching us. I am only watching her. The girl I was dancing with takes her cue and stands off to the side. I am smiling. I've rehearsed this a thousand times. Stay calm Henry, you've got this. I say to myself. She comes near me and kisses me on each cheek. She's staring directly in my eyes. I see a flash of fear and then it's all candy floss and bubble gum. She's mouths the words, "I've missed you. How are you?" I say out loud to her, "I've thought a lot about you too." I'm smiling, even though I want to choke her. I take her hand and lift it up high and say "you're looking gorgeous." It's a great shot for the press. She giggles or at least it seems like she does. "Oh Mr. Henry, you've always been such a charmer." I pull her close to me and we start swaying to the music. "I really have missed you" I whisper in her ear. She pulls back and looks at me. "I've missed you too, Mr. Henry" and there's actually a tear in her eye. We start swaying again our bodies locked together. Maybe I'm wrong, I start to think, maybe she was controlled by Amos. I get a flash of her in the hospital bed with that baby. That was not a strong confident woman. Maybe it was all him? Maybe he used to beat her like my father? I wouldn't be fucking surprised. I'm so confused. Then I remember the notes. No, she wouldn't leave notes like that. Or would she? Poppy pulls back from me once the press leaves. "Why didn't you want to see me?" she has her head cocked to one side.

"Oh, Poppy. It wasn't that I didn't want to see you. I was just afraid and embarrassed. I haven't been in a good spot," I say.

"Well I think you are even more handsome that when we were on the show," she smiles at me. I forget everything. I take a hold of her chin and tilt her head up towards mine and we kiss, a slow wet sensual kiss. She wraps her arms around the back of my neck and we slowly sway from side to side.

How easily I fall. I try to remind myself that the whole point of this was to make her pay. But now I'm not sure what she would be paying for. If Amos was really a fucking snake, then he deserved to die. It's really hard to imagine that someone could be such a fucking evil bitch and be so fucking beautiful at the same time. There's a softness to her beauty, a down-to-earth realness. Her freckles, the tilt of her head, the softness and waves of her hair. She's not the kind of girl that wears much makeup every day. She can laugh at herself. It's how every boy has imagined Cinderella. Cinderella couldn't be evil. There's no way Poppy can be an absolute psychopath. No fucking way. Maybe I should just flat out ask her. Now how would I phrase that? "Hey Poppy, did Amos beat the fuck out of you or at the very least control you to the point that you were so frightened of him that the only way out was to kill him as self-defense or did you just slit his throat in cold blood cause your some weird evil nasty bitch? Or maybe it wasn't you that killed him at all but some sketchy coke dealer who he owed a whack of cash to? Tell me?" Fuck it. I'm not opening that can of worms. There's nothing in how she is with me that rings alarms or tells me she is evil. I promise myself that I will find out what happened, and if she is in fact evil, that I will find her weakness, and she will be destroyed. But in the meantime, can't I enjoy her? Enjoy the most beautiful mystery in this life, Poppy Aver.

We start to date. Call me crazy, but a catch up turns into another and another, and then one day we are out and she introduces me as her boyfriend and I feel my heart explode with pride. I can't help it.

We laugh a lot. We cook together. We lay by the fire and take turns reading each other chapters from the newest Grisham novel. Of course I can't hear when she reads, but I watch her mouth move. Sometimes I read her lips and sometimes I just watch the movement. We are even starting to have our own little inside jokes. We've been invited on numerous news shows together and they are always trying to dig deeper and find out more about our relationship but we are staying private or as private as we can be. All of this screams 'trust'. It's starting to feel like something real, something solid. I think about the early days when Junip and I were first married. It feels similar to that. It's a good feeling and maybe I just need to remind myself that I am worthy of good feelings. Just like Junip tried to tell me. I am allowed to feel good.

Admittedly we do have some days that are a little less

good than others. It' not all unicorns and rainbows but our bad days are little things that Poppy doesn't even seem to notice. Sometimes, I feel like she's a million miles away, or that she gets kind of broody for no reason. But Junip could be like that too sometimes. I shrug it off as 'female' thing and try to forget that she might be a monster. Yet, over time she starts to get a bit harsher and a bit more snappy or impatient. To be fair, I think some of that is natural in relationships, but I guess I just wanted the magic of the beginning to last a little bit longer. I guess we are just starting to figure out what we each need for our own personal space. Honestly, I could smother her to death but I make up shit that I have to do so that she doesn't get tired of me.

I'm so confused. I change my mind about what to do with her through the day, depending on how I feel about myself, depending on whether my head or my stupid-ass heart reigns. It's fucking horrible.

Her newest thing are these long solitary strolls in the vineyards, or if we're in Sydney at my apartment, she takes Clyde down to the beach for long solitary walks. She will head out in the late afternoon, and if I ask if she'd like company, she always refuses. She doesn't get back until after the sun has set. Often, I'll be in the kitchen cooking and I'll see her walking back and there's something very strong and formidable about her. Something stern and cold. I wonder if it's her reckoning with her past and having been a victim to Amos? Or if it's the opposite? Her trying to reconcile her own guilt, I don't know, all I know is that it's frightening. Then she'll come in and kiss me on the cheek and start chatting to me about her walk.

"Oh I found the saddest baby bird that was half mangled. I'm sure a cat had had a go at it. I just held it and stroked its poor little head and sang to it until it slowly passed away. Oh Henry it was beautiful and sad at the same time." Her stories would make me forget any misgivings I might be having, any doubts. She would talk about the neighbour and his sick wife and she would insist that we make food and she'd take it over to them. Poppy would start planning how we could have fruit trees around the house. And she would absentmindedly say 'we' as if it was understood. Her moods seemed to cater to whoever was around. I know we all do this to some degree but the switch in Poppy was both fascinating and frightening to watch. It was as if there was a whole other person inside her that nobody except Poppy was ever going to know. And here I was falling madly in love with her. I wasn't even sure if this was my choice. Or what exactly I was falling in love with.

Yet as time keeps moving, the cracks seem to grow deeper or widen. Soon she starts snapping at me or patronizes me. It's little things, but over time they collate and seem bigger and bigger. Once, I had asked what the herb was that she had come back from her walk with, bunched in her hand. "Oh, I thought you were a chef?" she had mocked, referring to all the cooking I do. She slammed the herbs on the kitchen table and walked past me, "They need washing, 'chef'."

Then there were times when I was opening up about

how lonely I was after the accident, how utterly isolating it feels at times not being able to hear. The Poppy I know would normally rub my back and ask questions or even try to make me laugh but this new or hidden Poppy gets irritated and impatient. "Don't you think loneliness is part of life. Everybody experiences it. You're not special, Mr. Henry."

"I know" I say, taken aback. "I wasn't trying to say that it wasn't part of life or that everyone doesn't experience it, but not everyone experiences going fucking deaf later in life." I'm frustrated as fuck. She isn't even looking at me as I speak, she's scrolling through her Instagram. Then she smiles up at me, all the butter melts everywhere in the world. Fuck that smile. It's as if I never snapped at her at all.

"That's true Henry, loneliness must be wider when you can't hear. Is it like it makes the rest of the world shrivel up? " We are sitting on opposite ends of the couch. She has her feet in my lap. I'm absentmindedly massaging her toes, bending them forwards and then back.

"Yes, that's it exactly" I say.

"Hmmm….well maybe it's about evolution? And not despair." I can't tell if she's mocking me as there's a hint of a challenge in her eyes.

"Ouch!" she says and pulls her foot away. I was bending her toes too far back. She keeps her knees bent and wraps her arms around them and rests her head on her knees.

"Sorry," I mumble, "You think loneliness is part of evolution? Like feeling horny is maybe connected to procreation and the continuance of human life, or loving your kid and thinking they're cute is connected to the need to care for them so they will survive, or jealousy or envy is maybe connected to a drive to succeed? What is loneliness connected to Poppy? Enlighten me." I feel my anger rising. This always amuses her. It's like she gets a little rush off upsetting me.

She doesn't respond at first. She sits in a kind of silence with me and we stare at each other. I start to feel fidgety and I'm not sure if she is going to snap, or if she's going to crawl into my lap and soothe me. I'm always guessing and on edge these days.

She picks up her wine glass and takes a big gulp. "Loneliness is about focusing on the self. It's a push to find yourself. It forces us into a space where we are challenged with who we are and what we are. It's exactly what happened to you. Look at how far you've come since your accident." She opens her arms wide and gestures around the room. She does this without a smile, without affection. I'd rather she had yelled – *you ungrateful sack of shit.*

And who the hell does she think she is? What she's gesturing to is hers, not mine. I'm not successful. I'm financially comfortable because I can't fucking hear and I capitalized on that, but that's her fault too. Everything is hers. It's like she possesses me and treats me like a thing, an object, not a man, not a person with feelings. I'm good if I'm matching her mood or doing what she wants or needs but the moment I step out of that role, I'm a burden, or worse I'm despised. She's not human. Who the hell am I spending time with? Why have I let this go on for so long?

"Oh Henry, don't be so serious all the time." She grabs the wine bottle off the floor and leans forward and tops of my glass. "We are the lucky ones, don't you get it?"

There's a silence and I wonder if she's trying to keep her mouth shut. Or if she's about to laugh and slap me playfully on the arm and say something like, 'Oh Mr. Henry, I'm so sorry you were so lonely. It's hard not to blame myself, but know you are enough and you will never be lonely again, not with me.'

Later, I'm lying in bed beside her. She's curled up on her side and I can hear her rhythmic breathing. She's fast asleep. Sometimes it is hard to believe she is human, to feel the rise and fall of her breasts when my arms are around her, and the smell of her sweet sweat when we make love.

I can't sleep, my head is spinning. It's a fucking joke, isn't it? I'm a fucking joke. I have all the truth in my hands, all the lies laid out but I'm choosing to remain inside this illusion. I'm choosing to remain delusional. They say love is blind. I think it's made me deaf, dumb and blind. I still want to figure her out though. I look down at her, she looks so small, so fragile, so beautifully perfectly perfect. All I want to do is protect her. To make her happy and safe, forever. This is crazy but I don't know how to stop it. I bend down and kiss her forehead. She lets out a little sigh. I slide down and curl up beside her.

The day of my surgery is fast approaching. In my good moments I'm ecstatic and hopeful. I think about what I want to hear first... music?... Poppy moaning with pleasure?...The ocean? Then in my bad moments I'm as nervous and frightened as hell. What if it doesn't work? What if I am to remain deaf forever? Or what if I have to get a cochlear implant that will barely imitate the hearing I had before? The thought is paralyzing. I'm well aware of everything that could go wrong. Then I have moments where I think that hearing will become intrusive on this silent cocoon I've built for myself. That I will be forced out of this comfort zone and my expectations and other people's expectations for me will change. I've spoken to a few people who are deaf at events and over social media, and as strange as it might sound, they are resolute that they don't want to hear. That being deaf is a blessing. It's fucked. It's like they are attaching to all the attraction that being a victim or being different brings. But I want to escape from this silent tomb that I've been living in no matter how intrusive sound might seem at first.

Poppy is wrapped in a blanket, sitting on the floor by the fire. I'm drinking wine and going through the pre-procedure instructions for my operation. It's in two days. I'm wired as fuck. I'm nervous and excited. I really think it's going to work. I watch Poppy's head bob up and down as she reaches for wine. There must be music playing. How fucking glorious, how fucking gloriously simple to be able to listen to music. Soon, so soon.

CHAPTER NINETEEN

(Poppy)

I have to keep an eye on Henry. I made a mistake with Amos. He was almost going to turn me in. I didn't find any evidence thank fucking god. There's that old saying, keep your friends close but your enemies closer. Not that Henry is my enemy but all his emotional outbursts are annoying as fuck.

Amos almost looked better dead – it's as if it was meant to be. No more of that annoying nervous energy fucking up the world. Stupid fuck.

The cops had knocked at my door a few days after his death. I was expecting this. I had plenty of time to rehearse this role. I let them in. There was a man and a woman. I was a bit surprised that it was a female cop. Surely smart women can find something more inspiring or meaningful to do? Plus those uniforms look like shit on a woman.

"Hello Miss Aver." And we commence with firm handshakes all around.

"Oh no, please just call me Poppy." And there's a warm smile that only goes between me and the male cop.

"Thanks for taking the time to see us. I'm Detective Stacey Jones and this is my partner Detective George Leonard." Stacey has razor straight bangs, a thin nose and lips, and little lines etched in around her mouth and between her eyes. Her fat ass looks as if it's fighting to escape her pants. I'd honestly recommend going up a size. George is a bit softer looking. He's got the lazy desk pudge around his middle and his chin. And those droopy eyelids that are just itching to retire.

"No problem. Please come in," I move aside and we make our way to the living room.

"Please sit down. Can I get either of you a coffee? I just made a fresh pot." George says sure and of course Stacey the bitch refuses. I go to fetch George a coffee. I'm unsure if this is an interrogation or they're just here to let me know what happened. I holler back to George, "Milk or sugar?"

"Yes, a bit of both, please." he hollers back. I return with a coffee for George and hand it to him.

"Can I just say, my wife is a huge fan of yours. She never misses an episode of The Eligibles." He's grinning. "She makes me watch it with her. I'm going to have to tell her you're a lot prettier in person even."

"Thank you, Detective. You are too kind. Is this to do

with the show and the car accident?" I play dumb as I take a chair opposite them. George looks over at Stacey. "No, no, we are actually here on a bit more of a serious note." George says.

Detective Jones is growing frustrated and impatient. Her eyes dart from George to myself.

"We are here about Amos Vern," she states.

I sit up a bit straighter and lean forward. I am so good at acting and feigning all the right moves. "Is he okay? Is he in some kind of trouble?" I respond with surprise and wide eyes.

"Unfortunately, it is a little more serious than that." I let out a little gasp. "Amos was killed in his home two days ago." Detective Jones is all cop.

"Sorry, what?" I say and fall back in my chair. "Oh my god. That is insane. Killed? As in murdered?" I make my eyes well up. My hand is over my mouth. I think about how I booked my domestic flight to Adelaide under a false name, just because I didn't want the paparazzi showing up. Why they don't check your ID, I don't know. Seems it was useful in more way than one.

"I'm sorry," says George. Detective Jones leans forward to pat my knee. It's an awkward move. I put my head in both my hands and start sobbing.

"I'm so sorry," I say, rubbing my eyes with the heel of my hands. "I don't know why I'm crying. I haven't seen Amos in years. It's just a shock."

"We figured as much," says George. Detective Jones doesn't take her eyes off me. *I'm so much better at this than you bitch*, I think to myself.

"It was so long ago," I say to George. I look down at my hands. "We lost a baby together." I feel my eyes welling up again. I look at Detective Jones and George. George looks down, "Yes, we have done our research, I'm so sorry. Just know we will keep all this information as private as possible."

Detective Jones has her pad and pen out. "I know this is hard. We are just wondering if you remember any names of Amos's friends? Or anyone who you think might have a grudge against him?" I mention a couple of names and keep apologizing that I can't help them anymore. We all shake hands and they thank me for my time. George asks me for a selfie for his wife. I can see Stacey grimacing. I say "Oh, I'm not sure if I look okay for a selfie, I've been crying."

"Oh my god, of course. That was rude of me to ask."

"Yes it really was. Sorry Poppy" says Stacey. The first time she's softened to me the whole time.

"It's okay, really. What's your wife' name?" I ask. I go to the desk and pull out a notepad and start writing a note for his wife. "Cheryl" he says, peeking over my shoulder. "Oh she's going to be so excited." He's grinning like a school boy. What a sweet man. I finally close the door. Thank fuck that is over. I give myself a pat on the back. "Good job, Poppy" I say out loud. Now the only one to worry about is Henry. Fuck.

I arrange for Henry's manager, Steve, to make sure Henry is at the next big event I'm at. It's a club opening in Bondi Beach. I tell Steve to make sure he doesn't bring a date. I wear my white pant suit and get a blow-wave and even paint my nails.

I catch Henry's eye almost as soon as he arrives, but he looks away. He joins a group of guys and turns his back to me. What the fuck... but I also find it kind of hot. I ignore him for a bit but then I see him take some short little slim brunette on to the dance floor. I feel like he's putting on a performance for me. I wonder what he knows. Okay, Mr. Henry Vedder, game on. I am going to make you mine. The media are going to love this. My Insta account is going to go through the roof. I slowly walk over towards the dance floor.

All I can say is that it was all a lot easier than I thought it would be.

I can tell that the reason he hasn't contacted me is to play it cool. That forced fucked up game that guys play. He thinks I'm putty in his hands. I can see his confidence return. He doesn't know that I actually have the power – and that's the splendour – the command beautiful women can instate when it comes to men in general. They would never think that someone who looks like me could ever be anything other than innocent and beautiful.

So my plan works and as far as the media is concerned, Henry and I are in a relationship and I suppose that we are. Catching up for a second time turns into a few days, and then weeks and between work commitments and travel we're seeing each other often. Surprisingly, being with Henry is actually really nice. It's not tiresome at all. He's good in bed, and the fact that he does whatever I say is beautiful. He's a little clingy and a bit too emotional but it's nothing I can't handle – I've had worse. I take time off from him as much as I can. He goes to the gym and does charity work he doesn't like people to know about, and I run the vineyard. If I'm in Sydney with him, I'll take Clyde for walks. Clyde is one of the first dogs I've met that isn't afraid of me. We have a special connection. Maybe he just gets that Henry loves me, or maybe he's smart enough to understand that I'm not just some flighty killer, but rather that I actually save the world from having to tolerate scum like Amos. That I'm brave and that putting self preservation first is the smart thing to do.

One day I'm down at the beach and Clyde does his business on the side of the pavement. I had forgotten to bring the little plastic doggie bags I usually do, so I just smiled apologetically around me and went to continue on my way – it's not like it was wham bam in the middle of the pavement. An older lady stopped me though. She was dressed in a tacky pink matching tracksuit and had an identical coloured hat. Trashy bitch. She was fat and her jowls flopped over the sides of her thin lips when she spoke, "That is very disrespectful." She had her finger out in front of her, wagging it at me.

"I'm so sorry, I usually bring bags with me but I forgot today," I'm all sweet and apologetic.

"I'm sure you have something in that bag of yours you can use. Your dog, your responsibility. I don't want my taxes cleaning up your dog's filth." She's mean and relentless.

I can see a couple of people looking at us and I really

don't want any of the attention. But fuck her. Stupid bitch.

I don't usually have banknotes on me, but the drug trade in Sydney still works in cash, and I do like to dabble when I go out. I was going to pick up some blow for Henry and I, so had a few hundred on me. "Actually I think I do have something." I pull a bunch of fifty-dollar bills out. I use more notes than I need to. I put them gently in the bin and the lady scoffs. Her jowls wag.

Clyde and I go sit on a park bench, and sure enough she begins to dig around for the notes in the trash. I can see she's trying to explain that she dropped something in there to passers-by. It's terrifyingly funny to watch and oh-so-satisfying.

When I get back to Henry's I want to tell him what happened. I want to tell him the story with a smile in my eyes, and then I want to laugh together about it while we cook dinner. But I know he'll think what I did was cruel and unnecessary. It reminds me of the vast valley stretching out between us. That I can never be too comfortable, that I must keep up the illusion of being the damsel, the victim, the woman who has triumphed over tragedy. The one-dimensional archetype of every man's fantasy. It is strange to catch myself wanting to impress Henry – wanting to be who he thinks I am, not just *pretending* to be.

I even start to think that maybe this could actually be a thing. But then that slippery fucking slope into 'domesticity' starts to rear its ugly fucking head. We're staying in bed longer, we're not going out as much, I've lost a little control over Tenacious, I'm not promoting the wines like I should be. I feel like I haven't learned anything useful in months. All Henry wants to do is hold hands, talk about feelings, go to the gym and cook food. I feel fat and bored as fuck. They always say it's girls that want to talk about their feelings but honestly I feel like it's guys. Henry never shuts up. And having conversations with a deaf dude takes a bit more work. It's this wishy-washy self-help personal growth bullshit fuelled by his slowly dwindling flaccid pack of antidepressants. Somebody shoot me in the head. I'm trying to teach him but he's not a quick study. Not every feeling has to be dissected and held onto. Practice the Tao you stupid motherfucker. You can't change anyone though. We are who we are. Henry is Henry. My god I hope he gets his hearing back. At least I won't have to look at him every time I talk to him. And it will be another great publicity boost.

I do care about Henry, don't get me wrong. He's good for my image but if this operation doesn't work, I don't know how much longer I can do this. All the wallowing is like a river that just keeps growing wider and deeper and I don't have the strength or the audacity to cross it or wade through it. When someone asks themselves if they're happy, usually that's when they cease to have the capacity to be just that. I'm not even sure that if he regained his hearing, I would be able to continue this "perfect coupling". I'll make up my mind after the operation is done and dusted and then I can call in a few favours if need be. The paparazzi owe me and to be honest I'm the one doing them the favour. If I want out, I'll set up a shot to make it look like he's cheating and that way I'm the winner and poor, poor Henry will just have to lose. I love planning shit like this. It gives me a chance to practice, rehearse and perfect my role. I'll make sure I confront him in public and I'll cry a little, but not ugly cry, and raise my voice, but not too much, and I'll walk out the restaurant or bar or wherever and leave him sitting there in dumb silence. Oh it will be good. I should get my agent to ramp up some auditions for me. I'm a natural.

It's late afternoon at the vineyard and I'm loading the dishwasher while Henry prepares the fire. The view from the kitchen window is insane. The sun is just starting to set over the courtyard and the entire estate is smeared in a watercolour of light and dark blues, purples and yellows. That alone feeling of connection and power wells up in me. There is no separation between me and all that is and the feeling permeates my whole being in a profound peace. It's the same feeling I have when I go camping.

"Poppy, the fire is ready. Are you cold?" Henry calls from the other room. His voice is like a wave and it's part of everything I'm feeling.

I walk into the room towards the fire. I smile at Henry and sit cross-legged on the floor in front of the hearth. Henry wraps a white knitted blanket around me, hands me a glass of red wine and kisses me on the forehead. I feel majestic and let out a long slow breath.

"I'm going to jump in the shower," says Henry. I smile up at him.

I stare at the fire. The flames lick and dance as if possessed. I take in the heat and breathe slowly in and out.

I am now confident and decisive and I know that letting Henry go is what I will need to do regardless of the outcome of his operation. Being certain of my decision brings me a sense of profound calm. I am in control of my destiny.

Henry comes back with a glass of wine in one hand and the opened bottle in the other. His hair is wet and casual slicked back, he's wearing light grey track pants and a tight white t-shirt. We've had an easy day and little Clyde is with us. I love that fucking dog. He's happy with me and like the rest of the world seems to want my love and adoration and approval. I really feel like as a species we are all at different stages of evolution and I was fortunate to be born extremely evolved.

Henry sits down beside me and I turn to him. "You're going to be able to hear tomorrow," I smile and mouth the words slowly like he needs me to.

"If all goes to plan. You realise how risky this is, right Poppy? I might never hear again," he looks down into his wine glass.

I lean over to lift his chin. "The doctors are amazing, Mr. Henry. You will be fine. More than fine." I take a deep breath, "You will soon be able to hear me speak again. Hear my orgasms, not just feel them." I've placed my hand on top of his pants and I feel his cock twitch underneath my touch.

"That I'm looking forward to." Henry leans in and gives me a slow and sensual kiss.

"I have to read the pre-procedure brochures baby," he says as he gets up, sets his glass of wine down on the coffee table and settles into the couch with his new cute-ass glasses on. He's fully absorbed in the pamphlets. I adjust myself so I'm slightly turned away and I rub Clyde's little belly.

"Mr. Henry, it's kind of hard to say this out in the open, but your being deaf is sort of my fault." I let out a little laugh. "I say sort of because really it's your own fucking fault. You were going to ruin the plan I had for our sweet little love story by blurting out your truth. Anyway, that's that and now you know my truth... how does it feel?" I snort to myself. I smile down at Clyde and he wags his tail. I take a long slow sip of my wine. I turn back to Henry with a smile on my face. He looks up at me.

"It says here I have to fast for twelve hours. What time is it now? Let's eat soon babe. I probably shouldn't be drinking either."

"Sounds good," I mouth to Henry.

"Fucking deaf cunt," I say to Clyde and he wags his tail at me.

CHAPTER TWENTY

(Henry)

I slowly start to wake up. I feel stoned. I reach for my ears. There're thick bandages wrapped around my whole head. I fall back asleep. I dream I'm in a crowded room and I'm standing by a door and I'm screaming at the top of my lungs but nobody can hear me. I'm going up to people and tapping on their shoulders but they can't feel me. I'm yelling 'what the fuck is wrong with you people?' And nothing. I start to panic. I'm yelling and crying and it's as if I don't exist. I start pulling at my hair. Then I feel someone grab my hands. They are pinning them to my side. I wake up and a nurse and a doctor are standing over me. The doctor is speaking, his lips are moving but I can't hear him. I'm confused, but then I see Poppy, she's crying and she comes over to the nurses side and takes me hand and kisses my cheek. She looks down at me and mouths, "it's not that it didn't work Henry. We don't know yet. There were complications; swelling. I'm so sorry."

I start to cry. The doctor and nurse leave us alone. Poppy stays by my side looking down at me with her head tilted to the side. She looks like she's playing a role. The stupid fucking empathetic girlfriend role. I fucking hate her. I hate everyone. I'm so fucking angry. I grind my teeth for a minute and I feel her hands leave mine. She must feel my anger. All of a sudden I start speaking and I can't stop. A swarm of bees leaving the hive of my fucked up mind.

"You fucking cunt. I went to Amos's place. His throat was slit like a pig that had just been slaughtered. I know it was you, Poppy. You fucking egomaniacal, psychopathic bitch. What the fuck is it with you? Is it *all* about the image, the lights, the cameras? What the fuck *are* you?" I can't look at her. I know if I do that those eyes, those lips, will tell a story that isn't right, isn't true. "I fucking thought I loved you but you're a shell, a carcass. You would rather kill a man and let another man drown in his guilt and remorse than be anywhere near the fucking truth. And you drove that car off the road, didn't you? You did this to me. You diabolic fucking cunt!! Fuck off! Get the fuck out of my life! You're evil, pure fucking evil."

I turn to face her. She's not there. My words had simply reverberated off of the empty hospital walls. The nurse pops her head in, "Are you okay? I heard you yelling?" I don't say anything. My tongue, my mouth are exhausted, whipped, from lashing out. I turn my head away. The nurse frowns, "Poppy went to get you the food she made for you, she'll be back soon, okay?" I don't hear anything.

It's like a never ending revolving door doors. I hurt, and she never pays. I love and she mocks. Never ending. Well fuck that shit. I recall that evil box of truths. The one piece I took with me back from Adelaide, stuffed in the bottom drawer in my cupboard in my Sydney apartment. That original plan was way better than a rage in a hospital bed. I've never been a bitter, revengeful type, but I want to see her squirm like I have, and to feel what I have. So it's time to execute the plan. Let it rain like the book of revelations.

CHAPTER TWENTY-ONE

(Poppy)

I was at the hospital all day during Henry's surgery. There were paparazzi outside and downstairs but they wouldn't let them onto his floor. I would sometimes wander downstairs for a tea or just to let them snap a couple of pictures of me looking sad and worried. Then at about 3pm the doctor came and told me that Henry was out of surgery but that they weren't feeling hopeful. I let out a little cry. Not too much though as I didn't want my eyes to get too puffy. They said Henry would be in recovery for a bit but that they would come and get me as soon as they thought he was waking up.

When I went into his room a doctor and a nurse were standing on either side of him, holding his arms down. Henry was crying. I moved over to the nurses side and took Henry's hand in mine. I kissed his cheek and looked him in the eyes and told him what the doctors had told me. He was so angry. He told the nurse and doctor to fuck off. I almost laughed out loud. I had to turn my face away. I told him I was going to heat up the food I'd made him, that he must be hungry. He was crying. I went to get the food, mainly to give him some space. I know I'd want that in his situation. Time to grieve.

When I got downstairs I was surrounded by the press. I cried and told them that things were not looking good and I asked them to please respect our privacy at this time. They backed away from me while I got Henry food. They kept snapping pictures. Hopefully some of them will turn out okay. I'm sure my picture will be all over the Daily Mail tomorrow.

I take him home and although he is sad, he tries to smile. He's really manning up. He is a little less desperate with me, less needy. A new Henry that I like much better. He doesn't ask for anything. He doesn't whine. He reads me interesting articles he's found: About the world's oldest monument in Turkey, the original novel written by Mary Shelley about Frankenstein, some other book he's reading concerning morality for atheists. He reads a lot. More than I do. I begin to wonder if he's smarter than I thought, but then I remind myself he's not smart enough to figure out who I really am or smart enough to know the reality of our situation. I'm in this strange ebb and flow with Henry. I can't figure out who he is or how I feel about him or what I want to do with him.

He's still on too many painkillers to actually get it up so we don't have sex, but we still make out. It's different now. The way he kisses me. It's with a kind of passionate anger. Like he's pressing against me with rage. I feel raw and open. I feel like in those few moments that it is okay to be me, all dark and exposed. But then we stop and he apologises. I tell him it's okay, that soon we will be fucking like usual. He kind of grimaces, looks sick. I guess he's embarrassed.

After one week Henry feels well enough to do interviews. The doctors had advised him to take it easy for at least four to six weeks but for whatever reason he's rearing to go. In his interviews Henry is all sunshine and roses. He's feeling optimistic and happy. A few weeks after his initial initial interviews we're at a massive event that has been organized by the Network. It's a huge concert with Amy Shark headlining. All proceeds are going to Better Hearing Australia (BHA). I find it ironic that that they've organized a music event but Henry tells me it's set-up for the hearing-impaired as well as us "normals". It's a sensory experience of motion and vibration, paired with some pretty epic visuals on multiple large screens that visual art students at the University of Sydney put together. It looks like Henry and I were the masterminds behind all of it, as our names are on all the promotional material. There's even a large cut out of us at the main entrance. We look like a set of cardboard greeters. Henry and I are really just rocking up, being the faces of the whole thing. Fans and the press are all over us. We also are having the chance to reconnect with other 'celebs' as nearly everyone from every season of The Eligibles is here. The event is epic.

After the second or third warm-up band plays, they ask us to come up on stage. The crowd cheers. It's quite humbling and quite powerful and for a moment I even think about Henry and wish that he could hear this. I have always wondered how it would feel playing in a band, listening to this every night, being 'wanted' by such a large crowd. It's intoxicating, all this joyful ecstatic energy, from all these people, being thrust at me like electricity. I knew we were going to be called on stage I just hadn't expected this level of enthusiasm. I didn't realize how much we were loved. I was loved. Henry and I are holding hands and smiling and waving out to the people. The ambassador from the charity briefly talks about how important these events are to help all the hearing impaired and then he talks about Henry. He mentions how brave Henry is and how hard it is being impaired later in life. I think it's kind of embarrassing though. He makes it sound like Henry's dying – or at least really rubbing in his pain. It's excruciating, but I stand there and smile like a good soldier. When he finally fucking finishes, we all give a big wave to the crowd. He walks off the stage but Henry and I start dancing on the stage as the band starts playing. Henry is swaying to the sound of the vibrations and I join along. One of the band members takes my arm and I lean towards him. He whispers to me, 'congratulations' and I hear the crowd scream uncontrollably. I have no idea what is going on but when I turn around, there is Henry, on one knee, a little blue ring case in his hand.

My heart is beating a million miles a minute. No... No!

Why the fuck would he be doing this? Surely he's not that stupid? I know it's been easier lately between us and to be honest I have thought about whether he would actually be good for my image, but what the fuck? I'm not ready for this. When he opens the box I nearly faint. I stagger back and the same band guy who took my arm earlier grabs my arm again to steady me. I feel like I'm going to pass out or throw up. The crowd is going wild. Henry is smiling up at me with an evil grin. The ring that he is presenting to me is the same fucking ugly pink and blue ring that Amos gave me five years ago. A million thoughts are spinning me, distracting me, killing me, all at once. How did he find the ring? Does he know everything? What else did he find? Then I have a flash and recall Amos telling me that Henry and him had planned to meet up. I had thought he was bluffing. That fucking asshole. Still, I searched the house for all of this stuff. How did Henry find it? Maybe Henry was there before me? If he was then maybe he doesn't know anything? Maybe this was part of Amos' plan? But what fucking plan? Did Amos have a plan? All this swirled around in my head in a nanosecond and Henry is still on one knee grinning up at me like a fucking cheshire cat. The band guy has handed him a mic.

"Poppy you are the most honest and kind person I have ever had the pleasure of meeting." The sarcasm bleeds out everywhere. "We have been through so much. Our lives intertwined like destiny." This at least is true. "When I first met you I felt like I already knew you, Pops." Because he did. Fucker. I can't believe this ring is here, that Henry is holding the fucking thing up towards me like a piece of kryptonite, or like Sauron's ring. A goddamn curse. "Poppy, I want to know you more every day. More than I even do now." I want to kick him in the fucking balls. "Will you do me the honour of becoming my wife?"

Wife? *Wife?* I know I don't have a choice here. He knows I don't have a choice, which is exactly why he's doing it. I know I look shocked. I know I don't have to hide it because the audience sees the shock as whatever they want it to be – joy, love, whatever. I meet his vehement stare with a look of rage and I smile. We are at war. Henry has no idea what he has done. I say yes and the crowd goes crazy. It's like some weird episode of the Game of Thrones. Henry puts the ring on my finger and leaps up and kisses me. When he hugs me I'm expecting him to whisper something in my ear, but all I feel is his hot breath and his heart beating next to mine.

I didn't think he had it in him, to do this. To pretend with me, to act or to be patient for his revenge. The neediness, the suffocation, was it all part of the rouse? How long has he known? Is this why he's been acting so mysterious since the hospital? Why he was kissing me with anger? Was he going to let me off and then decided against it?

Fuck, I've publicly said yes to marrying the fuckwit. And I can't back out without a cause or I'll ruin my career and public image. I look down at the ring with all the past trapped in its ugly little monster head. I have a flash of Amos lying on the couch with his throat slit. How long will I have to wear blood on my wedding finger? On my hands? Can't Henry see I was doing us all a favour by slitting Amos' throat. Idiot.

Henry and I leave the stage hand in hand. My head is spinning. People come up to congratulate us and gawk at my 'beautiful' ring. It all feels fake and contrived.

Then I start to think... maybe... maybe this is Henry's way of letting me know he knows everything but that I am safe? Is he marrying me to say we are in this together? Is he telling me that he is protecting me?

I'm more confused than ever and I vacillate between respect, abhorrence, love, and complete frustration for Henry as he swoons around me.

People are still surrounding us and I continue to smile and say thank you as my mind races. Maybe he finally understands that if it wasn't for me he'd still be that sad sorry fuck with a mediocre job and a mediocre wife, that Amos picked up at that yacht party. He's well-off and famous because of me. And he probably had the best sex he's ever had with the hottest woman he's ever had. I've seen pictures of his ex-wife. Her boobs are small and she has a hook in her nose. She's nowhere near as hot as me and she looks boring.

Everything I have done has only been to further my life. I have never set out to deliberately crush others. It's all Darwinian. It's instinctive to want to be at the top of the food chain.. Surely Henry sees that? Surely he understands it's not personal. I still don't know if he thinks he's fucking me over by marrying me. Surely, he knows that asking me to marry him doesn't just fuck me over, it fucks him over too.

I'm certain he doesn't have a plan beyond this.

"Yes, it's a beautiful ring. Thanks so much." I hug another stranger.

Henry is enjoying himself. He's fucking hell-bent on seeing me burn or at least squirm at whatever cost, just like Amos was.

Henry and I pose for a photograph. We look at each other and smile some weird plastic smile but we have both being smiling for cameras for so long that we have it down pat. No one would ever suspect anything but love.

Why the fuck is he so hung up on the truth? Why not just enjoy the ride? Why not just tell me that he knows? People who get stuck in the idiotic concept of justice usually end up poor and miserable just like my Mum. Her cross necklace and her search for redemption never brought her happiness. She only got a little happier after I gave her money. Then she found a man and a life. Enjoy the fucking ride people.

Henry has underestimated me with this maneuver. I always win, Henry. Always!

Still, he got me good tonight and I just want to leave this hub of smiling idiots. I ask him if we can go. I can't leave without him; the media would love it way too much. Fucking vultures.

He's so fucking pleased with himself. He's like a peacock strutting out the party with his arm around me. I feel sick. I can't believe this is happening to *me*. To me, Poppy-fucking-Aver! I throw up in the garden at the front and he pats my back and says, "There, there darling. A bit too much to drink, perhaps?" The paparazzi are swarming around us and taking pictures. I hate him. I fucking hate him and I will not let him ruin me.

We get in the car and I wipe my mouth. I take off the ring and put it between us. He picks it up and puts it in his jacket pocket, "I'll save this for later". Neither of us bothers to say anything else. Everything has already been said.

I'm exhausted. I don't know what to feel. I'm dithering between every feeling ever fucking felt by any human ever. They're nameless emotions. I don't like it – not being in control, the dizziness washing over me making it impossible to collect my thoughts. I stare out the car window and watch the lights blur and reflect back at me. I feel like a five-year-old who is sulking. I try to take deep breaths without Henry noticing, but my heart is beating too fast and I feel like I need to gulp the air in. I can feel him looking at me. I need oxygen in my blood, in my brain. I open the window and take a couple of gulps of air.

After a good ten minutes of trying to calm myself down, I can feel the overwhelming sense of fear and vulnerability start to fade away, and red hot anger take its place. I'm okay with red hot anger. It's more manageable. I know how to take that emotion and turn it into rationalization, into action.

From here on in we are fucking doing it on my terms. I'm not going to be written up in the press as the woman who ditched her deaf fiancé for no good reason. Not a chance in hell. Time to unleash the plan I had all along, the plan that this situation has just made even more glorious. Henry shouldn't have fucked with me.

We head back to my vineyard for the week as planned. At first we don't talk. It's a stalemate. We bump into each other occasionally in the kitchen, and one of us says, "Oh, sorry," as if we have always been polite strangers, as if we don't have a mutual friend that was slaughtered for both our benefit, as if we weren't complicit in a bank robbery, as if we aren't technically 'engaged'.

I don't yell at him and he doesn't call me some sort of evil bitch like I know he wants to. The charade is so fucked. Henry still climbs into my bed every night well after I have turned the lights out, and sometimes he even puts his arm around me and snores in my ear. He never sleeps in the spare bedroom. And I don't tell him to. It's as if he has never been safer or happier or more at peace. There is one night when he comes into the room and just sits on the other side of the bed for a while. I pretend to be asleep. He's drunk. I can tell by the way he's breathing. Henry rolls under the sheets and perches his chin on my shoulder and softly whispers in my ear, "Poppy... beautiful Poppy. Do you know... You are a vestigial and functionless part of the world? Do you know that? Like wisdom teeth or the appendix," he lets out a little laugh. "They hang around and eventually flare up or burst and the only thing society knows what to do when that happens, it to have them removed. To have them cut out."

I hold a gasp in my throat so he won't feel my movements, so he won't feel the shock coursing up my spine. I feel scared, like maybe he is about to gauche my face or chest with a piece of broken glass, but then Henry rolls off of me and rolls over and starts to snore.

I remind myself that he is a coward. An idiot. He was then, and he is now. I'm sure he knows as well as me that we can't keep this up forever. That the shit will eventually hit the fan – for him, for me, for us. Hopefully though, just for him.

There are a few paparazzi hanging around the skirts of the vineyard. Camping it out, waiting to get pictures. This means I have to wear that bloody fucking engagement ring at all times. The proposal has created even more public interest – we're the Nation's "golden couple". I'm getting emails from all over the country, designers wanting to create the perfect dress, magazines wanting interviews, cake makers, venues, florists, musicians – all wanting a piece of this stupid, exclusive wedding. Even my employees think it's real. Steve, Jen, Joanne, and a few tourists that are currently working and staying at the vineyard, make us an engagement cake. It's a beautifully decorated blueberry cheesecake. The blueberries remind me of our first date. When Henry and I were on The Eligibles, sitting on that beach blanket eating fruit and cheese while the camera crew swirled around us. That seems like a million years ago.

We cut the cake together and pretend. We laugh and even smash a little in each other's faces. We have an awkward moment where we catch one others eyes and kind of stop laughing and look down. Jen says it's cute.

She thinks our inhibited response to the party is bred out of shyness, out of love, but it's actually out of some fucked-up, all-knowing respect that we seem to have developed since truth threw up between us. Henry now makes me nervous. His happy slumber, his quiet nature, his inability to be frightened by me.

Because of the paparazzi waiting to catch us out, Henry decides to stay longer than he wants to. He says it's because he can't deal with them right now, but I think it's actually because he knows that when he leaves, it's all over. We're over. I'm getting on with running the vineyard, staying as busy as I can, while waiting for the opportunity I know will end all this shit, that will make me the winner. I need to be patient.

Henry reads, he cooks, he plays guitar. Clyde follows him around or sits by him with his little head on his paws, and his floppy ears bent over the sides of his big old-soul eyes. He's the one I'm going to miss. On about the fifth day Henry takes his guitar outside and starts to smash it to pieces on the side deck while Jen and I watch in shock from the office window. He screams as he does it until all he's holding in his hand is the head with bits of wood and string hanging off like flesh from a torn off limb. I tell Jen he's just trying to deal with not being able to hear again, that it's a process. She nods, tears fill her eyes. Once he's done with all the rage, he cleans up the pieces. Puts the larger bits in the big green trash bin. Sweeps up whatever's left and puts that in the bin too. Then Henry sits with his head in his hands and cries. It's a hallowing, wailing kind of cry. At first I figure that maybe he can't hear how loud and painful he sounds, but after a while it's evident that Henry just doesn't really care. I need him to calm down. When his wailing finally dies down a little, I bring him a glass of wine. I kneel down and place it beside him. He says thanks, and I leave.

Every afternoon I go for a long walk. I need it. It stabilizes me. It gives me the alone time I require. Away from the depressing energy that is Henry Vedder, away from the truth that is 'us'. I start thinking about how Henry is the only person that has ever really known me, and probably the only person who ever will. We have a connection to one another's darkness and fears. I have always thought that revealing one's true nature is not conducive to love, but maybe I'm wrong. Maybe we are safe here at the vineyard, maybe we can't hurt each other anymore than we already have, and maybe that makes us equals in some way.

Clyde has come with me today. He roams freely as we walk through the vineyard. The sun sits about five fingers from the horizon as we head down the slope further away from the house. I whistle for Clyde who has been rummaging in the dirt. He comes bouncing up to me and together we walk through the wooden gate and into the bushland behind. There are tyre marks right around the vineyard fence, probably from kids in the surrounding areas doing burnouts on their ATVs. I don't have a problem with it at all except that they leave beer cans everywhere. Fucking teenagers. Clyde is up ahead, running, his ears flopping up and down. . Suddenly, he stops at a little grey bush and starts barking frantically. As

I walk closer, I look down and a kangaroo is lying on the dirt mangled, it's legs are twisted and it's eyes are open and opaque. It's fur is matted on the side with brown and red blood and there's a large pool of blood on the ground. I'm guessing one of those fucktards hit the poor animal and left it to bleed out. Clyde is still barking and I tell him to hush. He whimpers and stands behind my legs. I can see something moving in the kangaroo's pouch. There's a little joey. I take my sweater off, tie the hood into a knot and then tie both the sweater arms and make my own pouch. I squat down and hold the sweater upside down while I reach my other hand into the dead kangaroo's pouch. The little guy leaps out without much help, head-first into the open sweater. Its long skinny legs are hanging out. The poor thing is shaking. I tuck his legs in and hold him close to my body. One leg pops back out and dangles freely as we walk. Clyde is wagging his tail and trying to peer up into the sweater. He lets out a couple of little barks as we make our way back towards the house. I'll have to call George, our local ranger. He always takes the injured animals I find. He gets them over to Morgan's Animal Hospital where they treat them through a fund set up from local donations. Afterwards, it's either on to a home, a sanctuary or back to the land. I've always loved animals. They're much better than humans.

When we get back to the house, Jen and Steve have their arms wrapped around each other on the veranda as they lean against the rail. They're talking to Henry, who is sitting at a little round table, whisky in hand. He's half a bottle in. I tense up, wondering what they are talking about. Yet, the sunset makes them look all mellow and happy and dreamy. Jen and Steve are sipping on some wine. Jen runs up to me when she sees the little joey's leg hanging out. "Oh my good Lord," she exclaims as she peaks into the sweater.

"Clyde found the little guy in his mama's pouch. The poor mum was dead," I frown as I look down at the little joey.

"Dead, how?" asks Jen.

"I think some of the kids around here have been doing burnouts again. Must've hit her I figure."

Jen shakes her head. She is stroking the little guy's foot as we reach Steve and Henry.

"Well we need to sort that out once and for all don't we?" Jen says, angrily.

"Yeah for sure. They were probably terrified too but they shouldn't have just left her there without calling someone. Can you call George for me, Steve?" I ask.

"Sure, sure." Steve answers. "It will have to wait until morning though, I know he's away seeing family this weekend." I hand the sweater with the Joey wrapped inside to Jen.

"I'll get him a pillowcase," says Jen. "And he can sleep next to me."

Henry lets out a chuckle. We all look down at him. He rolls his eyes and slumps a little further into his chair. "Is someone going to tell the deaf guy what's going on?" Steve looks at Henry and repeats the story. Henry isn't impressed.

"What the fuck Poppy? We were having a good evening." His speech is slightly slurred.

Jen looks and Steve look at me and then back at Henry. Nobody knows what to say.

Henry looks up at me and continues, "Oh, what? You actually give a shit about this roo? Seriously? You want to make sure he's happy and safe and warm? Like you wanted Amos to be happy and safe and warm? Like you want me to be happy and safe and warm? You think you're some kind of saint? You find the injured and you heal them?"

The three of us are stunned. Steve is kind of shuffling, it looks like he's about to say something but then he stops. Henry takes another swig of his whiskey and smirks.

"Surely you actually killed its mother just so you could look good right now. Probably strangled her to death, or maybe beat her to death with a shovel? Oh wait, no… a knife is your forte isn't it?" He sounds completely delusional. I want to take a shovel to his head to shut him the fuck up. "So what are you going to do with this poor creature you've kidnapped? Keep him around until he doesn't serve a purpose, is my guess. He can be all cute and you can post a picture with him on your Instagram, saying how you 'saved his life'. Then you can kill him too. Tell us Poppy. I want to know how much evil you can possibly manifest you fucking evil cunt."

Steve steps forward, "Hey… hey Henry, I think that's enough." He puts a hand on Henry's shoulder.

Henry laughs and jerks his shoulder from underneath Steve's grip. "Well if you say so Steve."

"It's okay you two," I say and I step in between Steve and Henry. I face away from Henry. "It's the meds and the booze. He's just really frustrated and sad. He was banking on this operation and he just needs to lash out. We've been through a lot lately, it's okay. It'll be okay. " I pick up the half empty bottle of whiskey. This shit has got to stop, I think to myself.

When Henry starts crying, Steve and Jen each give me a hug. "Are you sure you'll be okay?" Steve asks.

"Yeah... yeah... take the joey in." They give Henry a squeeze on the shoulder and then make their way back to the guest house. I stand there until they are out of sight and then I leave too. I'm so fucking angry.

Does Henry think his little crying outbursts will make me feel sorry for him? I can promise you they don't. Henry thinks he's some kind of saint or victim in all of this. I noticed he omitted any mention of himself and his own crimes in his little drunken outburst. He's so far from saint-like. Does he willingly forget that he participated in a bank robbery and watched as I 'allegedly' got raped? Or that he left a dead guy on his couch, ransacked his house and never called the cops? Everyone with half a brain knows that evil is both active and passive. It's not just action that causes shit, sometimes it's fucking inaction. It's like Henry thinks his drunken self-righteous cerebration somehow makes it real. That he's blameless and I'm what... just an evil cunt? As if! As if thinking that you're good *makes* you good. Stupid dick. Moral thoughts aren't some kind of Batman that feed the poor or fight crimes and injustice. The only thing his thoughts have morphed into, are his own fucking perception of being some sort of superhero or victim. I pour the half bottle of whiskey down the kitchen sink. I have to keep this shit away from Henry. Fuck, he basically told Steve and Jen about Amos. Good fucking thing I've got half a brain and thought to blame his outburst on his recent operation and his meds.

He needs to wise the fuck up. There's an actual news story about a woman, Kitty Genovese, who was raped, and then murdered at the front of an apartment block in New York city. All the residents watched it happen without intervening, without calling the cops, without feeling responsible. They were all waiting for someone else to do something. It's called the 'Bystanders Effect'. Henry is every one of those residents, one of those bystanders. He's not contributing anything good to society. He's not reporting anyone. He's just sitting there with his whisky blaming everyone else, and particularly me, for his own fucking mistakes. He's fucking lucky I killed Amos. He was the only other person who knew that he robbed that bank.

Fuck, this world is messed up, I think to myself as I wander towards the bedroom. My mind is spinning.

Look at the state of the environment. We all complain and whine and watch documentaries about global warming and our oceans, and about the corporate big-dogs and their need for wealth above all else. There're countless articles and conversations about the burning of fossil fuels for transportation, the connection between animal production and methane emission, and chemical fertilizers on croplands. But really isn't the truth that despite our education and our empathetic sighs we all contribute to this destruction? I mean, I do. I eat the animals and their by-products despite having 'intellectual' conversation with 'intellectual' people about it.

Unless we want to live off the grid, it takes a fuck ton of effort to not make the fat-fatter and wealthy-wealthier. *What the hell am I thinking about the environment for?* I've got Henry to worry about. I strip down and hop in the shower. My mind keeps racing.

Henry... fucking Henry who spent the money from the robbery on his own gains. Henry who covered up what he thought was an even worse crime, my "rape", is the same Henry who fucked a hundred women in Sydney, without probably remembering any of their names. . Henry who still wanted to date me even though he blames me for the murder of Amos. Murder, such a weighty word. There should be a different word when we are simply eliminating the scum of the world. Henry even pretended on radio and TV that he doesn't mind his disability, that he's strong and that others can be too, thereby setting people up for feelings of failure and self loathing if they 'fail' in their struggles. It's like the onslaught and marketing of 'self-help' books. People should think about the damage that they actually cause.

Henry is a liar, a coward, a pussy, a sham. His guilt doesn't change anything. Maybe to him I'm the corporate asshole and he's the people, but he's been riding on my coat-tails for so long with barely a word of complaint. I don't feel any ounce of sorry for that man.

It's the first night Henry doesn't sleep in my room. He stays in the spare room and I'm grateful.

The next day, Henry's nurse comes to see him. I ask her if I can have a quiet word with her.

"How's he doing today?" I ask.

"There's no change in his hearing, though some of the swelling has subsided." she says.

I tear up a little. "He's not talking to me, he's so depressed." I continue.

"Hmm... Is he sleeping a lot and refusing to speak with people?" she asks.

"He's drinking a lot and lashing out," I start to cry. "Oh poor, Henry."

"If you think it's necessary, I can recommend the doctor prescribe some anti-depressants. You'd have to make sure he doesn't drink though. I'm sure he'll come around. He's a strong man. I've heard him speak on the radio." I cringe inside. He's already on antidepressants. And he's a fucking loser.

"It's such a blow," she continues, "many people live with much worse. Remember the doctor said he still may hear once all the swelling goes down," she pats my arm.

I cry a little harder. "I don't know," I say. "Maybe we should call Junip. She was the only person that could get through to Henry last time after the accident. What do you think?" I give her my best wide eyes.

"Maybe you're right. It certainly wouldn't hurt and he needs support to handle this."

"I have her number. I'm not sure she'll talk to me. Would you call her?" I ask.

"Sure," says the nurse and pats my hand. "Sure."

The plan is being put into place. I've told Henry I need some space, and he seems relieved. I don't think he thought of much else besides presenting me with Amos's ring.

I've gotten in touch with my paparazzi boys and let them know that Henry will be going back to his home in Bondi soon. I casually let it drop that there is something off with him and that I think maybe he is getting cold feet after proposing and that I think that maybe there is someone else. That maybe there has always been someone else.

That does the trick. They camp outside his apartment and bam, Junip shows up. They get pictures of Henry and Junip hugging and kissing one another's cheeks, and her entering the apartment block, and the headlines are fantastic: "Henry Vedder is with his Ex-wife. Where's Poppy?" "Was their Marriage Ever Really Over?" "It was Poppy who stood by Henry but Henry Returns to the arms of his EX". It's fucking perfect. I'm brilliant. You couldn't write this stuff any better. The best headline "Henry cheats on Poppy with EX-WIFE." Fucking brilliant.

The backlash is fantastic. No one can understand why Henry would cheat on someone so beautiful. Someone who stood by his side and cared for him. The press is having a field day. I lay low. I issue one statement requesting my privacy during this 'difficult time'. I know that Henry, even with all that he said to me, will not go to the police. He'd only fuck himself over – and as much as he might not want to admit it I know he loves the attention of the press. He will act exactly how I want him to act. I'm the one in control Mr. Henry – don't ever fucking forget it. He'll probably spiral into his depressed drunken slutty self again but hopefully he knows it's best to keep his mouth shut. The engagement is over. Shit, maybe even he's relieved like I am. Go get on with your life Henry Vedder. Leave me alone.

What's that saying? You close one door and another one opens? Two months after the bitter break up, guess who gets in contact? Gabriel! The sex god from South America. I guess his little family meddling engagement girl didn't work out so well. Settling or settling down is often not all it's cracked up to be. We started sending dirty texts a few weeks back and had a couple of pretty racy Face-Time calls and now he's coming to Australia. I'm going to finally get properly laid. I can't wait. I had been hanging low for the past months, playing the poor rejected card. It's actually been nice to have some alone time. But enough time has passed and it will be great to emerge on the scene again with a sweet sexy hot exotic piece of ass. Nobody would expect a woman like me to stay home for too long. That would be such a waste.

Gabriel arrives, and it is pure bliss. We spend a week at

the vineyard just banging our brains out. Then he takes off into Melbourne for a week to sort out some business he's been working on. I didn't really pay attention. I'm just glad that he's being so independent – I missed that in a partner. He's read all the tabloids, so he's pretty much up to speed on my life. Yet, to make him feel good and to keep him hard I told him that Henry was just another poor attempt at finding a substitute for him. He loved it.

When he came back from Melbourne, he had bought and arranged to have a motorcycle delivered, a Triumph MY17 Rocket III. As soon as it arrived, we took off on an overnight trip for some camping under the stars.

I'd forgotten how smart Gabriel was. We curled up naked in a sleeping bag and started to talk politics and law as we slowly sipped wine by the fire I had made. It was nice to have him with me camping. Usually I'd do this stuff by myself. It felt so liberating to be with a man who could actually fucking hear what I had to say, and who not only knew how to fuck a woman but also knew how to have a damn conversation. Gabriel didn't digress into a shit bag of emotional barfing, crying and clinginess. The closest he got to that side of life was telling me what an ass he was for trying to control me before. He told me that after he lost me being with a 'local' girl was when he realized that the 'story' I created for us was the one he wanted. He didn't say it exactly like that but he most definitely made it clear I had been right and he was wrong. I finally felt that I was with someone who understood how to be with me.

The media is loving us. The most recent shots are of

Gabriel and I at the beach in Bondi. They look fantastic and really capture the fun we are having. The public adores us. They are only using shots of us canoodling and laughing. He's so damn handsome and his dark hair and eyes really compliment my light long wavy beach hair and freckles. We are so perfect together. We haven't announced anything 'officially' yet but I've had my agent book us in as a couple to an upcoming charity event. That will seal the deal as far as the press goes.

Gabriel and I had a long talk about him staying in Australia. He let me know that he had put out some feelers before leaving home, just in case. Soon, he's offered a job at one of the best law firms in Melbourne. We are both stoked. They just need to finish up the paper-work for his Visa. They assure us that because of all his experience back home and because he's multilingual that it won't be a problem. His specialty is defamation cases which might be good for me with all the press I get. People can get jealous and bitter when you're hot and famous. It's a shame really, I worked hard for this. I wish they would spend more time creating their own lives than worrying about mine. I've had the odd callous remark published about me but I've been very careful about how I curate the press and handle the paparazzi. I'm a pro, but I guess you never know and it's always good to have a lawyer on your team.

I'm still in contact with all the producers and the network executives from the show. I gave them the best ratings they've ever had and they really want me to be part of a show again, some kind of spin-off. They have never had an ending where the Eligible didn't end up with someone. I don't want to be their play thing anymore though. I've done that and going back to do it again isn't right for the future I have planned.

I've started looking into getting my own production company. My own reality show that I'll curate, not star in. It means I'll still be tethered to a network, but if I'm going to do this I sure as hell want to have all the power and praise, instead of just being the "talent". I can't tell the network the entire idea for my new reality show concept yet though. There are a few things I have to do first, to set it in place. Plans that will set the show up to be an international success.

It's great having Gabriel as it's free legal advice any time I need it. He's already told me countless times now that he's madly in love with me which is exactly as it should be. I know that I have him. That he'll do what I say no matter what. Plus I have a little dirt on Gabriel too. It's always good to have back-up. I tell him I love him too and maybe I actually can if he doesn't fall down that clingy, overprotective, mushy rabbit hole.

CHAPTER TWENTY-TWO

(Henry)

My whole wretched plan went even better than I thought it would. You should've seen Poppy's face. First when I was on one knee in front of hundreds of people, and then again when I opened the jack-in-the-box to her dirty truth. I thought she was going to throw up. She went white under that stupid fake smile, and I felt her trembling when I hugged her. Poppy did end up throwing up – it was at that point that I felt a little bad, but I was feeling way too smug and proud of myself to say anything.

I didn't really think much past asking her to marry me. It was more about the shock and awe. The public spectacle. It was as if I was trying to imitate her own awe-inducing acts. I mean, I'm not going to marry the evil wench, am I? I just wanted her to know that I knew about her and Amos, and that I could fuck her over as much as she's fucked me over. Well, sort of. I wasn't really sure what to do next. But she didn't know that.

Going back to the vineyard was strange. We had to hang together because of the paparazzi that surrounded us. Neither of us could be bothered to pretend that we were a couple. We were being polite to each other for the sake of the staff. I felt like everything had been said. That everything was finally out in the open. I didn't have it in me to ask for any more answers. I think we both knew she didn't have any, that there're no excuses, that she's simply some sort of fucked up narcissistic psychopath. There was definitely still part of me that was still a little scared of her. The image of Amos, slumped on that dirty red couch, the fact she had slit a man's throat. I wondered if she felt like slitting mine. I knew I was safe for the moment though. There were too many eyes on us. She also had to know that I was never going to say anything. I was unfortunately caught up in all her fucked up shit. And how would killing me help her? Really, this is the best plan I had, the best thing I could think of to really to fuck with her. It felt good to be the one in control even if it was just for a moment.

After barely a week, I realise that I really have no control at all. That again, it's me that has to deal with the fallout of this whole situation, not Poppy. She's untouchable. She's stoic and relaxed. She is silent. The only outbursts have come from me. I can't think properly with her dark energy swirling courteously around me all day. I need my space again. My nurse comes to check on my progress. The swelling has gone down a bit but I still haven't recovered any of my hearing. I use the disappointment of that visit to tell Poppy that I'm going to head home for a bit. She doesn't give a shit. She barely acknowledges me. The next day I pack up my stuff and drive back to Sydney with Clyde. We drive in silence and I let the coastline fill my soul where music normally would. I finally feel like I can breathe.

When I finally reach home Ruben is there to greet Clyde and I. He had been looking after my place while I was away. He's a good friend. We give each other a hug and he gives me a pat on the back. It's great to see him.

"Hey man, congratulations on your engagement. You snagged yourself a smoking fiance," he says. I wish to God I could tell him the truth, talk to him, figure this shit out, but instead I simply say, "Thanks man. I'm one lucky fella," and I smile that smile I'm so used to smiling. Will this fiction ever end?

Ruben can't stick around and I'm tired. We make plans to meet up later in the week. I throw my bags down on the bed and fill Clyde's bowl with water and food. Maybe I'll tell Ruben that I'm not sure about Poppy anymore. That things weren't good out at the winery. That I think that maybe we only work when we are under the spotlight. Maybe he can help me figure out how to get out of this.

The next day, who shows up out of the blue with a casserole and a kiss on the cheek? Junip. She says she's here for work but I really feel that Junip is here to check up on me. She's the most comforting constant thread in my life. Our friendship is like family. We keep our distance but she comes around every time the shit hits the fan. Her husband Dave sounds pretty cool. It's obvious from what Junip says that he doesn't see me as a threat. He's pretty down to earth. Dave is an electrician. He has a daughter from a previous relationship, Madison, who is eight and stays with them half the time. Junip just adores her. You can see it in her eyes when she's talking about her. It makes me so happy even though I feel a small twinge of jealousy. She has what we were never able to create together.

I'm glad Junip is here. I need her. Although I can't actually tell her anything, it's a reminder that things can be simple and good, and maybe they will be again someday for me too.

With Poppy, I started to feel like I hated all women. There was just so much bullshit, but Junip brings me back home, back down to reality. She makes me realize that Poppy isn't a woman, she's a fucking monster. I can't believe I spent so many years feeling guilt and remorse for that 'poor girl at the bank', or that I had a crush on the 'adventurous Instagram girl' I was following for years. The useless guilt ruined my marriage. If I had known the truth all along, maybe Junip and I would still be together. Then I fell for the wide-eyed, easy-going, flirtatious woman from The Eligibles, but the worst, and I can't believe I'm actually admitting this, well at least to myself. I actually thought I loved the woman I was with out at the vineyard even after I knew her all her secrets. I was so conflicted and confused out there. She was so composed. I got so wasted one day and I lashed out at her in front of Steve and Jen. It was bad. She did nothing. She said nothing. She was so cold. She has... had, such a hold on me. What a desperate and shit place to be in where I was able to rationalize Poppy the killer as Poppy the victim. As I was driving home, I realized that we grow up on stories where women are the ones that need saving, and that as men we are supposed to protect them. It's so hard to believe that they can be the villains and that maybe it's us men that need protecting. And maybe in some fucked up way I was trying to save my mother, something I was never able to do as a child. It's such a mess and I want out. I don't want to wander into that place of lies and deception anymore. I need to figure out how to free myself completely from her.

Junip taps me on the shoulder. I didn't realize I had been staring out the window. I turn to face her. "Are you going to show me your place?" she asks. She has Clyde in her arms, he's trying to lick her face and I can see she is giggling. I exhale. I always feel safe around Junip.

After I show her around, we sit down at the kitchen table and I make us each a coffee. I finally tell her that I'm sorry. That I'm sorry for the way that our marriage ended. That I'm sorry that I let her down as a husband and that although being young and foolish isn't an excuse, I had thought that it was 'things' that made someone happy and that if I could buy us all the 'things' that we would be happy. I don't tell her 'how' I ended up being able to do that. Junip doesn't need to ever know about the Amos' or Poppy's of this world.

"How stubborn you are Henry. And thank you for your apology. But if none of that would have happened I wouldn't be where I am now and I am so, so happy." I can tell she means it.

"You being happy, Junip, makes me happy. I get that we all have our own journeys that are special and unique to us. And knowing that makes me happy, happy for you and happy for me."

I tell her that she doesn't have to worry about me this time. That I feel okay and that I know that I understand now that our first happiness comes from a love and acceptance of ourselves no matter what and that once we forgive ourselves for being 'human' then we are capable of real love and the happiness that that brings. My eyes are welling up and I chuckle. My decade late apology. Junip holds my hands across the table. I look down. I'm still not sure if I mean the 'happy for me' part yet.

We talk about my operation and the fact that I might be deaf for the rest of my life, and that if it doesn't I'll need an implant. The doctors haven't completely ruled out my ability to hear as I heal from the operation but they are not very hopeful. I'm way more pragmatic this time and I truly believe all will work out as it is meant to.

The paparazzi pictures come out the next day. I bet I know who is behind that. It doesn't look good for me but I really don't give a fuck. I'm so tired of the bullshit. I'm more worried about Junip and her husband Dave, that it might affect their relationship. I shoot her a text but she sends a message back letting me know that they both just laughed. She said Dave was razzing her, calling her a celebrity. There's a wee pinch that Dave didn't even feel the slightest bit of jealousy but the feeling was super fleeting. Of course, I have the opportunity to respond to the claims, to say it wasn't what it looked like, but I just want the whole saga to be over and this is my out. Don't confirm or deny.

There's no slippery slope into the abyss of drugs and alcohol this time around, although I'm still taking my antidepressants, trying to be responsible with my medication. At least I'm trying my best. It's more about meditation, the gym and Clyde and I doing our chill thing. On the weekends I might have a glass or two of wine or a finger of scotch but nothing crazy. I'm thinking about what kind of work I would actually like to do.

Ruben and I have been hanging out a fair bit. We've hooked up at the gym this morning. It's good motivation for me. Ruben is in great shape. He's seen all the headlines, but he believes me when I tell him that I didn't cheat on Poppy. He thinks she just took me seeing Junip the wrong way and things went bad.

"It's all for the best, man," I say. "Things hadn't been so good out at the winery". I don't go into any details and he doesn't ask. "And I'm on a sex-fast." I add.

"What the fuck is that?" Ruben laughs.

"Haha… I'm taking a few months off. Just trying to steady the ship my friend. Just trying to steady the ship." I head over to the free weights.

I know he actually gets it and supports me. He's a good

guy and a lot of the humour he had on the show was just his way of protecting himself.

I haven't turned into a monk though and on weekends Ruben and I will go out and hit the town. I still like flirting and stuff but I'm just not bringing anybody home. I used to use sex the same way I used drugs, simply to numb the pain. I feel shitty about that. I didn't even know their names half the time. There's a saying that the external world is simply mirroring what's going on in our internal world. I'm starting to believe that.

The months go by and I've got a pretty good routine down and I'm feeling stronger in all areas of my life. I have a couple of flings after my 'dry spell' but nothing serious.

I still attend a bunch of events even though I still really want to step out of this reality and into something new. They make it hard though with all the free shit they throw at you. Maybe I'll take some time travelling, soon. It would definitely be a good way to create more distance and to really clear my head. I know Ruben would hang with Clyde.

Tonight, however, I am booked in to attend a big hotel opening. It's a huge event. There will be hundreds of people there and one of those fucking people is going to be Poppy. There's been pictures of her recently in the press with her old Chilean boyfriend, Gabriel. She was probably in touch with him the whole time we were hooked up. Steve, my agent has warned me to be on my best behaviour. The press still thinks I'm a cheating dog and Poppy has somehow wrangled it so that she is the one that's been hard done by. She's such a fucking bitch. I wonder what the press would think if they knew she was a fucking calculating cold-blooded murderer? Steve has told me to stay away from women, to stay away from booze and that it would be great if I can get one good publicity shot with Poppy where we look like good old mates. I've roped Ruben into being my date. I feel like if I have my bud with me I'll be less likely to fuck this up.

Ruben and I roll up in a limo, which wasn't my choice, Steve sorted that one out. It feels wanky but I'm trying not to care. I just want to get through the night and then hopefully get on a plane and get the fuck out of Australia for a while.

There's press everywhere. All of a sudden there's a camera in front of my face and someone is asking if I have seen Poppy. I brush them off without saying a word and Ruben and I head straight for the bar. It's strange again to be in such a crowded space without being able to hear. I've gotten used to it in my day-to-day life but this is the biggest gala I've attended since 'popping the question'.

"Hi," I smile at the bartender. "Can I get a double shot of Glenfiddich? Ruben?" I turn to Ruben. He has no idea about any of the real pressure or bullshit that is flying around in my world. To him, we are just a couple of hot bachelors out on the town and out to have a good time.

"Sounds good mate, I'll take the same." Ruben puts an arm around my shoulder. "Fuck this is going to be a good night." I never have to remind Ruben to look at me when he talks. He has no idea how much that fucking means to me. We down our scotch and Ruben orders us a couple of beers before we start wandering among the crowds.

There're trays of hors d'oeuvres and champagne floating around everywhere. I'm on my third glass of champers when I spot Poppy with her new-slash-old fucking boy-toy, Gabriel. They are hanging in the back corner of the main ballroom. They are doing all the 'right' things for the cameras – holding hands, kissing, laughing — basically all the same shit we used to do with each other. I wonder if he knows that she's a cold-blooded killer or if he is just another poor schmuck serving some purpose in her ever so carefully curated life. I wonder what she is trying to get from him – what purpose he serves? Poor fucker.

The rest of the night is a bit of a blur. Someone gave me a pill of some kind. I don't think I even asked what it was. I was back in the vortex and when the pill was handed to me, I just licked it up and swallowed. I remember throwing up in the toilets, dancing with some chick from another reality TV show. I have a blurry memory of her taking my pants off in handicap wash-room and sucking me off. I don't even know if I was hard. I remember drinking more and more and when the barman wouldn't serve me, other people getting drinks for me. I remember whispering in Poppy's ear, "cunt" when we happened to be at the bar next to one another. She smiled and said, "Thank you, wishing the best for you too Henry." I remember being in some room with coke lines spread on the table and Ruben saying to me, "What the fuck Henry! What the fuck are you talking about?" And then that's it. I completely black out.

I wake up early in the morning on Bondi Beach and I have no fucking idea how I got here. Fuck. I thought I was passed all this shit. I hoist myself up on one elbow. I'm still in my tux, my fucking mouth feels like a dry sewer. I squint into the rising sun and listen to the waves and try to get my bearings. It must be 5 or 6am.

Wait.

I can hear the waves.

I can hear the fucking waves!

Oh my god! It's quiet, but it's there. I jump up and look around. There's no one on the beach near me. I see someone off in the distance walking towards me but I can't tell if it's a man or a woman. I yell at the top of my lungs.

"I CAN HEAR THE FUCKING WAVES." I'm looking around like an excited boy who just got their first brand new bike. I want to show it to everyone. Tears are streaming down my face. I head towards the water. I take my socks and shoes off and strip down to my trunks and jump in the ocean. The cool water feels so fucking good. I feel so alive. I'm laughing my head off and splashing water everywhere. I can hear the fucking waves!

(Poppy)

Ruben walks over to me at the party. I'm with Gabriel. He

yanks me by my arm and pulls me aside. I'm about to tell him to stop, to give Gabriel the look that says *save me*, but then I see a madness in Ruben's eyes, a fear.

"I need to talk to you. Now." Ruben shouts over the noise. Gabe has stepped forward. It's instinctive. I let him know it's okay and I follow Ruben across the room and out the front door into the night. It's cold outside, but Ruben was marching and I didn't think to grab my coat from the cloak room. Ruben still hasn't said anything as he walks down the front entrance steps, along the side driveway, and around to the back. I'm frantically following him in my heels. It is dim and dank and smells like drunks and garbage. Ruben stops at the end of the complex' driveway and I stand in front of him. The only entrance back into the building is a metal red door that I assume is some sort of service entrance. Above the outside of the door is a single bulb glaring yellow inside a metal cage. There are soggy mops leaning up against the concrete and there is no sound aside from the rever- beration of the bass from the party pumping up my heels. The large green skip bins pushed up against the back concrete wall are overflowing with bottles. It stinks. There's even a skinny cat with chewed off ears by the bin legs, licking up beer that has dripped from the broken beer bottles. The poor thing is too tired and too emaci- ated to care that we are there. I really want to go and pick it up and take it home but I'm aware enough to know that I need to focus, to focus on Ruben and what he has to say. It's so still out here. It's like a movie that has stopped playing. It is the antithesis of the chaos inside. It feels a little rapey, but I know Ruben well enough to trust him.

"What's going on Ruben? Where's Henry?" I ask.

"Henry has lost the plot. He's wandered down to the beach drunk as fuck. I can't control him. The media will do whatever they do."

And why is this my problem, I'm thinking to myself, but instead I say, "Maybe we should go find him and make sure he's okay?" I'm hoping to God that's what this conversation is about but I don't quite believe that that is it.

"He'll be okay. But it seems like he's got a good reason to be so fucked up. Poppy," I brace myself. "He's been saying some very serious things. Some really fucked up serious things."

I feel my heart jump up into my throat. I try to play it cool.

"Like what Ruben?"

"Do you know an Amos? Henry says you murdered him. That you were covering up another crime." Ruben is staring at me. "Murdered?"

"Ruben for fuck sakes," I interrupt him. "He's drunk and probably high. . Hallucinating. We have no idea what he's taken," I say.

Ruben runs his hands over his face and back over his hair as he stretches back, lets out a moan The cat scurries past us. I can hear its nails scratching against the gravel as it disappears into the darkness. Poor kitty.

"Poppy, I fucking googled this guy Amos. He was actually killed a few months ago. They don't know who did it. I mean... fuck, this is crazy."

I laugh, "Do you really think I could kill someone Ruben? Really?" I spread my arms open wide. "I have no idea what's going on in Henry's world. *We* have no idea. Just like you said, Henry has lost the plot. He's drunk. Uncontrollable."

"He also says you set up paparazzi shots to make him look like he was cheating. That's a lot easier to believe. Can you admit to that?" Ruben has his arms folded. The single bulb is casting shadows on Ruben's face and in the darkness I can see his knotted eyebrows and the crease etched in between his eyes. . His eyes look wet but I don't know what they're wet with -- Confusion? Fear?

I try to laugh, but it catches on the lump in my throat. "Come on Ruben, this is crazy. I'm done with Henry's bullshit. You should be too. We know better than this. Henry has been messed up on meds for a long time now."

Ruben laughs. I feel scared. "I talked to my media guys, Poppy. You *did* set it up. DON'T FUCKING LIE TO ME! We're past that!" His eyes are wide open, arms outstretched in disbelief.

I'm silent, trying to figure out my options here. Ruben and I have always connected. You could almost call us friends, an Insta message here and there, a screenshot exchange of Daily Mail articles, a good laugh at the craziness of our lives. When we see each other at events we play, tease, talk. He's a Poppy fan and I'm a Ruben fan. In this crazy world of celebritydom we've always had each other's backs.

What the fuck has Henry done? And how the fuck do I dissolve this?

Ruben puts his hands on my shoulders so he can look at me in the eyes. His hands are soft on my skin. Warm. Tender. Not threatening at all.

"I need an honest answer with this one, okay? Did you deliberately cause the car accident that made Henry deaf?" I look down. *I can't believe this is happening.* Ruben grips my shoulders a little tighter and starts yelling, "POPPY FUCKING LOOK AT ME. WHAT THE FUCK IS HAPPENING HERE?! ANSWER THE FUCKING QUESTIONS, MY GOD!" He lets go of me and starts pacing. He kicks the green bin. It lets out a reverberating clang. I close my eyes and try to breathe.

He paces up and down. He's ranting. "What do I do here? Do I call the Police? Did you know Amos? How did Henry know Amos? Why would he say you killed him? Just tell me something I can believe so I can let this go. What. The. Fuck. Is. Going. On?!" He hits the bin once more and then turns towards me and starts shaking my shoulders.

I'm about to unleash on him when we hear quick, heavy footsteps coming up the drive. Headlights slice past the alleyway and illuminates a silhouette with clenched fists walking towards us. Whoever it is, is picking up speed. I feel a sucking in my gut, as if coils are wrapped around my frame, cracking the air and life from my ribs like a python. Is that Henry? Has he finally come for his revenge? Are they going to hurt me? Kill me??

. . .

Then I see it is not Henry at all, it is Gabriel. *My saviour, Gabriel.* There is a rage in his walk. His shoulders expanding like a lion on the prowl. He grabs Ruben in one swoop by the back of the shirt and throws him down hard. Ruben slides across the gravel, groans, his head cracking against the ground as he comes to a stop. There is a small second of silence as Ruben, confused, reaches his fingers up to touch his bloodied head. "What the fuck! He yells as he sees the blood on his hand. !" Gabriel walks towards him, rage heaving, as Ruben deliriously stretches out to pick up a broken beer bottle, clenching the neck between his fist.

"Don't you fucking touch me!!" Ruben says, his voice trembling. He's propped on one elbow and with his other hand he is holding the broken bottle up in the air. pines of cut glass are catching the reflection from the yellow light.

"Shut the fuck up! You hurt my lady and I hurt you! Asshole!" Gabriel is drunk, slurring.

Ah, Gabriel. So sweet. So loyal. I can't help but feel a little turned on in this fucked up situation.

"Both of you, stop it! Right now!" I yell, knowing full well that I don't mean it. I actually need the opposite to happen. Gabriel pauses though, my little lost, obedient pup. He looks at me as if waiting for a command. Ruben takes the opportunity to rise up on his feet although he is a little unsteady. Gabriel's eyes turn back to him as Ruben spits "Poppy, is Gabriel part of this too? You sick, twisted FUCKS! It will ALL come out, all of it! How could I be so delusional?"

Gabriel screams and lunges at Ruben with balled fists

and swings, missing him by an inch. I try to come between them, my palms stretched out, motioning for them to stop, but I am pushed to the ground by Ruben's free hand. My ass and elbows land first, I can feel the sting of the fall, the blood. I start crying, wailing, and my hands cover my face. I'm lying on my back on the ground. "This is all a misunderstanding! Stop it, stop it, stop it! Don't hurt each other, don't hurt me Ruben! Please don't hurt me!"

Ruben looks down at me, his eyes widen. He is aghast that he has just pushed me, Poppy Aver, to the ground. He falls to his knees, at my side with his face perched over mine. One of his hands is on my cheek, wiping my tears away, and the other is still loosely holding the broken beer bottle by my side. "I'm sorry Pops, I didn't mean to hurt you, I just want some answers. I'm so damn confused." I look Ruben in the eyes and take note of his vulnerability. Then I immediately know that he has to die, and that it is Henry's fault. Henry's fault for opening his big mouth and telling an innocent man *our* truth. *Why would he do that? Why would he be so selfish?*

In one quick swoop I grab hold of Rueben's fist that is clenching the bottle and try to push the glass into the space just above his collarbone. He's pushes back and he's much, much stronger than me. I hoist myself up with my other arm and my face is close to Ruben's as I try to push. I can feel his breath on me. We lock eyes. He bites my bottom lip and rips my flesh. I cry out. Ruben is yelling, screaming out meaningless, guttural curses. Then I feel Gabriel's hand reach from behind Ruben. Then comes the hot wet stickiness of blood squirting and sludging out everywhere. Ruben's eyes lock with mine. He's in shock. He's gasping as he chokes on his own blood. His eyeballs are bloodshot and start to turn upwards. He falls on top of me, slumped and drowning as death wrings out his life.. I'm soaked in his blood. My hair is soaked, my dress. I wiggle myself out from under him and sit against the concrete wall, gasping for air. Gabriel has his hands pushed against his scalp, as if he is trying to free his brain from his skull. He's hyperventilating.

"Oh my god. Poppy. Poppy. What fuck have we done, Poppy? I thought he was trying to kill you. I went blank. I went mad. I had to save you… oh my god."

I take a deep breath. "Gabriel, calm down. Take a deep breath. I've got this. Stop. Listen to me. Just do what I say."

-

The Police show up three mornings later at my Melbourne apartment. The same two as last time. Detective Leonard, the fat, pudgy schmuck, who was a little obsessed with me on our first meeting. Today he doesn't look so kind. He's all business, and when he does meet my gaze, he's cold and stern. There's a power in his eyes that makes me uncomfortable. Stacey handcuffs me and says, "You're arrested on the charge of first degree murder in the death of Ruben McIntosh." As she recites my rights, I'm certain she's trying to hold back a smile. Stupid bitch.

Gabriel starts arguing with the Police as we planned, and in the end they agree to let him come with me to the station. When I'm taken outside the paparazzi are clicking and flashing and clamouring over each other to get the best shot. There are four police cars surrounding the property as if trying to contain the horror that is Poppy Aver. Questions are hurled at me: "Did you kill Ruben McIntosh?" "Poppy have you been formally charged?" "Poppy, are you involved in an ongoing murder investigation?" " Where's Henry?" These Fuckers wait like vultures for this kind of chaos, happily licking up the entrails of a gruesome story.

I also feel the excitement well up in me. This is the beginning of my most glorious project yet. The last stage of the plan that will make Poppy Productions not just a company, but a fucking social movement. See, I'm about to be the next Amanda Knox, except I'll be bigger than Amanda. The world will know my name. There'll be vitriol, venomous bile that will be thrown at me by the media and the white, patriarchal law enforcers and it'll prompt nationwide and international interest and conversation. My story, with its end-game arrangements, will entertain the masses, will cause shock and awe to the nth degree.

I just hope Henry will comply because this is all banking on him being my puppet and him being smart enough to put self-preservation before truth.

As they lower me into the back of a cruiser, I remember what he whispered into my ear that one night at the vineyard, saying something about society eventually cutting me out like an ugly, cancerous mole. Ha! All I know is that if I'm going to be dislodged permanently from this free world, so is he. He'll have the option to save me, or to go down with me. He's the one who put us in this mess in the first place.

Let the games begin.

End.

AUTHOR'S NOTE

Episode Eight is based around a Reality TV show, so I'm often asked how much of the book is autobiographical since I've been on two of these suckers. It *is* a work of fiction, and even though many of the emotional dilemmas the characters experience in the aftermath of their show participation are borrowed from my own struggles, it is in no sense a kaleidoscope of my life. There are so many ideas, so many borrowed emotions and experiences from myself and other people, so many shattered specks that have made the mural of *Episode Eight* come into existence! I believe the personal and external conflicts in the book explore universal human themes of identity, love, loyalty, loss, and self-preservation.

As most of you may know, in 'reality' TV there is behind-the-scenes producing to create eccentric characters we love to watch. This involves intense psychological and emotional manipulation when it comes to the contestants. As reality TV D-grade fuckwits (I own up to being one of them), we are unwittingly (and sometimes wittingly) coached and edited into roles to create a dramatic effect that often has no resemblance to the true storyline, personality, or feeling at the time. Our contracts ensure this is the case.

Henry's hearing loss was a conscious metaphor for the sense of loss I felt coming off *The Bachelor*. My life was no longer my own and although it is often expressed that as TV personalities or public figures we should know what we are getting into, the reality is that public scrutiny and public attacks on one's character are at first extremely hard to deal with.

By the time I went on my second show, *Bachelor in Paradise*, I had grown a much thicker skin and was able to allow public criticism to wash over me and enjoy the experience. I am extremely grateful for having had the privilege of working in TV, and the crew were amazing with me. Although I have multi-faceted feelings about the 'adventure', I was lucky enough to be given the opportunity to be exactly who I am, both in personality and sexuality (not every contestant came out feeling like this).

Nevertheless, the whole experience had me tap into the darker sides of my own ego. For a while there was no room left for vulnerability, friendship, trust or love. I was entrenched in the tyranny of my own self, hiding behind a protective shield.

Today, after a lot of mistakes and some hard-truths, I'm trying to open myself back up to vulnerability. Exploring the characters of Poppy and Henry has helped me to do this. Poppy represents an entrenchment in the darker side of the ego, whereas Henry is perhaps more fluid and struggles to come to terms with his reality. *Will people think differently of me? Will expectations of me change? Who am I?* Without a strong foundation or support it is hard to 'survive' the initial changes brought about by very public experiences.

Then there is the extension of reality TV, outside the controlled and manipulated environment of production, to society as a whole. How is this type of TV shaping our social culture and ourselves? Why do we watch this "shit"? Why do we love it so much? Why do we think we're clever for our ability to laugh at its stupidity, even though we're still moved by the drama?

Popular entertainment can either mirror socio-cultural attitudes or shift them.

Archetypal gendered fantasy stories have worked entertainment wonders for ages. I was a church kid, and most of the stories I grew up with, told me men were meant to be one way and women another. If you watched Disney when you were a kid, maybe it was similar. So many dating shows foster the same ideals and stereotypes. The backdrop has changed but it is still some weird fantasy-world that is firmly ingrained in societies gendered norms.

The character of Henry in particular was driven by his preconceived idea of what the 'male role' is. He has unresolved childhood issues related to his father's abuse of his mother and his regressive or delusional guilt about his inability to protect his mother. There are obvious power and dependency issues related to his past. So much of what Henry grapples with as an adult are directly linked to him trying to uplift or empower his 'masculine self-esteem' that was castrated as a youth. He oscillates between 'bangable' women who are objectified because of their beauty, and revering the more approachable woman, Junip. This oscillation between extreme and limited characterisations of women is the external manifestation of Henry's internal self-loathing. For Henry, Junip has no flaws and she becomes a moral compass to his 'out of control' reality. She is the needle by which Henry measures all that is wrong with himself. His view that he needed to be a 'provider' for his wife Junip, and without excessive provision she would be unhappy, was the catalyst for all of Henry's further struggles. Without any awareness, Henry views women as weak and he intrinsically believes that if men don't protect women, they will get hurt. First it was his mother, then his wife, Junip, and finally Poppy.

I do believe the world is moving into a space of more interdependence between the sexes. We are coming to understand that we foster the most dynamic relationships when we abolish our gender stereotypes and work and play together

Do or can dating shows foster this interdependence? Is there hope that alternative sexual preferences will become accepted? Or do they simply uphold gender stereotypes? Or are they ego driven modalities where fame, money and love are sought after at any cost?

The character of Poppy, with her own set of gender stereotypes personifies the latter of these questions. She believes that men are controlled by their innate desires for sex, and animalistic and irrational instincts to be "the man". She therefore believes that she is smarter than the men she manipulates. Poppy believes she can get what she wants by momentarily allowing men to get what they want from her. She carefully curates a reality where everyone is a stepping stone or a tool to the fulfillment of her desires. She projects to society an unattainable blue-print of perfection and what she thinks it means to be a successful Australian woman, and she will do whatever is possible, to continue that false illusion.

Is she a psychopath? Is she just enchanted by social power? Or is she a reflection of the extreme version of our influencer-driven society?

It is all too easy to belittle and laugh at the fame-hungry and the Facetune-vain on IG, who flog false exis-tences on your Instagram (I interchange between both, admittedly) than to look at the deeper impact such 'false feeds' have on our society. Whether your community of followers is twenty or twenty million, is it not all the same ego?

Most social media influencers, at some point, wish they could get off the hamster wheel and understand their souls rather than their Instagram statistics - but "work is work" – and we continue to sign promotional contracts at (sometimes) the expense of our true identities.

I once had an ideal love like Henry and Junip. We were married when I was eighteen. The marriage lasted six years. He taught me to drive, to cook, to love. We didn't have social media. We didn't drink or take drugs. In our downtime we read history and philosophy books to one another. We went freediving. We watched David Attenborough documentaries on Sunday afternoons until we fell asleep in each other's arms. We cooked food for friends and family. He supported me while I went to Uni. We went vegan and gave charity milking goats for Christmas to unapproving family members. He'd go surfing, and I'd go diving. We were faithful emotionally and physically and didn't feel the need for jealousy. We'd camp under the stars on regular occasion. He'd tell me I was perfect as I was, all white and brunette. Not better with a tan, not better blonde, not better with botox.

Chris was a surfer, like Junip. I'd think of him out in the water, basking in the glory of the ocean and the beauty of the world. That's what I cared about. His happiness. Him coming home salty and cold from the ocean and putting his cold feet between my warm sleepy thighs that big smile and those surfers arms around me. I'd count the dark freckles on his tanned back and in his eyes, lick the salt off his neck and play with his chest hair, pinch his nipples. As he grew into his late twenties, the laugh wrinkles around his eyes made me happy. We were happy getting older even though we were still young. Happy in the simplicity of our love without social media or fame and all the ills it brings.

How quickly we digressed. I digressed. How quickly the world can suck you up and spit you out. How quickly I believed the bullshit of the world because of my own fucked up ego. How quickly we can all become everything we proclaim we hate in the world. How quickly I became my own fucked-up version of Henry and Poppy.

Love in a world driven by social-media and RTV ideals is just a fucked up game of jenga, really. You both make moves cautiously until one of you fucks up and it's like, *oh well, game over. Should we play again or nah?*

Episode Nine is coming very soon. I'm hoping to remove a few egos in this one. Probably not mine though as that one is holding on for dear life.

Megan Marx

ACKNOWLEDGMENTS

Bev Hotchkiss for being clever and warm. For teaching me so much about the written word. For making this book better. You inspire me.

Mum, for supporting me every step of the way. Even when I was burdensome and lost. Instead of telling me who I should be, we'd drink wine and talk about the world, and you'd tell me you were proud of me. You were a saving hand when I was drowning. Your love lifted me up.

Chris, for being my Junip.

Elora Murger, for feeding my ego at regular intervals even when I'm being sorry-for-myself. For being funny, and kind, and my best friend. For women supporting women. For being the strength I want to be.

Jake Ellis, for reading every word with passion. For telling me to ignore my fears. For kissing my forehead when I was up til 3am in the zone. We didn't 'work out' but there are no regrets. Thank you for the love.

Jason Holm, for supporting my dreams and crazy ideas. For making me see that no idea or darkness is too wild for this world.

Guilt, for the desire for redemption. For the power of pain.